A KET i LE
OF FISH

ALI BACON

With warmest wishes

Ali B

Nomine Choir
2019

Published in 2012

FeedARead.com Publishing – Arts Council funded

A CIP catalogue record for this title is available
from the British Library.

For my family

Acknowledgements

Thanks are due to all the writing friends who made comments and suggestions on the many drafts of this novel, especially the hugely supportive and talented members of Bristol Women Writers, and Sylvia Dyer who provided encouragement long before Thornberry Publishing was born. For all her advice, thanks also to my big sister Dorothy, who could have written many novels but decided she would rather be a reader, and to Barbara whose guided tour of Edinburgh several years ago was part of the inspiration. Finally to Geoff and Penny, for never complaining (well hardly ever) at how much time it all took.

Cover design

Disclaimer

Some of the places in this novel are real. The characters and the events are entirely fictitious.

CHAPTER ONE

It's hardly the distant past, but things were different then. In 2007 only the cool and arty were on MySpace. Facebook was barely a rumour. Life went on, for the most part, in the cliquey huddles of dim school corridors, around the draughty entrances to shopping precincts or, on special occasions, at the corner table in Hot Shots Italian Coffee Bar.

And this was a special occasion. From April we'd been counting down the days. Our last exam, our last sports day and finally, yesterday, our last last-day-of-term. School was officially over. Faye and I were ready for take-off.

Between us on the fake marble table was an entire lipstick collection; not the stub ends from our grubby make-up bags, but a complete new set of testers, the cases still gleaming, the colours ranked in order from palest pink to crimson, each tip chiselled to a sharp edge. I'd borrowed them from Mum's Avon cupboard. She knew I borrowed things and I knew she knew. Back then, that's how it was between us.

Faye was deep in concentration. I watched as her hand hovered, hesitated and dropped with hawk-like precision on number fourteen, Wicked Plum. She picked it up and twisted the end so that its waxy length was revealed. It was a good choice.

"Go for it," I said.

She took out a heart-shaped mirror, drew a careful outline around her top lip and filled it in. Pressing her lips together to set the colour, she gave me an extravagant purple pout.

"What d'ye think?"

"Nice," I said. It was. Dead nice. Dead Faye. "You should wear it. Tomorrow."

"You reckon?"

I nodded. Tomorrow Faye's dad was driving us to a summer camp in the Highlands where we'd be paid to round up kids and keep them out of trouble. We'd be away from home for six whole weeks. And after that, there was uni.

Faye leaned forward, peering at my own mouth. "What's yours?"

Suddenly, Sugar Ice felt like a cop-out. Okay for meeting Faye to celebrate the end of school, but not for the start of the rest of my life. The lipsticks stood erect in their black plastic caddy like rockets on a launch pad. Before I could change my mind, I made a grab for Faye's mirror, and obliterated the pearly pink undercoat with a manic layer of Showstopper Red.

"Get you!" Faye hooted. "Hot or what?"

Behind me, the outside door swished open. Faye, facing the street, gave me a kick under the table. I scooped the lipstick collection into my canvas bag just as Laura Patterson sauntered in. It would have made her day to have spotted me doling out Avon booty when her gang could afford the big brands.

2

Laura was at the head of a three-girl posse. "Hi, Faye, hi Ailsa!" She swanned past, swinging a carrier bag, its upmarket logo in full view. At the counter she nudged the girl next to her in an exaggerated way. Their heads inclined towards each other. Over the whoosh and gurgle of the milk steamer, the words "Ailsa Robertson" and "saddo" were clearly audible, followed by muffled laughter.

Faye was watching them. She fixed me with a look. "Pay no attention, Ails. It's time we were out of here."

This scene, this town, this life.

On the street outside, we did a high five then fell silent, contemplating our so-called High Street in the fag-end of a Saturday afternoon.

Faye said, "Come back to mine. Help me pack."

I shook my head. "I said I'd get our tea. I'll have to go up to Kingsgate for it."

Faye rolled her eyes. "All right then. I'll let you off. But remember, tomorrow I'm taking you away from all this." And she gave me a push to send me on my way.

I was used to being in charge of tea, not to mention dinner and breakfast too. Mum wasn't an invalid, but she suffered from allergies that varied with the season, or sometimes the day of the week. Sunlight usually made them worse. On a Thursday night, her pal Liz took her to do a weekly shop, but I did the rest. Even when it was cloudy like today, she preferred to be at home with a cupboard-full of pills and potions for company. She described her weird collection of ailments as ME, a convenient label that to most people signalled hypochondria – in other words, a head-case.

But that summer Mum was better, better than she had been for ages. And so I was going off with Faye, away from home at last. And if Laura was going to call me names, I really didn't care. After today, there would be no more housework and no more running messages for six whole weeks, and so when Mum had said, "I fancy some fish for our tea, for a change," I was surprised, but I didn't argue.

I jogged past the string of estate agents and charity shops until I came to the fistful of concrete and glass that was Kingsgate shopping centre. Before I turned inside, I stopped to take in the view. From this corner, where the High Street became East Port and the New Row ran all the way down to the Nethertown, I could see the red triangles of the Forth Bridge poking above the Ferry Hills, and next to them the grey lattice towers of the road bridge. Arthur's Seat and Edinburgh looked only a stone's throw away. In between and out of sight was the sea, or rather the estuary, where the silver links of the Forth emerged from valleys and mudflats to bump up against the choppy grey waters of the North Sea. That's where the fish came from.

When Mum bought fish it came in a plastic tray, wrapped in film, or frozen into an unappetising brick. But when Dad took off and Mum fell ill, I had lived with Gran. Every week, Gran took a plate from her cupboard, a white one with a faded snowflake pattern, and sent me out to the fish van for "two haddock, not too big." The van came from along the coast. The fish, when it was cooked, flaked open like the top of a lacy wave.

Gran preferred herring, but the herring had been stolen by greedy fishermen from other countries. Gran

4

had been stolen too, struck down by a heart attack when I was twelve, but the plate had found its way into the kitchen cupboard at home, where it guarded its fishy inheritance like a seashell keeps its echo of the sea.

On a recent and more crucial shopping mission (new life, new wardrobe), I had spied two additions to the shopping centre. The Dunfermline Deli sounded like a contradiction in terms, but by now even the east of Scotland was experiencing a bit of a gastronomic renaissance. Next to the deli was a real live fishmonger's shop. The sign above it read: Catch of the Day, then in smaller letters: brought to you by Mackay & Son, purveyors of quality fish and game.

The Mackays had always had a fish shop, and in the days when it was still in the High Street, Gran had taken me there. Not for the fish ("not as fresh as off the van") but to call on her crony, Mrs Mackay. Mrs Mackay, with her pebble-thick specs and chest as big as any man's, had scared me half to death. While she asked me how I was getting on at school, she folded her hands across her blue-and-white striped stomach and looked at me as if I were an undersized haddock that she might choose to save or toss back in the water. But old Mrs Mackay was long gone. As I drew level with the shop, I saw that the business had skipped a generation. Inside was her grandson, Ian Mackay, wiping down the counter with a damp cloth, very much alive.

CHAPTER TWO

I knew Ian Mackay from primary school, where he had
been in the class above. His knees were dimpled with
puppy fat and his hands, when he was sent from the
next room with jotters or pencils, felt damp. At break-
times he could be found fighting in the playground over
football cards or He-Man figures. At some point he'd
left St Leonard's and since then he'd been off my radar,
probably at a fee-paying school in Edinburgh. That's
where kids went if the parents were well-off, or didn't
think their precious could cut it amongst the locals.

Ian was still big, though with a more solid and
dependable look than when he was five. He had thick
brown hair that moved across his forehead. His
complexion was ruddy, but in a healthy way, from
being outside and doing stuff like rugby or hockey.
There was no one else in the shop and from the way he
was patrolling the counter, flicking it from time to time
with a blue cloth, I guessed he liked it that way. When
he saw me, he nodded and I nodded back,
acknowledging our previous acquaintance and
dispensing with it.

If I was tongue-tied, it wasn't Ian himself so much as the gleaming display in front of him. I was accustomed to fish in tidy packages. Here they were laid out in rows: naked, open-eyed, and undeniably dead. The fillets weren't so bad, tidy white triangles, some of them frilled in grey. In between there were sprigs of plastic parsley whose garish emerald distracted from the reality of deceased sea-life. Behind them were thick steaks with flesh and bone exposed under the scaly skin, and whole fish, slick and grey with upturned eyes. These were bedded in ice crystals, but the cold hadn't stopped the blood showing around the gills. Here and there on the counter were wedges of fresh lemon. We never had lemon at home. It gave Mum mouth ulcers.

"What'll it be today?" Ian said. His mouth was defiantly red amongst the dead things.

"Two haddock, not too big."

He reached into the cabinet and flipped two white fillets onto a paper and weighed them before lifting them off, wrapping them and tying a deft knot in the bag. I was grateful for the two layers of paper between me and the fish.

"Anything else?"

I was struck by how many kinds of fish there were in the window and how few of them I could name. As far as I knew, since herring had become too tasty for their own good, the sea around here yielded up only white fish. But I was morbidly curious about Ian Mackay's counter display.

"What are these?" I pointed to the whole fish, the ones with the eyes. Even in death, their skins shone with arcs of iridescence.

"Bonny, aren't they? They're trout, wild, not farmed. We don't often get them."

I shook my head, unable to ignore the bloody places where the hook had pierced.

"They'll no bite," he said and it made me laugh, the idea of the dead fish leaping off the counter.

"How can you touch them?"

"What do you mean?"

"Well, they must be… slimy."

His forearms were beefy, his wrists stood out red above the translucent gloves that made me think of my last visit to the dentist.

Ian clicked his tongue. "Och, away, they're no slimy at all." He picked one up and held it out to me. For a minute I thought he might try sticking it in my face or down my neck, like he would have at school. I backed away but Ian laughed and put the fish back in its place. "They're fine to touch. All of them."

"Where do you get them?"

"Trout and salmon we get from a wholesaler. The rest's from Pittenweem."

I paid for the haddock. "My gran used to buy fish from a van."

He was wiping down his counter again, an even rhythm. He took pride in its spotless state. "That's handy. Maybe we should give it a try, a mobile fish shop."

Behind the till against the wall there was a bench with a marble top and on it a whole salmon. He followed my gaze. "You can touch it if you want. See what it feels like."

The salmon's eye had a brightness to it, and its body was plump and weighty. Compared to the skinny trout and the anaemic fillets it was massive. I felt drawn to it like I had been drawn to the parapet when Faye and I went up the Scott Monument and I'd had to stop at the second gallery. Sidling round the end of Ian Mackay's counter, I decided that in fish terms this was level four, the farthest you could go.

"You'd better have these." Ian handed me a pair of the thin latex gloves. "Health and Safety."

I stretched them over my fingers before I laid my hand on the fish's scales. Even with the gloves on, I could feel the fish was cold but dry. Like he said, not slimy at all.

"It's a special order," Ian said, "for a wedding."

I could picture a page in a magazine, the salmon arranged on a platter, prettified with overlapping slices of cucumber. I hoped Ian's salmon would be left unadorned, except maybe for a sprig of parsley, the real kind, or a lemon. That way it might retain some of its dignity.

"Is this what you're going to do?" I asked him, indicating the bright but limited surroundings of the fish shop.

"Looks like it. What about you?"

"I've a summer job, up north, then I'm going to Edinburgh." By staying for a sixth year, my grades should be in the bag. English literature beckoned, not to mention the parties.

"Student life, eh? Can't be bad."

"Here's hoping."

"See you then."

"See you."

I felt him watch me all the way out of the door.

Outside, I caught a girl's face reflected back at me from the window of the shop opposite, a confident face, made brash by bright red lipstick. My own.

I fished for a tissue to rub off the waxy bloom of Showstopper Red then thought better of it. What did I care if Ian Mackay thought I looked like a tart? Soon I would have bigger fish to fry.

As I expected, the house was quiet. Saturday mornings are busy in the depilation trade because women who work all week save beauty treatments for weekends. But even with the worst of her ailments at bay, a whole day's work was too much for Mum. It wasn't unusual for her to go to bed on a Saturday afternoon.

The lipstick caddy was still in my bag. Mum didn't mind me borrowing them for a while but I had to put them back now. The cupboard where she kept them was in the room next to the front door. It had a nameplate on it, the kind that kids have on a bedroom, white plastic with black letters and a bunch of flowers in the corner. Except this one didn't say *Gemma* or *Becky* or even *Ailsa,* but *Treatment Room.*

I opened the door and went in, skirting the trolley with its jars of paste and the other gunk Mum used to remove hair from places where it wasn't wanted. The sticky scent that pervaded the house was at its strongest here. Vertical blinds, put up for privacy, kept out most of the natural light. What was left was subtly altered by the peach coloured walls to create a sickly orange glow.

Mum had stopped offering to do my legs for me because she knew I would refuse. She made the occasional comment on the money I spent on depilatory creams, reminding me she used hypoallergenic lotions,

10

with the implication I was dousing myself in chemicals. But the idea of her doing it? Faye and I agreed it just wasn't on.

I could remember when we had a real front room, with easy chairs and a bookcase. Mum sat with me there in the afternoons, with the sun coming in and people going past outside. We watched cartoons on our only TV until Dad came home and the air changed: the outside world came in. Mum left us there together while she went to make the tea. Dad picked me up and twirled me around. We laughed together when the TV presenters fell over or got covered in mud. Then Dad read to me from my favourite books, even though we both knew the endings. He was funny and happy and then he was gone. I was only six. Since then, it hadn't been much fun for anybody.

Now the big TV was in the back room but there was an old portable in here so that Mum and her "girls", as she called them, had something to take their minds off what was going on. Its cold grey eye watched as I opened the wall press and replaced the lipsticks.

I closed the door behind me and went through to the back room, thinking Mum might like a cup of tea when she woke, but I'd only just put the kettle on when I heard something from upstairs; not a cry exactly, just a bit of a noise, a scrabbling, a grunt. I closed my eyes. *Please, God, not today.*

"Ailsa, are you there?"

I wasn't asking for a miracle. I didn't expect Mum to be cured, only to be well enough so that I could get away for a while, for the particular while that started tomorrow.

CHAPTER THREE

Mum was on the top landing on all fours. Her hair had fallen forward in an unwashed hank so that the ends of it brushed the carpet and I could see the nape of her neck exposed to daylight. Between her creased green t-shirt and washed-out denims there was another strip of flesh on view, smooth and white. In the doorway to her room a bedside table was lying on its side. A mug had rolled from it onto the floor, its contents making a dark stain on the blue bedroom carpet. She must have got out of bed and grabbed for it as she fell over. I guessed the noises off were the sounds Mum made as she had got up from the floor into this ungainly kneeling position. She had only called out when she failed to get any further.

The attack must have come on just as she'd woken from her nap. Maybe she had seen the date on the bedside clock and some subliminal alarm system kicked in, sending a message down the neural pathway that nudged her ME into angry wakefulness. Not that she intended it. It was just the way things were.

I watched her inching her way towards the stairs, her lumpy toes poking out from under the jeans, knowing there was no way she was going to make it to our downstairs bathroom, not in one piece, not in any number of pieces.

"What on earth are you doing?" I said.

"Och, Ailsa. I'm sorry, I'll be all right. In a minute." She had to stop then to get her breath back, and so I wasn't taken in. I put my arms under hers and managed to sit her up so she could negotiate the stairs on her backside. Then I heaved her into the bathroom, sat her on the loo and closed the door on her. I'd never actually had to wipe her bum, but who knew what the next day might bring?

I went back up to my own room. On the chair I'd already laid out the outfit I was planning to wear the next day. I folded the new skirt back into its bag. The label was still on. With any luck I could get my money back.

Upstairs in the spare room there was a second-hand exercise bike Mum had bought a year ago in a moment of optimism and which I had appropriated. It had a speed dial and a calorie counter on it to show how much energy you were using. As I waited for Mum to sort herself out, I hitched myself onto it. The numbers clicked over, slowly at first until I built up a rhythm. The sweat was gathering in my oxters and the waistband of my jeans was getting damp. But no matter how hard I pedalled, the scenery refused to change.

By evening Mum was better but still in bed. Her face was flushed an angry red and she said she felt stiff all over. I knew she would sleep for a while, and so I left some water. There was a phone next to the bed.

"Ring me if you want to get up," I told her.

"Where are you going?"

13

"I have to see Faye."

Mum said nothing, but pulled the duvet up to her shoulders and rolled over to face the wall.

Downstairs, I changed the answerphone message to say that Smoothies Home Beauty Treatments would be closed until further notice. I imagined the customers adding Veet to their shopping list, or sneaking into the bathroom and borrowing a razor. Maybe they'd notice how much money they were saving. Maybe they wouldn't come back, and the front room could revert to somewhere more normal. But we needed the money. And Mum needed to feel useful. The Treatment Room, like Mum's illness, was here to stay.

At Faye's house I pressed the bell.

However much fun Dad had been, I blamed him for Mum being ill. The day he left, Auntie Moira came to get me from school. At home, Mum was in the front room, the old front room, with Gran.

"So?" Auntie Moira said.

Gran's mouth was in a straight line, like when she thought she'd been overcharged at the local shop. She shook her head. Mum was silent, looking at the dead white burners of the gas fire.

"But he's away?" Auntie Moira said.

Gran nodded. "Oh aye. He's away all right."

"Good," Auntie Moira said. "Good riddance."

And he never came back. That was when Mum had had some kind of breakdown and I went to stay with Gran. The day I came home for good, not just for a visit, was six months later. The gas fire was on and Mum was next to it, her arms wrapped around her knees. She said, "Hello, pet," and put her arms out for a

14

hug. Gran gave me a wee push across the knobbly green carpet. I was glad when Mum let go, because she didn't feel quite the same as before. She smelled different and had a limp feel, like a jumper that had been washed too many times.

After that, when Dad was gone and I was back at home, I was invited out to tea with girls I barely knew. Girls like Laura Patterson. When I got there, her mum was so nice to me I felt like I had to eat all of the sausage pie that was Laura's special favourite. It sat in my stomach under a layer of jelly until Laura's dad arrived home and was introduced. He gave me a funny look, as if I had something that would be embarrassing to mention, like a big birthmark or a bad case of BO. At this point the sausage stuff heaved itself over Laura's best t-shirt. Laura cried and was wiped down. Mum was duly summoned and I was sent on my way.

The trouble was, Mum had always been a bit miserable. Dad was the one who had taken me places, shown me things. He'd had too much life to hang around. Mum had stayed there, trapped in the grey cloud of our misfortune.

I might have been there too, if it hadn't been for Faye. Faye joined my class in Primary Five. She was tall and skinny with big eyes and a school jumper that looked too new. On her first day, our teacher told her to sit next to me. We had our packed lunch together in the dinner hall, where we swapped crisps because Faye's mum had given her a kind she didn't like. I said that my mum did that sometimes, forgot the things I didn't like. The next morning I waited for Faye in the playground and we went in together.

When Faye's mum and dad had settled in to their new house, I was invited for tea where there were sandwiches and no funny looks. Afterwards, Faye and I sat on her pony-covered duvet and agreed on all the important things in life, like wanting a cat but not a dog, and preferring *Matilda* to *The Witches*. Since then we had been a team.

In Faye's room the pony duvet had gone, but not much else had changed: the dressing table still had a wonky leg and was stained with mascara; there was still a lingering smell of the cheap perfume spilled when we were twelve, mixed with the toasty warmth that seeped upstairs from the kitchen.

"What's up?" Faye was sitting on the bed with her knees hunched up. She was still wearing the purple lipstick but its outline had gone crooked. She knew it was bad news.

"Fuck," she said, when I told her. "So did you get the doctor?"

"No point. She'll be okay in a couple of days."

Faye put her elbows on her knees and cupped her pointed chin in her hands so that she looked like a pixie. "So couldn't you just come?"

"You know how it is. She'll probably be like this off and on for a couple of months."

Faye moved up to let me sit next to her but she was still hugging her knees, keeping herself separate, signalling her disapproval. "So what now?"

"You can go."

"I will. But what about you?"

I shrugged. "I'll get another job I suppose. Around here. Save some money."

I waited for Faye's reaction. The time was always going to come when we would go our separate ways, but neither of us had thought it would be now, before the fun had even begun.

Faye got up from the bed. In the dressing table mirror she repaired the damage to the crooked lipstick. "So what about Edinburgh?"

She had only asked what I was thinking. If I couldn't go away for a six-week trip, how was Mum going to manage without me for a term?

"I could come back at weekends," I said. "But I don't know. I might just stay at home."

Faye rubbed off what was left of the lipstick. "It won't be the same."

Too right it wouldn't. Faye was going to Napier rather than the old university, but we had wangled it so we could share a flat. "Double whammy," Faye had said only the previous week. "Between us we'll have all Edinburgh sewn up." If I opted out of the flat it would mean a daily commute by train, missing out on new friends, night life, on everything I'd been looking forward to.

"September's a long way off," I said, preferring not to think about it.

Faye lay down next to me again. "Don't let the bastards grind you down." She meant Laura Patterson and the others.

"I'll survive," I said. "Sticks and stones."

"Yer dad was a prick to do a runner."

I shrugged. "He'll have a new life now. A new family." I looked around for a change of subject. On Faye's bookshelves I could see the old brown photo

17

album she had shown me when we were kids. "Can I look?"

"If you like."

Only a few pages had been filled. All of the photos included a boy, James, Faye's wee brother. The last one had a group photo with a caption that read: Dunblane Primary School, Christmas 1995.

Everybody knew about Dunblane. "A bonny place," Gran had called it. Then a pervert burst into a school gym and shot down the kids. James was one of them. I shivered just thinking about it.

"Do you still think about him?"

Faye had followed my gaze. "James? Not really."

They did an annual pilgrimage to Dunblane. Faye said it was to limit the pain, keep it in one place.

"Do you still go there, every year?"

"No. Mum and Dad go, but not me."

Faye didn't talk about James, like I didn't talk about Dad. It was something we had in common, that someone had gone away and not come back. But there was no where I could go to visit Dad, any time of year.

Faye's mum, Vi, was calling from downstairs, asking if I wanted to stay for my tea. Vi was nothing at all like my mum, but tall with curly hair and a liking for short skirts. I knew if I stayed there would be jaunty remarks about the expedition north.

"Don't worry," Faye said. "I'll tell them about it tomorrow."

I hugged her and got up to leave. "Don't do anything I wouldn't do," I said.

That was just a joke. Faye had missed a year at school because of James and was a year older than me. She was the one who'd had dates with boys and

18

reported back for my edification. She was the one who knew what was what. I could just see her with one of those fitness trainers, or some shy highlander with hidden depths. When she got back, things would be different. I was going to have to manage on my own.

CHAPTER FOUR

A week later, Lorraine was back at work, and I had got myself a job in the filling station down on the main road. Life didn't seem so bad. Texts arrived from Faye most days complaining about the weather, the rowdy kids or the voracious midges. Mrs Reedie, the owner of the garage, left me on my own most of the time, so when it was quiet I could work through my reading list for Module 1: The American Novel. In fact, I had a copy of *On the Road* propped on the chewing gum stand when I saw a white van draw up at the pumps. The van had blue writing on the side: Mackay & Son – Quality Fish.

I watched as Ian Mackay got out, filled up with petrol and walked towards me across the forecourt. He carried his weight without embarrassment. Maybe a bit of ballast helped if you were carrying crates on a dockside or standing next to a fridge all day. It was only as he laid a Mars Bar and a packet of mints on the counter that he recognised me and did a double take.

"What are you doing here?"

"What does it look like?"

The sarcasm was lost on Ian, who stuffed his wallet and the sweeties into the pocket of a navy gilet. "How was the haddock?" he said.

"Em… Nice. We enjoyed it." After Mum's fall the haddock had been forgotten. I had chucked it in the bin the following day, which now seemed a lifetime away, but I certainly didn't feel like explaining all of this to Ian Mackay.

Ian looked out of the window towards his van, as if checking the coast was clear. "Do you work here every day?"

An alarm bell rang in my head. This sounded like the prelude to a date, something I'd been waiting for since at least Third Year at school, but now that one might be coming up, I wasn't so sure. Ian Mackay wasn't exactly catch of the day. I picked up my book to remind myself, and Ian, that my life had some higher purpose.

"I get Sundays off and another day in the week," I said.

"I could take you to Pittenweem, next time I go for the fish. It's early though."

From this distance Ian Mackay didn't actually smell of fish, and how many offers was I likely to get?

"What day do you go?" I asked.

"Depends. I take turns with my dad. When are you next off?"

"Thursday next week, but—"

"Thursday it is then."

At least he was decisive. We arranged to meet at the garage. He swung off and into his van and let off the brake, his eyes on the passing traffic. At the last minute I dashed out and stopped him.

21

"Have you fish with you?"

"I do that. I've just been for them."

I asked for two haddock and he didn't charge me. It made me feel better about chucking out the last lot.

Back at home, I plonked the fish on the kitchen worktop.

"I got haddock – fresh."

"Where from?"

"Ian Mackay came into the garage for petrol."

She raised her eyebrows. "Was it dear?" She was reaching for her purse to pay me back.

"It's okay. My treat."

When it was cooked, the haddock was good.

"Nice," Mum said. She ate it quickly. She was definitely getting better.

"Did he go to an Edinburgh school, Ian Mackay?" I asked.

She frowned. "I don't know. I dare say they could have afforded it, but they left the town for a while. Opened a shop in Cowdenbeath."

Ian's disappearance and his accent – more Beath High than Royal High – were explained.

Mum was still trawling the database of trivia brought in by her clients. "They bought a house in Hillside when they came back." Her tone implied a good address. "I didn't know you knew him."

"He was at St Leonard's."

"So what's he doing now?"

"I think he's staying in the shop."

She shrugged. "Funny job for a man."

I passed on Ian's career choice. I'd already had a letter from Edinburgh, confirming my term-time address and telling me how to matriculate. Mum was adamant she could manage without me. Liz and Auntie Moira and a few of our less judgemental neighbours were all lining up to help, or so she said. For me, going to Edinburgh would be a fresh start. In Edinburgh, I reasoned, no one would know about my ailing mother and my defecting or defective Dad. But it might be a risk too. Edinburgh was full of people from home. What if someone crawled out of the woodwork to spoil things? Sometimes I wondered if being stuck here with Mum might be an easier option. There was a lot to be said for knowing where you were and who you were with.

Five a.m. wasn't an hour I was accustomed to seeing in any weather, and on that Thursday there was a sneaky mist blotting out the sun and working its way through my thin cotton cardi. A trip along the coast was losing its appeal. Not wanting to risk contaminating my new trainers with fish guts, I'd chosen to wear flip-flops. I looked down at my bare toes, as pink as newly defrosted prawns.

The garage forecourt was deserted; Mrs Reedie didn't open until seven. I considered the possibility that Ian wouldn't turn up, that I was just a joke he'd share in the East Port Bar, or wherever fish-men hang out on a Friday night. But before I had time to send a face-saving text to say I'd changed my mind, the van rolled up and stopped next to me. Ian slid the door open.

"Hiya," he said. I climbed in and huddled on the seat next to him, hugging myself for warmth. He pointed to a silver thermos next to the gearbox. "Help yerself."

I shook my head. He had the heater on, and so I started to thaw out.

"How long will it take?" I swallowed down a sour taste in my mouth. I wasn't sure how long I could breathe in the combination of engine oil, stale tobacco and a popular men's deodorant. Ian, I felt sure, didn't smoke, but the nicotine was probably ingrained in the van's ancient upholstery. Underneath it all, a distinctly fishy aroma completed the cocktail.

"Should be there in an hour or so. I'll be busy when we get there, but I'll take ye for breakfast later on."

"Okay." I took a cautious breath and concentrated on the scenery.

As we bowled along to Kirkcaldy, I guessed there were corners of the road where the sea could be glimpsed, but the mist kept everything under wraps. The M90 divides Fife like a big zip, but this was an older road with more branches and forks. When we turned away from the coast we were soon in farming country. This was the golden edge of Fife, its black heart hidden away behind us. Leven, Lundin Links, Elie; the signposts went scudding past. Stooks of corn and occasional splashes of oilseed rape wavered behind the low cloud. I dragged up some memory of a geography lesson and a day-trip from school to a big harbour with a museum at one end.

"Why Pittenweem?" I asked him. "Isn't Anstruther bigger?"

Ian laughed. "What century are you in? There's been no fishing out of Anstruther for years. Pittenweem's the only market left."

He pronounced it "Anster". I could have asked him about the dearth of herring, but since I was already behind with the fishing news, I decided not to risk showing further ignorance. He put on the local radio station so we didn't talk much more until the DJ made a joke about the local football team. Our laughter mingling in the stuffy air of the van came as a shock.

Ian parked close to the dockside and now the whole world was a stink of fish and a shriek of seagulls. He jumped out of the van.

"Will I come with you?" I asked.

He looked at me and saw the problem. I would be in the way.

"I could just stay here."

"I'll be an hour, at least." He weighed the keys in his hand and then handed them to me. "Okay. If you want to go out, just leave the van open."

I watched him and his workman's body as he shouldered his way through the crowd. He seemed older here, doing deals, running a business, not just a schoolboy.

After ten minutes I'd had enough of the radio and needed some air. It was as grey and chilly as before, but I jumped out of the van and walked away from the harbour, climbing up through narrow streets with closed curtains and dark shop windows. When I reached the top, I looked back to watch the town wake from its sleep.

There was a disc of light, still smudged by cloud, hanging over where I knew the sea should be, and soon I could make out a line; the place where sky became water and water sky. As the sun broke through, the sea condensed into something darker and more mobile, nudging up against the harbour wall, making its presence felt. I reminded myself that this wasn't the seaside of sandcastles and boat trips round the bay. This sea was rich and dangerous, a maverick who might be for you or against you.

I set off back down the hill, and as I lurched into a half-run down the cobbles, the mist dissolved and the scene moved from insipid greyscale to a full colour display. I was like Dorothy waking up in the land of Oz. Sun bounced off the crowded quay and made rainbows in puddles of water and petrol. Everywhere was frantic with the call of birds and the shouts of stallholders. Everywhere slippery with fish.

I was relieved to find Ian in the crowd and he seemed pleased enough to see me. He took me round the stalls without embarrassment, showing me the catch: haddock, cod, whiting. The prices were falling, the best stuff had already gone. Incredibly, I'd got used to the smell.

"Come on then," he said. "I'm clamouring for a cup."

We walked along the harbour and passed two cafés before he stopped at a third. It was busy, and someone nodded to him, but I guessed this wasn't his usual haunt. He wouldn't go there with a girl. At the counter he ordered bacon and eggs and a bacon roll for me. In the melamine cubicle that smelled of floor-polish and stewed tea, I was struck by his bright-eyed cleanliness. His hair was soft and floppy. He must have showered before he left.

"What do you think then?" he asked, mopping up egg yolk with a crust of toast. I probably looked blank and so he carried on. "Better than sitting in an office all day, if you ask me."

I was impressed by his energy. Anyone I knew who wasn't going to uni was looking for a cushy billet in a bank or a call-centre and enough money to get rat-arsed at weekends.

"You wouldn't have to get up so early," I said.

"It's not every day. Dad and me take it in turns."

A shop's less boring if it's your own, and Ian and his dad were their own supply-chain, in thrall to the weather, the sea, and maybe the EU, but still knowing where the fish came from, making their own deliveries. Mrs Reedie sat warm and comfy in the back room of the garage, but had no say over the big oil companies that brought the petrol or the prices they charged.

I looked at my watch, feeling Ian's eyes on me.

"How's your mother?" he asked.

This was what people asked me. Not "What music do you like?" or "Do you fancy a shag?" but "How's your mother?" I imagined the scene in the front room chez Mackay: "You know her mother's not well. Never has been, since her man left." The *not well* would have been said with a look, implying possible mental problems, but that's as far as it would have gone. His question to me was genuine enough.

"Not too bad," I replied. "She's up and down."

"Do you have to look after her?"

"Sometimes. Usually she's okay."

"But you're going to Edinburgh."

"Yeah, can't wait."

Ian took this in. He was looking at me pretty full on and I was struck again by his mouth. The word "sensuous" crossed my mind but was quickly followed by "lascivious", and lascivious for some reason the one that stayed.

"So," he said, "what pictures do you like?"

At least we'd got past the mother question. I shrugged. "I don't go much."

"Come on, what did you see last?"

I mentioned a chick flick I saw with Faye, probably what he expected. "What about you?"

He named a sci-fi sequel. "We could go to something, if you like. You could choose."

Before I could answer, he went to the counter and paid the bill.

"Are ye right then?" He had a heavy watch that was loose on his chubby wrist. "I have to get back."

When we came out of the café, the sun was warm on my face. I stuck my hands in the pockets of my cardi and started to jump over puddles, until one jump fell short and my flip-flops went *splat* right in it. I must have been a sight, showered in mucky water. I wiped myself off with a tissue and Ian laughed.

Back at the van, Ian opened the door and flung the sweater he'd taken off in the café onto the passenger seat. Then he remembered about me. As I climbed in, he picked up the sweater to let me sit down. Since there was nowhere else to put it, I took it from him and folded it on my lap.

On the way back we passed a sign for Largo.

"We went to Largo once," I said, picturing a wide sweeping bay, a pier, and the tide coming in over rocks that poked up from a swirl of sea.

"On holiday?"

"I was only wee."

Five maybe, the last holiday with Dad. After the first day, Mum hadn't gone to the beach. She had stayed in the stuffy caravan with its blue and yellow curtains and brown shiny walls. "I can't go like this," she had said. "Look at my face." When they got back, Dad had said, "Still off-colour?" making a joke of it. Mum had laughed. "You can say that again."

On the beach we had met a girl who took me to play on the rocks where I teetered on a rough ledge, damp and slippery. The next rock was safe and dry, encrusted with limpets, but it looked like a long way away. I had to jump but couldn't make myself let go. Dad had said not to get my shoes wet or Mum would be cross. The girl was already on the other side. "Come on, Ailsa, jump!" I couldn't be left behind and so I did, the leap of faith, and just made it, feet skidding over seaweed, mischievous waves licking at my heels. "There you are, it was easy, wasn't it?" A hand, gritty with sand and salt, grabbed mine and dragged me off to some other adventure. I was heady with the wind and the sea and the jumping across. Nancy. My first friend. I hadn't thought of her in years.

"Could we go?" I asked Ian. "Just for a look." The memory had come from nowhere. Like a shell or a piece of driftwood brought back from the beach, it had been carefully packed away and then forgotten. But now that I'd found it I wanted more. I wanted to get out the whole treasure trove and look at it again.

Ian waggled his wrist on the steering wheel so that the face of the watch was towards him.

"To Largo? Havena'e really time. We could go another day, if you like." He put his foot down.

As we bowled along past Leven, his jumper grew warm on my legs, like a cat asleep in the sun.

29

CHAPTER FIVE

A Fiat Punto in a shade of yellow reminiscent of puke was parked outside our house. I'd forgotten it was Liz's day off work. I hoped she and Mum would be safely tucked up in the Treatment Room, but they were in the back, drinking coffee and ruminating over the latest Avon catalogue. When I walked in, conversation ceased. Liz had her jeans rolled up to her knees and was bending forward to run her hand over each knobbly shin, admiring Mum's handiwork. I guessed that Mum had spilled the beans about my trip with Ian

"So!" Liz sat up, letting her boobs settle back into the black balcony bra visible under a lime t-shirt. I looked pointedly at the amount of wrinkled cleavage still showing, but it took a lot to put Liz off her stride. "How was the fishing trip?"

She was oblivious to her own double entendre, but I caught Mum's eye. At that time we could still share the odd joke.

"Fine." I headed for the kitchen on the pretext of making a drink and lurked there until I heard Liz leave.

I don't know why it was that Liz and I didn't get on. We'd taken up our respective positions a long time ago, and it was easier to keep up our mutual distaste than to cease hostilities.

When I went back in, Mum, who had got used to me and Liz misbehaving, was clearing away the mugs. "Did you have a good time?" she said.

"It was cold. It got warmer when the sun came out."

"Are you seeing him again?"

"Well, he asked me to the pictures. Sort of."

"And what did you say?"

I wasn't sure what I'd said. "Depends what's on."

Mum wasn't fooled. She threw me a copy of the *Press*. "You'd better get looking then."

I could tell she was pleased I'd found myself some company. I decided I was pleased too. I studied the cinema guide with a lot more interest than I could usually muster.

On the mantelpiece I also clocked a letter in a white envelope. Despite the fact we didn't talk about Dad, he did send us money. These thick white envelopes turned up from time to time from a solicitor's office in Edinburgh. Mum called them "paperwork" and put them away as soon as she had read them. Like her, I accepted this arrangement. It was enough to keep us from a state of penury and provide the odd extra. Once she looked really pleased and said, "Just as well we have a sugar daddy." I assumed he had upped our allowance or whatever it was. If Mum was happy with the money, so was I. It was easier not to think about the rest, although Largo had reminded me that there had been what felt like two dads: the nice one who had held me up to the window and taken me swimming, and the other one, who made everybody angry, especially Mum.

In the afternoon Mum had more customers so I took myself off to the public library. This was somewhere that Faye and I usually avoided, but with four examples of the Great American Novel still to go, it made more sense than spending my hard-earned cash.

Of course, this wasn't just any public library but, as every teacher was at pains to remind us, the very first of its kind, provided by the largess of local hero, Andrew Carnegie. Under the Victorian turrets, the entrance hall was smaller than I remembered, but still full of its own importance. I scuffed my trainers experimentally, feeling Gran's eyes on my back as I toyed with the possibility of a forbidden slide across the chequered squares of the marble floor.

At the end of the hall was a staircase with a polished wooden rail, and under the bend in the stairs, a space used for exhibitions. Part of it was given over to council business, planning applications and announcements on bright red and blue pin-boards, but my eye was drawn to the old-fashioned glass cases at the back. A closer look and I saw that they were full of stuff about the High School. There was some anniversary coming up, and in the first case, opposite the door to the library proper, there were documents connected with the founding of the school, back in the mists of time. Next to these were photographs of the buildings the school had occupied, ending with the one that until a week ago had been the centre of my limited universe.

Not any more. Whatever the future held, school was in the past. Maybe that made it more interesting. I passed on the historical stuff and made for the cases farther in. This part of the display covered the century just past and housed a collection of school magazines from about 1920. They had been left open at pages that gave away their period: photos of boys in shorts that went right to the knee, carrying gasmasks or ancient cricket bats, depending on the decade.

I looked along the display until I got to the Eighties and stepped closer to where I could see a group photo: *Staff and pupils on the annual school trip abroad.* On the facing page, some keener had written up a trip to Brittany to make it sound fun and educational, when, as everyone knew, these things could only be one or the other. But it was the photo that caught my eye. In front of a rabble of around thirty kids, there were six teachers, all named in the caption underneath. Three women in the middle were French teachers, two men on the left were from Geography, and on the right, standing together, were Mr Tom Robertson (Art and Design) and Miss Lorraine Ferguson (History).

I felt my colour rise. If Mum had photos of Dad she kept them locked away. Occasionally one turned up and was snatched away from view. This photo, a snapshot with the colours washed to hazy pastel, was a hidden treasure. I lingered over it, tasting forbidden fruit.

At least I recognised him. The time we'd spent together had left its imprint after all, or else I was seeing a version of myself: hair darker than mine but with the same unruly wave, and a nose that was almost too long. In the photo his face was pale, but I knew that this was a trick of the light. He had been olive skinned, almost sallow. "Not like you, with your rosy cheeks," he had said once, holding me up to the mirror in the hallway, his long brown face next to my round pink one. I blinked away the picture, refusing to cry in this most

33

public of places. But the memory lingered in the soft scratch of his face on mine, the knowledge as I gasped and flapped across the swimming pool on a Sunday morning that his hand wouldn't leave the strap of my swimsuit until the very minute I was ready to go it alone.

Mum stood beside Tom Robertson in the photo, plump and cheerful. Her emerald jumper was the brightest thing on the photograph and she wore wire-rimmed sunglasses that must have been in vogue at the time. Her hair was tied back but a few strands had come loose and she was raising a hand to brush them away. She looked good. This Lorraine had disappeared as completely as Tom. In fact, she had been the first to leave, waving goodbye as Dad and I set out on some expedition, stepping out with the sun at our backs, playing games with our shadows to make them grow or disappear. When we went to the park she would say, "No thanks. You two go. I'll stay here." On the beach it was Dad who took me to find wee fishes for my bucket. Mum was off somewhere, keeping to the shade. I had been a daddy's girl, and proud of it.

Why had he left? Any time I had asked, Gran had said, "Wheesht now, don't upset your mum." After a while, I gave up.

I pictured Mum as she had edged downstairs two weeks ago, clinging to the banister, and then looked again at the photo of the old Lorraine. They were standing together, Mum and Dad, but not particularly close. They didn't look like a couple. Was it the start of it for them? The freedom of a school trip, getting to know each other, taking a chance after the kids were safely tucked up in their cramped dormitory bedrooms.

34

I turned away. Sex and parents did not go together. And why did he never write to me or even send a birthday card? Other people had absent fathers who reappeared from time to time or sent big presents at Christmas. If Dad had found a better life, could he not afford to share any of it with me? I stuck my hands deep into the pockets of my long cardi to where biscuit crumbs and old bus tickets had got stuck in the knobbly seam. "He's away," Gran had said, meaning gone and not coming back.

The door to the street swung open and in the draught I found myself shivering. I needed to get a grip. Dad had done nothing worse than find himself somebody better than Mum, somebody who went out and did stuff and didn't get laid up with mystery ailments. I allowed myself a moment's anger that when Dad had gone off to a new life he had left me behind, then I turned on my heel and marched into the library.

Back at home, I postponed the next novel in favour of redoing my toenails in the back room, which is where Mum found me when her appointments ended. She sat down in the chair opposite, the chemical hit of nail-polish remover drowned out by the aura of sugar paste and aloe vera lotion that clung to the white coat she wore for work. This scent, oppressive but soothing, signified situation normal, if normal was a word that could ever be used of Mum. Nothing with her was ever straightforward. Despite eating erratically, she always seemed to be overweight. Even though she looked the picture of health, with colour in her cheeks, she always claimed to be "done".

She sank down in the chair with the kind of sigh that suggested she'd just done an army assault course instead of whipping the fluff off a stubborn upper lip.

"Did they have what you needed, at the library?"

"Some of it. Enough for now." I wanted to shake her into life. "They have a display on in the entrance, old school magazines and stuff."

"What, the High School?"

I nodded. "There's a picture of you there. And Dad." Mentioning Dad always felt like kicking Mum, especially when she was already down. But she just looked puzzled.

"Are you sure?"

"Och, yes. It was you all right. And him."

Mum studied the contents of her mug, but there were no tea leaves to read. "I can't think when that would have been."

She couldn't wriggle away. I knew exactly. "Nineteen eighty-nine. On a school trip."

I had thought this might elicit a reaction, a smile of nostalgia, a grimace of what hell it had been with all those kids, but Mum's face barely changed when she said, "Oh. Right enough. I suppose there would have been a photo."

"So how was it? The trip?" Annoyance at missing my summer of adventure, and at Mum's passivity, was prodding me into places I would usually avoid.

Mum shrugged. "It was a long time ago."

"So was that when you and Dad, when you first, you know…?"

This time Mum was shocked. "What? Oh, with your dad. Well, I suppose so. Not on the trip, not then, but around that time." She drew her white coat around her like a hermit crab retreating into its shell.

It really got to me that she actually couldn't care less. For her it was all over. Well, she might be content to shuffle up and down stairs, waiting for me to come home, but I had other ideas. I took the mug out of her hand so quickly it made her jump.

"You know," I said, "you looked really good in that photo. I would hardly have recognised you."

Mum was struggling to keep up with my mood swings. "There's none of us getting any younger."

"It's not about getting old," I told her. "It's about getting better."

Her complexion flushed again in the way it did, the redness unfurling over her face like the wings of a butterfly. "Do you think I want to be like this?"

"Well, sometimes I wonder. Since you never do anything about it."

Now she was as riled as I was. "Like what? You know I've been seeing that herbalist, taking the stuff he recommends. I've been a lot better."

"Until it mattered. Until I was going away."

That shut her up. Her face sagged and I was left feeling bad.

"I'm sorry."

"No. Don't be," she said. "It's not right. It's not fair on you."

"I'm fine. I have a job. I'll get the reading done."

Mum pushed a non-existent strand of hair from her forehead. Was it the same one I'd seen in the photo?

"Okay. But you're still to go to Edinburgh in September. I'll go and see a doctor."

That made me sit up all right. Mum had fallen out with conventional medicine a long time ago.

"A real one?"

She nodded. "Liz says there's a new one just come. She's meant to be good. Might be worth a try. And if it keeps you happy."

Happiness, I thought, was relative. But this could be a start.

In the presence of the opposite sex, I usually either talked a load of shite or fell into some kind of verbal paralysis, but with Ian I felt that if I had something to say I could say it. If not, I could cope with a reasonably companionable silence. For me this was progress. By the time we'd arrived at the multiplex the following week, it was as if we'd been seeing each other for ages. I deduced that this was because sex hadn't really entered the arena – not yet, anyway. He certainly didn't make a move in the pictures, but took my hand as we walked back to the car park. When he stopped next to the car and kissed me, it took me by surprise. But I was hardly going to object. He had paid, after all. And he didn't push it. A suggestion of tongues, as if to say "next time?" And I thought next time would be fine. Did I fancy him? Not in a big way, but I wondered how full tongues would feel, and what would come after that.

When Faye came home for results day, I told her about Ian. It made a much bigger impression than our more than adequate grades.

"Bloody hell, Ails," she said. "When did all this happen?"

I could tell she was a bit miffed that I'd achieved the feat of getting a boyfriend without her help.

"Nothing has happened," I told her, though this wasn't strictly true.

"How did you meet him?" she asked.

I told her about the shop and going to Pittenweem. "He's going to take me to Largo some time."

"What's at Largo?"

"Oh, you know. A beach."

Faye obviously didn't see the attraction of a downbeat seaside village. "Hmm." She used a biscuit to make a pattern in the foam of her coffee. "A car's an advantage, even a fish-van I suppose. And if they own the business at least he shouldn't be skint."

She gave me a précis of her time in the camp and a boy she met who was going to Napier too.

"I did quite fancy him," she admitted. "He's called Gavin." She leaned towards me and said in my ear, "We had a bit of a snog. I quite liked it."

"There you are then. You're leaving me for a man. I had to take action."

Faye didn't contradict me.

"So," she said, "when do I get to meet him?"

A month ago she would have walked straight up the town and staked out Catch of the Day, with me hovering at a distance, waiting for the verdict. But that was then. We had upped our game.

"We should go for a drink," I said. "The three of us."

It was only then I realised it might be a bit much to expect that Faye, my sister-in arms, and Ian, the boy I'd picked as my social get-out-of-jail card, would actually get on with one another.

CHAPTER SIX

At home, Mum was in the Treatment Room, taking the paper cover off the bed and crumpling it into the big bin with the flip-up lid.

"Hiya," she said, quite jaunty for that time of night. She took a new sheet out of the drawer and laid it over the thin white mattress. She was moving freely, not stiff like she often was.

"How did it go?" I asked her. It was the day of her doctor's appointment.

"Good," she replied. "Dr Archibald was very nice." She wiped over the side table where the paste warmer sat. You could still feel a slight heat from it and from the sun that shone late into the room through the slatted blinds, creating a dappled orange glow.

I wondered if the doctor had gone beyond the social niceties. "Did she have anything useful to say?"

"Well, she wants me to go back on steroids."

This didn't sound particularly encouraging. Bad experiences with steroids in the past had sent Mum running to the health shop and all things alternative.

"And what did you say to that?"

"Well, I told her I didn't like it, but she said it was only a temporary measure until she gets to the root of the problem. She took some blood tests. She listened."

"So, what is she testing you for?"

"She mentioned immune system."

Mum sounded perfectly calm. A noise like an air-raid siren went off in my head *Immune system.* "Well, that's a new one," I said, trying to replicate Mum's composure.

"That's what I thought," she said, like new meant good. "What about you? How was Faye?" Mum didn't like Faye much, which annoyed me just like it annoyed her that I didn't like Liz.

"She's all right."

"Only all right?"

"We're going out tonight for a drink, with Ian. She's moving into the flat next week."

"And what about you. When will you go?"

I had been too busy working out the possibilities with Ian to think about moving. Faye's term started a week before mine. By the time I got to Edinburgh it would feel like Faye's flat, shared with others from Napier. Faye might not appreciate having me in tow. And what about Gavin, where would he fit in? For once, I realised I wanted Mum's opinion, to know what she wanted for me.

"I could still stay at home. Get the train across for uni. What do you think?"

Mum stood up from tidying the bed and frowned at me. "I'm all right here. You please yourself."

I was back on the slippery rock, but was I ready to jump?

41

It was after eight on the Saturday night when Faye and I fought our way across the lounge of the East Port Bar. We paused for breath. "There he is," I said.

My voice tailed off. Ian was in the opposite corner, his hand on a pint. I'd had nearly a month to get used to Ian, but now I saw him through Faye's eyes: a shopkeeper wearing an opened neck shirt, a guy who could do with losing at least a stone. The confidence that sprang from having a boyfriend, any boyfriend, began to ooze away. It didn't help that sitting next to him was a guy I didn't know. The stranger was dark-haired with the shadow of stubble along his jaw. He wore a black jacket over a t-shirt; the kind of style statement Ian wouldn't even notice, never mind aspire to. Faye and I sat down.

"Do you know Andy?" Ian asked.

I shook my head. Faye's nails (dark green alternating with purple) didn't really go with her wispy blue smock, or the turquoise leggings that finished at her knees, but Faye never did care what anybody else thought. She gave Ian a minimal nod of greeting, then looked pointedly around the room as if to confirm her status as a free agent.

Andy flashed a smile. "What can I get you, girls?" His jeans were skinny and his trainers had a recognisable logo. I guessed he wasn't in the fish business. He took the order and went to the bar.

"Who's he?" I hissed at Ian. I didn't like it that he had felt the need for reinforcements, however easy on the eye.

"Andy Chalmers. Comes from Torryburn."

The people I knew from Torryburn lived in the cramped council houses built for miners. Clearly, the village had a more gentrified side.

Andy arrived back with the round. He was older than us, two or three years, I thought. "You girls from the High School then?" This was his way of indicating he had gone elsewhere. "My brother started at the High," he said, "but then my folks saw the light."

He ignored the way his joke fell flat. He asked what plans we had. When Faye said she was going to Napier University, he called it "The Tech". He said he already had a law degree. Now he was doing Law School.

"In Edinburgh?"

He nodded. "Part-time, though. Get some cash along the way."

The way he said *cash.* A shorter *a*, almost posh.

"All mapped out then," Faye said, "your brilliant career."

I didn't know what was getting to her. Maybe the absent Gavin meant more than she had let on. Ian gave me a look that said "Why did she have to come?"

Soon Faye decided she needed a fag and I went out with her to the patio where smokers jostled and chatted or just stared out into the dark. Faye lit up and stood with one leg resting against the wall behind her. She exhaled with feeling.

"No offence, Ails, but this is shite."

"Yeah, sorry. I didn't know he was bringing Andy. I've never seen him before in my life."

"Well, I have." Faye flicked ash on the floor. "He went out with Rachel Green's sister. He was all over her. They slept together then he gave her the heave-ho. Thinks he's God's gift."

43

I tried not to be impressed by Faye's fund of gossip or Andy's sexual adventures.

"Look," I said, "just go if you like. I'll make an excuse."

"Och, Ails, I feel a traitor. But you don't really need me here, do you?"

I gave Faye a push. "Just go, *yah dirty rat*." Vi was big on old films. Faye responded with a bony hug. "Cheers, Ails," and squirmed away between the smokers.

Back in the bar I sat down again. Ian and Andy were unfazed by Faye's disappearing act. Perhaps they'd expected it.

"Sudden illness in the family?" Andy enquired.

"Something like that."

"And you're off to uni too then?"

"Yeah, next month."

His close-cut black hair was flecked with the occasional strand of white. He'd look good as a barrister. His eyes were light grey.

"So what subject are you doing?" I was flattered by his interest but he was less than impressed with my reply. "English? What'll you do with that then?"

I shrugged. "I might teach. My mum was a teacher. And my dad." I felt an unusual desire to stick up for the teaching profession.

Andy was underwhelmed. "A family of English teachers? Is there a name for that?"

I could feel myself getting hot. "My mum taught history."

"And yer father?"

I could have kicked myself for getting into this conversation. "Art." I tried not to watch Andy too closely, wondering if he knew much about my family history, such as it was.

"Well," Ian came to my rescue. He might not have been a candidate for Mensa, but he knew when a change of subject was required. "Her dad's off the scene and good riddance." He then asked Andy some football related question and they were off. I was happy to keep stumm.

History and art. I could have done history; but art? Never. I hated it, even the smell of the art room with its dried up paint brushes turned me off. I thought of the photo of Dad in the library. Whatever traits I'd inherited, an artistic streak wasn't one of them. I had hated those lessons, with Jenny Carstairs looking over my shoulder, exuding a musty blend of French perfume and art room dust as I gouged or moulded or slapped some paint around. "Och, that's a very good effort, Ailsa."

Jenny had been there for years and by then was head of the department. She would have known Dad, probably been his boss. Her interest in me was another example of the sympathy vote, the consolation prize for being the daughter of Tom Robertson and his skeery wife.

Andy was making a move. "I'll leave you two lovebirds to it." He shrugged on his jacket. "See you, Ian. Nice to meet you… Ailsa." He left a tiny gap before my name, filing me away for future reference. I was gratified, then felt a stab of guilt.

I rounded on Ian. "Why on earth did you ask him along? Faye was really pissed off."

Ian drew back and lifted his hands in self-defence, as if I were a firework with the touch-paper lit. "Keep

45

the heid! I never asked him to come. I was here early and he bought me a pint. His dad's a friend of my dad. I don't really know him that well."

He went to the bar and brought another drink. When he came back I apologised but he was already laughing. "Bloody hell," he said, "I can see I'll have to watch myself with you."

We sat in silence until the awkwardness left by Faye and Andy got lost in the beery gloom.

"Andy's brother, how old is he?" I asked. He might have been at the High when Dad was there. I was interested in how much Andy might know about Dad, assuming he had made the connection.

"No idea. Older than Andy. Lives through in Glasgow." He finished his drink. "Sorry about Faye. I expect we'll get on better next time."

Ian was nice that way. He would try to get on with Faye, for my sake. But how much did Faye really matter?

He took me home in the van and we lingered over our customary kiss, tongues in a fight to the death. Despite its bad moments, the evening in the bar had had its effect. In my mind I turned over some of my recent discoveries. Andy slept with girls; Faye had gone nearly all the way. Ian's hand was on the hem of my vest top, poised to lift it. This was where I would always wriggle away and bring things to a swift conclusion.

Tonight I stayed put. Ian's hand darted under my t-shirt and found my bra with the speed of a heat-seeking missile. When his thumb brushed my nipple, it felt like an electric shock. The reaction sent a signal back to Ian and he did it again, flicking the switch, over and over.

Oh God, I was getting the hang of this all right. I forced myself to push him away.

Ian took it like a man. No arguments. He leaned over and kissed me, nice and soft.

"When can I see you?" But his voice was hoarse, as if he meant "When can we do it?"

I wanted to take his hand and put it back where it had been, or maybe somewhere else, lower, warmer, wetter. I was having trouble finding a reply, but he had one of his own.

"My mum and dad are away next weekend," he said. "We could go back to our place." His hand was in the small of my back, keeping me against him. I blotted out the thought of an empty house with big soft beds and Ian ready to please me.

"Maybe," I said. "Soon."

This time I ran for the house.

In bed, I touched my breast where Ian had and a few other places for good measure. I thought of Andy Chalmers' nice tight arse. Law School was in Edinburgh. That would make him a student too, and one with more money and contacts than me or Faye. Then I pictured Ian's puppy dog eyes if I took off for Edinburgh now, just when he thought he was getting me into bed.

CHAPTER SEVEN

Of all my childhood fantasies, my favourite was the one where Mum found happiness with a doctor, a doctor who loved her enough to go off and find a miracle cure. But the doctor in my mixed-up head had a habit of morphing into Dad, and so the dream came to an abrupt and unsatisfactory end. How rubbish is that, not even to have a decent fantasy? At least with Dr Archibald I wouldn't have to worry about romantic entanglements. And I thought a woman might be easier to talk to.

The houses in the street were set back from the road with long front gardens, all of them doctors or dentists or solicitors. I recognised the one I was looking for by the mossy path that led up to the door and the sundial that stood on the lawn. This contraption had always given me the creeps. On a sunny day it might have had a purpose, but in the shade its long finger was robbed of a purpose, its numerals meaningless and arcane.

Inside, my name was ticked off in a reception area, recently carpeted (judging by the smell) in blue and beige. There was still a stained glass window at the turn of the baronial stair and squeaky floorboards in the top corridor. A door led into the waiting room and I knew that another came out from the surgery into a back corridor, so that patients entering from the waiting room seemed to disappear completely. I think that might be why I'd always tried to stay healthy, the idea of going in there and not coming out.

When I was called in, a woman with a heavy face and frizzy hair was staring at a screen and typing. The desk was bare of everything except doctorly accessories: a stethoscope, a blood-pressure gauge, and a calendar from a pharmaceutical company. A nameplate told me this was Dr Helen Archibald. I sat down on one of the hard chairs, aware of a narrow bed behind me with a curtain rail around it. The doctor finished typing on her PC before looking up. The thick lenses in her glasses made her eyes look huge.

"Yes?"

She didn't argue with my request for contraception, but brought up a new screen with many boxes to be ticked. This process was followed by a lengthy lecture and a clutch of leaflets on everything from chlamydia to German Measles. Eventually a prescription was printed out.

"Actually, there was something else." I didn't quite know how to put it. I'd answered all her questions without hesitation, but I had a bigger one.

"I'm worried about my mum. She said you were doing tests."

This at least made it sound like I was a concerned daughter rather than shit-scared on my own behalf.

Helen Archibald frowned, presumably putting me and Mum together for the first time. "Really, Ailsa. I can't discuss details of another patient, even a relative."

I'd been relying on the old confidentiality thing to stop her blabbing to Mum about my visit, but now realised it worked both ways.

"But what if it's something that affects me. And people I... have contact with." *Immune system.* I knew the score. I could live with Mum and not catch anything, but what if she'd had it before I was born?

Helen Archibald looked puzzled. "Sorry? I'm not following, I'm afraid." She glanced up at the clock on the wall. I was over-running my time.

"Mum mentioned immune system. If she's HIV, I could be too."

HIV. Just saying the word gave it an awful reality. Luckily the doctor was unfazed, although she gave a big blink, and her eyebrows went up above the frames of her glasses. "Oh dear, I see now."

But she wasn't laughing. In fact I got the impression it was something she should have thought of herself and I'd just reminded her. She frowned and tapped her pudgy fingers on the edge of her keyboard as she considered which words to use.

"Right," she said. "There are very many conditions associated with the immune system of which AIDS is certainly one, but I have no reason to think it's something you personally should worry about. And from the information you've given me, there's no reason to think you're carrying any sexually transmitted infection." She sat back, happy with her textbook response. "Though you should, of course, be aware of symptoms that might indicate such an infection in you or a sexual partner."

"But what about Mum?"

She sighed, as if ruing the day she took the Hippocratic oath. "If your mother had AIDS, it would almost certainly be revealed in the tests I'm doing, but that's not what I expect to find."

Dr A got up and showed me out towards the back stairs. I was pleased neither Mum's future nor my own was under imminent threat. And soon I was going to make Ian happy, very happy indeed. With a skip in my step I turned back past the waiting room, just so that any one left in there would know I had got out alive.

Faye's term at Napier started earlier than mine at the university. She would move into the flat first and check out the other flatmates before I arrived the following weekend. She'd already packed most of her stuff and her room looked abandoned, the familiar posters barely clinging to the walls on dried up Blu-Tack. She had bought some vodka and poured me a shot. She lit up a fag too, but I passed on the offer.

"Can I take my bike?" I asked.

Faye looked doubtful. "I don't think there'll be room. I don't know why you do it anyway."

"To reduce the size of my arse."

"Och, it's fine, it's a fine arse."

"Is not."

"Is so."

Faye jumped off the bed and pulled me up with her so that we could see ourselves in the mirror. She was still like a stick and, despite the hours of pedalling, I still had a bosom and a bum.

Faye sighed. "You're gonna knock them dead, girl."

I was going to argue and then I thought of Ian. He was living proof that someone fancied me. I thought of

Andy Chalmers and the way his grey eyes had held mine as he left the bar. Would others do the same? Not proven.

Faye raised her shot glass and called a toast, "Freedom!" then flopped back on the bed. I took a swig without speaking and did the same, but Faye must have read my mind. She got up on her elbow and looked down at me. "Ails, you're not gonna run out on me, are you?"

"No fear. It's just I might come back sometimes, to see Ian. Just for the odd weekend. We're getting on okay."

I was taking the Pill now. Faye probably was too, but no one was mentioning it, as if we were both shy of the topic.

Faye sighed. "Ails, you've got this all wrong. You need to dump him. Plenty more fish in the…" A burp wrapped the rest of the sentence in vodka gases.

I looked away. Part of me thought the same. Edinburgh would be full of men with rangy shoulders and cute bums. Andy Chalmers was out of my league, but there might be boys who would grow up just like him. Part of me couldn't wait to get out of here. But then there was Ian with his comfy embrace, his big brown eyes, and the promise of a soft rug to lie on.

We had two more shots each. Faye reached out and took my hand.

"You need to cut loose. Forget fish-boy. Home-boy. Boy of the big bum. You can do better."

"Yeh, you're right."

Soon Faye was out for the count. I lay there, trying to imagine myself in Edinburgh, at a party, the kind where you could be anyone you liked, where sex would be on offer straight away, on a narrow bed or hard carpet tiles. Excitement, danger even. I wanted some of that.

With Faye's elbow in my back I couldn't sleep, not properly. I hadn't seen Andy since the night in the pub, but I had been thinking about Jenny Carstairs. In our time, Faye and I had done quite a bit of speculating as to what Dad had done and who he'd done it with. Jenny had been high on the list. Faye said that teachers having an affair were bound to cause a stramash. "He would have been for the chop, just for that."

But Jenny Carstairs, if it had been her, had kept her job until only a few years ago when she had left of her own volition to "do art for real", as she had said at the customary send-off. So why had she been nice to me? "You're father would be proud of you, you know." What did I have to be proud of? For managing to grow up without him? For staying with Mum? For trying to paint a picture? Had I imagined the next thing she had said? "You're father would be proud of you, you know. Don't believe all you hear."

I slept for a while but woke up in the night, shivering with cold and a hangover. I shook Faye and said I was going home.

On the way the streets were deserted. Only two cars passed and when they did, I found myself stepping back into the shadows, cowering against the walls of high buildings. At least Edinburgh wouldn't be like this. There would be places to go and people to go with. Wouldn't there?

I pushed open the front door. At the top of the stairs, out of habit, I stopped and listened to the rhythm of Mum's breathing.

Monday. My job had finished. Ian sent me a text: "*What night are you free?*"

Mum watched me read it. "Problem?"

I snapped the phone shut. "No."

"Started your packing?"

"No rush. I'll start tomorrow." I looked around for something to do and picked up the library books I'd had since the day Faye left for the camp. "I'll take these back. Get them out of the way. I'll go and see Ian on the way back."

In the few weeks since I'd been to the library, the exhibition had changed and the foyer was full of paintings mounted on coloured display boards. It was a competition for local schools and these were the finalists. The outright winner would be chosen by "celebrated local artist" Jenni Carstairs. With an "i". Jenny had done art for real after all. It felt like an omen. The truth about Dad, the good, the bad or the ugly, couldn't be that hard to find. It was just that I'd never had the guts to look for it.

Inside, I returned the novels and asked the librarian if I could look at old copies of the *Press*.

The woman wasn't in a mood to help. "It's online from nineteen ninety-seven. The computers are over there."

Dad wasn't going to be in the local paper after he had left, but to keep her happy I went online and did a Google search for Dad. Among the nine thousand and ninety-nine Tom Robertsons there was one artist working in Carolina, aged thirty, and posting on Myspace. No such luck. I went back to the desk.

"I need the years before that. Probably nineteen ninety-five or nineteen ninety-six." The woman disappeared and a younger guy came out. He said I'd have to use microfilm. The films and the reader were in a separate room.

He left me alone there with the reels for the years in question. There was a handle that birled the film until you got to the right place, like an old fruit machine but without the cherries. As I sped through the weekly issues, a hundred pictures flashed past: traffic accidents, house fires, wedding photos.

This was stupid. There had to be an index. I wound all the way to the end and found it there. *Robertson, Thomas. November 29th, 2b, December 6th 4c.*

Page two. It must have been something big to be near the front. I had to rewind back to November and turned it too fast so that I went too far, then changed direction again until the thing juddered to a halt on the right date. I found page two. None of the headlines looked likely. Maybe I'd always been kidding myself. I was going to check the index again when one of them caught my eye, and not in a good way.

CHAPTER EIGHT

"High School teacher on sexual assault charge"

It looked like a tabloid headline, but this was the local rag. My grip on the winding handle tightened until the sweat made my fingers slide off. It was way before my time, but it made me feel sick, even before I got to the name.

"Art teacher Tom Robertson of 36 Erskine Place appeared before magistrates on a charge of indecently assaulting and raping a thirteen year-old pupil at her home. The girl cannot be named for legal reasons."

Tom Robertson was my dad. He had held me up to the window to look at the birds, taken me swimming, read books and done puzzles. But all the time he had been… And the address, our address, the place we called home. He hadn't just abused a girl, he'd dragged us into it too. He might as well have marked the house with a cross, the kind that meant "unclean".

Things were sliding into place, a jigsaw of blue skies and treats and smiles turning into a slimy mess. The way people looked at me, the way they never mentioned Dad. It wasn't because of Mum. Well, not in the way I had thought. People pitied me, not because

Mum was a freak, but because of Dad. Laura Patterson's family, Jenni Carstairs, nearly everyone I could think of had only ever taken pity on the daughter of a rapist, a kiddyfiddler. Let's not pretend: a paedophile.

There was a movement behind me.

"Are you all right?" It was the library man.

I moved the film on so that he couldn't see what I'd been reading.

"We're locking up early," he said. "But you can have another five minutes."

"Thanks." I didn't turn round. My cheeks were wet with tears.

The girl had been thirteen. She would have been in the Third Year. At thirteen, Faye and I liked Take That and played their albums in Faye's room at full volume, dancing and shouting out the words until Vi knocked on the door, yelling at us to keep the noise down. Boys were objects of speculation rather than experience. Faye thought Robin Gourlay had a cute bum and nice eyelashes, but went out with him and reported back on sweaty hands and bad breath. I had a crush on Mr Aitken who taught maths. If he asked me a question I blushed and couldn't get the words out. When he bumped into me in a crowded corridor my stomach lurched. But what if the bump had been deliberate? What if his hand, patting my shoulder in apology had hesitated, suggested a caress?

I made myself go back and read the whole report again, but nothing had changed. It had been no trick of the light, or nightmare that would disappear in the blink of an eye. Dad was still there on the page, accused of the same crime.

57

I moved the film on to the second entry, heavy-hearted. But by the sixth of December, only a week later, Tom Robertson was old news. On page four I read that the case had failed through lack of evidence; the charges had been dropped. So he hadn't been sent down. He'd gone on with his life and paid for his guilt through the Edinburgh lawyer.

Outside, I banged my hand against the iron railing that flanked the library steps until my knuckles were red. I let the wind blow away my tears, leaving my skin taut and sore. I'd been stupid. I'd wanted to believe that Dad was a good guy, when all along the truth had been lying there, for anybody to see. As for evidence, I had read about how women panicked and took a bath, or how juries just took the side of the man. Rape happened all the time, convictions were as rare as hen's teeth.

I broke into a run, along Canmore Street, down the New Row and left past the doctor's into the public park. It was mostly downhill and I'd barely broken sweat. Mothers with buggies were loitering by the swings. I didn't want company and turned to the path that bordered the railway line, just in time to see the back of the Edinburgh train as it pulled away.

Edinburgh. I could cut and run and make a fresh start just like I had planned all along. Nothing had to change, not really. I could go home and start packing right now. A train came from the other direction and went past me heading to the towns of Fife – Kelty, Cardenden, Cowdenbeath. I brushed the thought of Ian aside. Before long Ian would know too, if he didn't already. That's how it worked. Too bad. I liked him, but I wouldn't be coming back. I would go on the run to a new life, with new people.

Faye. Like litter on a railway track, she derailed my thoughts as they sped away to imagined freedom. Faye had never liked Dad, or what she knew of him. She had sussed something was wrong, warned me against digging too deeply, winkling out the truth. Now I'd have to tell her she'd been right. The thought of putting it into words turned my stomach.

But Faye was already gone. Maybe Faye didn't need to know. And that would be better. Anyone who knew might tell someone who didn't. Not out of mischief, but just in a careless remark, a cheeky response when the drink was flowing. These things happened. It would be easier if things with Faye stayed just as they were. In Edinburgh we'd have better things to think about than parents.

Rounding the corner towards home, I slowed to a walk. Mum had been here in this house when it happened, when it hit the papers. Maybe Dad had still been here too. No wonder she kept herself to herself. Who could blame her?

I couldn't deny I'd resented Mum's illness and the burden it laid on me. I'd suspected her of playing helpless or making up symptoms. But now I knew it was for real. Never mind the girl that Tom had raped. Mum, saddled with a kid and struck down by ailments, mental or physical, was his real victim.

Before I opened the door, I tried to compose myself. For her it was over and done with. What was the point in raking it all up?

She was in the back, reading the paper, her white coat thrown over the arm of a chair. On an impulse I went over and put my arms around her heavy shoulders, absorbing the sticky sweetness left behind by the last treatment session.

She laughed in surprise. "What's this about?"

"Nothing. Just hope the tests come good. It's time they sorted you out."

"The doctor rang me."

"And?"

"So far the tests are inconclusive. She's giving me more steroids – different ones – and doing more tests. Something that's hard to pin down, she says."

I went upstairs and started opening cupboards and drawers and then lay down on the bed, too overwhelmed to think about going anywhere. Even if I'd been able to read, I'd left myself without any books. I turned my face to the pillow and gave in to the pictures of Dad that were teeming through my head, on the rampage, like a virus out of control. Sleazy images of girls with older men, salacious poses, words I barely understood, *cunnilingus*, *pederasty*, they all came to life now that I had someone to attach them to.

Think about something else. Someone else.

Ian.

Ian was good-hearted, comfortable and eager as a puppy. I curled my thoughts against him like a lamb seeking shelter from the storm.

But Ian would have to go. His parents might have told him already. If not, someone else would spread the poison. Some crony of his mum's, or a mate out to cause mischief. A mate like Andy Chalmers, whom I had thought might fancy me. Did Andy know? Did Dad's notoriety actually make me more interesting? Anything was possible.

It was easier thinking about the night in the East Port than thinking about Dad. What had been said about him? I wished I'd paid more attention. It had come up, I was sure, but Ian had deflected the conversation. Come to think of it, any other time Dad had been mentioned, Ian had always changed the subject.

I sat up, clutching the pillow against me. It didn't matter if Andy knew or not. If Andy had tried telling Ian, Ian would change the subject. Because Ian already knew.

The knowledge rushed in at me like a new gust of wind. The grapevine had got to him already. But the wind was less chill than it should be. Instead of a gale that knocked down everything in its path, it was getting warmer; a friendly breeze that melted ice and drove winter away.

Ian knew alright, but Ian didn't care. It didn't matter to him that Dad was a scumbag. Only that I should be protected from him, from other people's comments. With Ian I was safe.

Now the breeze was freshening and tossing stuff around. Faye and Edinburgh. I had thought it was best to get away, to be where no one knew about me or Tom or anything he had done. But that would never work. The truth would come out, sooner or later. Things would fall apart. I had been with Ian for a while now and everything was fine, it was great. There was nothing more to be known.

Later I watched as Mum cooked lunch. I guessed that this doctor had given her some kind of hope. Some days, like today, she moved more easily. But she was laboured and stiff compared to anyone else of her age.

61

"Let me do that," I said.

"Do what?"

"Make the dinner."

She stood back to let me take over peeling the carrots. "What's this in aid of?"

"I'm not going to Edinburgh."

Her reaction was silent but tangible, a wave of negative energy in the air. I rushed to counteract it. "I mean, I'll go to uni. But I'll stay at home with you."

"How can you?"

"It's what you did, didn't you? And there are plenty of trains."

"I suppose." She had reclaimed the carrots and the knife and was attacking them with extra vigour. "But I thought you wanted to be away."

"Staying here I'll save money. And probably get more work done."

She clapped the lid on the pan and lit the gas under it. "Is this about Ian?"

"Well, a bit. He's nice. We get on." And we were about to get on a lot better. "But in the week we'll both be busy. I'll mainly see him at weekends."

"Well… if it's what you want."

I stepped up behind her. This hugging thing was surprisingly easy. I held her again and rested my cheek on hers.

"I suppose. If you're sure. It'll be nice to have you here."

Elation flowed over me. I had so nearly got it wrong. Maybe finding out about Dad had been no bad thing. "I'll ring up today and sort out the flat. They'll find someone else for it."

"What does Faye think about this?"

It looked like our auld alliance had come to an end. But Faye had never liked Ian, and soon she'd have new friends of her own. My mind was made up. "I'll tell her now. She'll understand."

A voice inside warned me: *like hell she will.*

CHAPTER NINE

Once I had started at uni I gave up the exercise bike. It took me ten minutes exactly to run up to the station in time for the early train, and at the other end, fifteen more over the High Street and past the National Library up to George Square. On the way back I might come along Chambers Street and down the Bridges followed by a run down Waverley Steps; either way it was enough exercise for me.

The train was an experience in itself. Mixed in with the commuters there were other students, most of them older, some doing part-time degrees. One woman, Barbara, was on my course. She had done an Access course at night school just to be accepted. She'd split up with her husband and had two kids whom she left with her mum. Whichever of us was first at the station bought two coffees-to-go, milk no sugar. We often got the same train home, and on a Friday we celebrated with Danish pastries.

Barbara had a different perspective. It was as if she had come to her own opinions instead of just absorbing them from teachers or TV. She told me about her ex who had a go at her for spending time reading. I told her about Mum and Ian and Faye. "Go your own way," she told me.

Every night as the train swung round the bend past the gasworks I could see the outline of the High School fading into the dusk. I'd been there for six years but it seemed like a long time ago. Maybe I was getting to be like Barbara, already a mature student. At home, I had my tea and then switched on the computer. As long as I nipped in to the library now and then, I could get most of the work done here.

For the first few weeks I was too busy to see much of Ian, but one Thursday he rang up and said his mum and dad were going away again for a weekend break. We could go out for a meal on Saturday night and back to his place. I hadn't told him about the Pill in so many words, but some things don't need saying.

I wore the most expensive perfume in Mum's collection and my very best undies. Anticipating future action, I tried not to eat too much, but it all slipped down too easily.

Outside the restaurant he hooked his pinkie round mine. "Come on," he said, "let's get back."

In Ian's hallway a gust of floral room-fragrance eclipsed any lingering memory of the Bengal Brasserie. In the lounge, he switched on wall lights to reveal a sideboard and bookcase crowded with coloured glass concoctions and china figurines. Photos of Ian – the only child – beamed at me from every wall.

I took off my shoes, dipping my toes into the thick pile carpet. "Nice." I was trying to ignore the visual assault and the aftertaste of curry in my throat.

Ian put his arms around me. "Mmm, I think so too."

As we kissed I let his mouth wander down my neck towards my cleavage where he pulled back my top and sent his tongue foraging under my bra.

This moment had been a long time coming. I didn't want to let it go, but something wasn't working.

"Put the lights out," I said, hoping darkness would distract me from the décor. Ian did as asked and led me to the sofa, where he lifted my arms and removed my top altogether. I lay down and he sank his face into my naked bosom with a groan of satisfaction. I lay there stroking his hair and feeling his hard-on, wishing away the rising tide of nausea.

"Sorry!" I threw him off me and ran for the downstairs loo where I was soon on my knees, staring at another Airwick dispenser and ridding myself of a large portion of chicken jalfrezi.

Outside Ian was asking if I was okay.

"In a minute," I said when I thought I could. "I'm just clearing up."

I managed to leave the place respectable. At least the curry had missed the fluffy toilet-seat cover and the matching apricot towels, but I still felt queasy. There was nothing for it but to go home.

In the van, we were both silent: Ian disappointed, me bloody furious. Here I was, young, free, single and still a virgin. Worst of all, I could find nothing and no one to blame other than my own greed. The restaurant, as Ian reminded me, had a five-star food hygiene certificate and was clearly beyond reproach.

"Sorry," I said when I could find my voice. "When do your folks get back?"

"Tomorrow afternoon."

"Right."

He shifted at the wheel. "I saw Andy Chalmers today. He's having a party."

"In Edinburgh?"

"No. In Torryburn. End of the month."

It had come to light in the intervening weeks that Andy was the son of Eddie Chalmers, a local builder well known for charitable donations and contesting planning decisions. Andy Chalmers wasn't just good looking but well-off too. But this didn't sound like a family affair, and it was high time I had my share of partying.

On the Saturday afternoon before the party, I went up to the shop to see Ian. It was one of those November days when daylight struggles to disperse a constant smir of rain. Christmas lights hung in lifeless black garlands over the High Street. It was mild but it was winter all right, not a crisp and optimistic winter but the damp variety where everyone has flu by February.

Mackay's was as busy as hell. Either people were stocking up their freezers or they were getting all their omega three in advance of the forthcoming turkeyfest. The smell of fish was strong but satisfyingly fresh, better than the more human aromas I could make out from the throng of customers.

Ian and Gordon, his dad, were hard at it, but there was still a queue. I could also see that they didn't have a system, probably because they didn't usually need one. They could have done with another body, but I guessed Rhona Mackay didn't wrap fish on a Saturday or any other day of the week. "She's very smart," Mum had said, which I somehow assumed referred to her fashion sense rather than her intellect.

I went behind the counter and the men were so busy they hardly noticed. "You two just wrap it up and write the price on," I said. "I'll do the till." It wasn't as fancy as the one I had used at the garage but I could see how it worked.

Gordon Mackay barely looked round. "You'll need an overall," he said. I found one at the back, through the door that lead to the storeroom. Pulling it on and adding the natty white cap that hung with it, I tried not to feel I was morphing into old Mrs Mackay.

For an hour or so they passed me neat packets of cold fish. I rang up the money and handed them over. It was clean work and it made me think of the trip to Pittenweem. I was part of the food chain now. When somebody came to collect an order, Ian went to the fridge in the storeroom and came back with a whole salmon. "You'll have tae wrap this one," he said to me. He laid it in my arms. "Weigh it and use that cling-film."

I put the fish down. Its cold eye was looking at me and so I didn't like to cover its face. In the end, I left the head exposed and wrapped the whole lot loosely in plain white paper.

At four o'clock Gordon disappeared into the back and brought back mugs of tea, handing one each to me and Ian. "She's a worker all right," he said.

Ian was gulping down the tea. Gordon turned to me. "We could do with you on a Saturday. The other girl's just left."

I looked at Ian and he shrugged. "Up to you," he said.

"Sometimes I have uni work."

Gordon nodded. "See what you think. Between now and Christmas we'll be pushed, that's for sure."

The end of term was only one essay away. "Okay, I could do it till then."

"Great," Gordon said.

I was still hanging up my hat when Gordon came and slipped a couple of tenners into my hand, which I thought was pretty good for two hours. An alliance with the Mackays might have its advantages.

"I hear you're off to the Chalmers' tonight," Gordon said. "I'll give you a lift out there if you like. You can get a taxi back."

Ian winked at me over Gordon's head, indicating he and Rhona had little idea of what Andy's party might entail. "Thanks, Dad, that'll be great."

I was sadly deficient in party experience, but I reckoned that this one would be the real deal. Thanks to my shift as a fishmonger I even had some cash, so I nipped into the shopping centre and got something I thought would make a bit of a statement. My chosen outfit was short, black and didn't leave much to the imagination.

At home I had some silver sandals and an assortment of funky jewellery. I got out the curling tongs and put my hair up at one side and let it hang down at the other. I didn't hold back with the make-up.

I told myself I wanted Ian to know I was making an effort. I was also thinking about Andy Chalmers. All through my first term I'd been keeping my eyes peeled for him in Edinburgh, but trainee lawyers were clearly a breed apart. I'd never as much as bumped into him.

I had a quick swig of vodka to get me in the mood, and when I heard a car pull up outside, teetered downstairs. A glance through the glass door showed I'd got it wrong. The car on kerb belonged to a neighbour.

Mum called from the back where she was checking her Avon orders. I had no option but to go in and sit down.

When she saw me Mum raised her eyebrows, but then, most people would have.

"Oh aye, off to have a good time, I see."

The scene around her was horribly familiar. At Christmas the usual toiletries were supplemented with cuddly toys, novelty clocks, fluffy slippers and an assortment of lurid underwear. Anything that was over-ordered or didn't get paid for found a home in my Christmas stocking. This is why I was rarely short of a teddy bear key-ring or a black bra embellished with pink hearts.

She was still looking me up and down. "I just hope Ian's ready for it."

I felt the need to elaborate. "We're going to a party, at Torryburn."

"Torryburn?" She looked up, biro poised over her list. "Who do you know there?"

I was startled. "Andy Chalmers. Ian knows him. We had a drink a week or two ago." I could have added "What's it to you?"

The bell rang. "That'll be them." I got up to go.

"Tell Ian to come in and say hello."

"He'll not want to wait."

"Just ask him in," Mum said. "I'll not bite." I reminded myself this was my first boyfriend. Maybe she was right to take a stand.

I was gratified to see that Ian had on a good coat and looked every bit the son of local business. He took one look at me and gave a quiet wolf whistle. I dragged him inside. "Mum says come in, it'll only be a minute."

I took him as far as the living room door where he nodded, "Hiya, Mrs Robertson."

"Come in, Ian. It's about time we said hello. I hear you're off to Torryburn."

"Uh-huh. Dad's outside. He's giving us a lift."

"The Chalmers boys are older than you, aren't they?"

"That's right, but Eddie and my dad are in the Rotary."

"And will they be there, Eddie and Irene?"

"No, it's just Andy. His mum and dad are away."

"Och, yes," she said. "I didn't think. Enjoy yourselves, anyway. I can see Ailsa's in the mood."

It was Mum's mood I was worried about, but it looked like she'd said her piece. She went back to her pile of Christmas tat and I got Ian out of there as fast as I could. But it had been disconcerting. Since when had Mum been on first name terms with the Chalmers family?

CHAPTER TEN

Gordon turned off the main road into what was barely more than a lane.

"Just drop us here," Ian said. "We'll walk up."

The car drew up next to stone gateposts. Ian took my arm as I stepped gingerly off the tarred road onto a gravel drive pock-marked with weeds.

I wasn't dressed for a trek. "How far is it?"

"It's only up here," he said. "Didn't want Dad nosing around."

The house was stone-built, three storeys high with big bay windows on both sides of the ground floor and attic windows in the top. It wasn't quite on the scale of the doctor's surgery but not far off. If there had been a garden it had disappeared under the gravel that widened in front of the house to provide a big parking space, currently empty. A modern double garage was tucked to one side, surrounded by dark shrubbery. I imagined a gleaming Merc or BMW tucked up safely in there while Eddie and Irene had a taxi to the airport.

When Ian rang the bell it had a persistent mechanical buzz that sounded too loud in the misty night air. The house was in total darkness.

"Not exactly jumping, is it?" It was still blowing through rain, so I cooried in against Ian. "Maybe they've gone to the pub?" I said, hoping we might do the same.

The rattle of a loud but unhealthy engine emerged from the rhythmic whine of traffic on the main road and two cars tore up the drive, scrambling to a halt on the gravel beside us. Andy Chalmers rolled down the window of a mini.

"Ian, you're early, man."

Before he could answer, Andy and the girl beside him heaved themselves out and went round to the boot, which Andy opened to reveal a stash of cans and bottles. He was wearing a long scarf over a shirt and had a fag in his mouth. He handed me a pack of cans without even looking at me and handed the next lot to Ian. Behind us, the occupants of the other car were going through the same routine, chums of Andy's who had been tempted across the Bridge by the thought of booze and free central heating.

Andy went round the corner of the house and let us in through a back door, where a narrow scullery led into an impressively modern kitchen in country-house style.

Andy was in charge and enjoying it. He started stacking cans on an island unit.

"Get to it then, children. Let's get this show on the road."

Apart from Ian and me, there were three blokes and two girls. The blonde girl who'd come in with Andy was wearing jeans and a lacy top. Her glossy mouth had a discontented curl, as if Fife on a Saturday night wasn't her idea of fun. The other one had spiky hair and leggings under a denim skirt and made me think of

Faye. I pulled my long cardi around my smart frock so as not to look overdressed, and took a swig from the can offered by Ian.

There was a barrage of phoning and texting as people arrived in groups, all at the back door. The place got warmer; the drink flowed. I stopped caring that my hair had unravelled in the rain and my shoes were OTT. This was a crowd and I was in it. When people spoke to me I said I was a student at Edinburgh, which I was, though maybe not in the way they thought. After a while, Andy disappeared with the blonde girl. The sound of a new indie band came welling into the kitchen.

"Come on," Ian said.

The other room was dark and filled with music but we were the first to arrive. Straight away he put his arms around me and we started a clumsy slow dance in which he pressed himself against me and kissed my neck. Looking over his shoulder I saw we were in one of the rooms with the big bay windows. The long curtains were open, and above the tall trees that surrounded the house there was enough light reflected from the orangey sky for me to make out leather furniture and a huge mirror over a fireplace. In it, I watched Ian and me turning in wonky circles. Compared to Rhona's lounge, there was a tasteful absence of clutter. I breathed in the tang of leather and well-polished wood, the smell of money. On the walls there were framed landscapes, but not the usual views of hills and valleys. These were modern and blotchy with chunky shapes in the foreground. When there was a break in the music I broke away from Ian to take a closer look.

One of them showed rocks, big rocks, like standing stones. Another was of flat fields with swathes of grey and yellow grass that looked like an angry sea. I guessed they might be originals. In the corner of each there were initials, a professional signature. Ian was beside me.

"Who's I.C.?" As soon as I said it, I realised. "Irene Chalmers, I suppose."

I'd never set eyes on Andy's mother, but I imagined her florid and bosomy, drifting around in bright colours, playing the amateur artist. She'd probably done evening classes, or gone on one of those painting holidays abroad. I was impressed, though. The paintings had a kind of strength. Better than I could have done, better than most people.

Ian squeezed my arm. "I need a piss. Don't go away."

I dropped into the leathery embrace of an armchair, leaned back and closed my eyes. I was no more than pleasantly drunk, but the night was young. I let myself drift in a warm sea of alcohol and music, wondering if Ian and I were going to have sex, and if so how we would do it.

"Miss Robertson, I presume?"

Even with my eyes closed, I knew it was Andy. I pictured myself, legs splayed and arms flung out, but resisted the impulse to move or open my eyes. There was no shame in being half cut.

"Yer man's abandoned you?"

I opened my eyes slowly. "Looks like it."

"Can't have that," Andy said and extended an arm. I hooked my fingers through his and let him pull me out of the chair.

We started dancing, not close, not even touching, just kind of weaving around each other. The music had changed to something slow and a bit retro. Andy was watching me but I danced for myself. Despite his presence I felt alone in the darkness. The old Ailsa, slumped in the chair with her eyes closed, was watching as this new one took her place, ready to let her hair down, ready to live.

I circled my hips and held my arms above my head, turning and swaying. On the periphery of my imagined circle, Andy seemed to catch my mood, holding out a hand for me to turn, but letting me choose the moves. I slid my arms down my sides and arched my back until I knew he'd stopped dancing and was just watching me. I liked that, holding the floor.

When I saw Ian at the door I didn't even think of stopping, but moved towards him, knowing the spotlight was still on me, and took his hand, drawing him into the dance, my dance, going through all the moves again, until Andy turned away and left the room, closing the door behind him.

As soon as we were alone, Ian took charge, backing me over to the wall and kissing me hard. Dancing in front of Andy had turned me on and now the need for sex was running through me like water. My legs no longer wanted to hold me up, but I had Ian on one side and the wall on the other. With one arm around my shoulders he used the other to hoist my skirt up over my bum and reach between my legs. He was breathing like a train. I felt for his flies and released him like I'd been doing it all my life, moving my pink lace thong aside to guide him in. He was wet and so was I. It was going to be fine.

"Wait." His voice came out like a growl, and he jerked away from me, delving in his pockets.

"No," I said. "It's okay. I'm sorted." I arched my back, my palms flat against the wall and lifted myself up for him. This was how I wanted it, hard and fast. As he buried himself in me he gave such a groan I thought it might be all over, but he steadied himself. I locked my hands around his neck and closed my eyes. The music had stopped and there was only the sound of our breathing, together and alone, welcoming the darkness, clambering towards the light at the end of this hot dark tunnel.

Just as I thought I might find what I was looking for, Ian gave a feral grunt that had to mean his journey was at an end.

"Christ," he said. Then, "Shit."

He grabbed me closer to him and I felt him slide out. My own breath was coming in gulps and I thought of reaching for him again but something told me my time was up. I clung to him, savouring what moment there had been. I was wondering how much noise we'd made when a car came up the drive, its lights strafing the room and illuminating everything in it, including us. We flattened ourselves against the wall.

"What the fuck," Ian said.

"It's all right. They didn't see," I told him. Or if they had they probably dismissed it as some kind of hallucination. His head was against my hair. He was saying "fuck" quietly, over and over, then he let me go. As I hopped around he produced a clean white hanky and held it out to me, like a knight returning a favour. I tried not to laugh, thinking of Rhona Mackay ironing the cotton square, little knowing what it would be used for.

"What's wrong?" Ian said.

I shook my head. "Nothing. I need the bog. Where is it?"

Before I left he grabbed my arm and kissed me. "I love you," he said.

In the upstairs bathroom I cleaned up and sprayed myself with perfume. I didn't know what to do with the hanky so stuffed it in my handbag, making a mental note not to pull it out at the wrong moment. When I came down, Ian was sitting on the bottom of the stairs.

He got up and put his arms around me and nuzzled my ear. "All right?"

"Fine." His smell was warm and familiar. It made me think of sex. Now I knew how it smelled, how it felt, and how it might feel again. I wondered how obvious it might be we'd been shagging, then gave up.

There was a whiff of charred pizza in the air and with my need for sex sated, I was famished. I dragged Ian off to the kitchen.

By the time we had eaten, it was after midnight and the party was in melt-down. Most folks had drifted into the lounge where Ian and I had made our mark, and were lolling around, bladdered, stoned or both. We curled up for a while on a sofa and soon I guessed from Ian's weight against me that he had fallen asleep. My mouth was dry as a stone, and so I disentangled myself and went back to the kitchen for some water. Crossing the hall, I heard noises from upstairs, subdued laughter, bumps and yelps, silences that went on just too long for comfort. I hoped Irene and Eddie had locked their bedroom door, or they could be in for a nasty shock when they got back from the Christmas markets of Cologne.

The kitchen was empty and I sat down with my glass at the table strewn with paper plates. The bin was overflowing with pizza wrapping and empty cans. I was thinking I'd wake Ian and suggest going home when Andy came in and sat down opposite, frowning at me with the concentration of the deeply drunk.

"Not much left," I said. A row of empty wine bottles by the sink was flanked by two unopened cans of cider, like sentries keeping guard.

"Bad show," Andy said. "Who the fuck's running this party anyway?" This was followed by a loud burp. "Sorry."

"No problem."

The sound of my voice nudged his brain cells into action. His smile was wolfish. "Did you two enjoy your dance?"

"We did, thank you."

"And to think I never had Ian down as much of a mover…" The drink had got the better of him. He shuffled over to the sink, drank some water and picked up one of the cans. He sat down again, blinking at me. "So, young Ailsa, what were we talking about?"

I was starting to get cold, like you do when you've sobered up. I didn't feel like the girl who'd been cavorting around earlier. "We weren't, really," I said.

"But we could."

"Could what?"

"Talk about you, and your man. How did you meet him?"

79

"Just in the town. What about you? Which part of Edinburgh are you in?"

"Marchmont. My dad bought a flat. Generous to a fault, you could say."

"Sounds like it."

He ran his tongue over his lips, his mouth presumably as dry as mine. "Don't be daft. He'll sell it when I move on and make a packet. How about you?"

"I stay at home."

He raised his eyebrows. "So you can see Ian?"

I shook my head. "We only started going out in the summer." I was implying Ian needn't be a permanent fixture, though the way things were going it was looking like he might be.

"It's a lot of travelling."

"It's not too bad. I've got used to it. My mum needs looking after. Sometimes."

Andy opened the cider and offered it to me.

I shook my head. "No thanks. We'll be away in a minute."

Andy took a swig. I got up from the table and headed for the door. As I passed him I leaned over and kissed him full on the mouth, my fingers brushing his hair, savouring its wiry texture. He tasted of booze.

"Good party," I said. I felt elated and powerful. Sex with Ian had given me the ability to dispense such casual intimacy. I walked out before Andy had time to react.

The hallway was deserted but the lights were on and I noticed that the door to the room opposite the lounge was open. By now I was curious about the Chalmers family or any family with so much money to spare. I put my head around the half-open door and took in what the light from the hallway revealed.

Like the room on the other side of the hallway, this one too had a bay window, but the furnishings were more homely. Amongst the framed photos on the mantelpiece, I made out a guy who looked a bit like Andy in academic garb holding a scroll, and another of kids in a garden, huddled on top of a blue pyramid climbing frame. Normal family stuff. On the wall next to the door there was a small painting, a crude watercolour showing a house, square on, two storeys high but with a single storey to one side painted in a lighter colour, obviously an addition. The only sign of human habitation was a milk bottle on the doorstep and next to it, a blue plastic bucket with a three spades in it, the kind kids take to the beach. I went closer to look. The picture was simple and stylised, the kind of house any child might paint. Next to the door there was a nameplate, its letters way out of proportion to the building. Lauder House. I took a long hard look at it. It was definitely familiar.

CHAPTER ELEVEN

Next morning, Dr Archibald stood at the door in a mud-green padded jacket, glaring at me through her pebble-thick lenses.

"What's the problem?"

I got out of her way. "She was fine last night. Now she can't move, I think she's having trouble breathing."

The doctor's habitual frown unbent as she put me in context, then she walked in, shouldering me aside. I'd been scared enough to ring the surgery and follow a chain of recorded instructions. The grumpy human voice at the end turned out to be Dr Archibald herself. My own throat had closed up and it took me a few seconds to get the words out, but the anxiety must have registered. She said she'd come round straight away.

I followed her upstairs, her backside swaying in front of me along with a black bag that looked roomy enough to contain everything deployed in an average episode of *Casualty*. I thought Mum might need all of it.

"She was okay last night," I said. Of course I hadn't seen her since early in the evening. When I'd got back I was still high on my fix of sexual gratification. The cheeky snog with Andy was the tang of lemon icing on a rich cake. I hadn't thought about checking on Mum. This morning she hadn't got up. When I went in she couldn't even turn over. Which was why I was now shivering with fear and guilt.

"She can't really talk," I told the doctor. "Her face is swollen." The remembered fear added anger to my voice. "She's a mess."

The doctor stopped at the top of the stairs. "Which room?" was all she said.

I hovered in the doorway of the bedroom, unwilling to surrender my patient. Mum's bed was adjacent to the door and she was turned the other way, almost completely concealed in the bedclothes. I knew her face was red and her eyes swollen shut. The doctor went around the bed and drew back the covers.

"Lorraine," she spoke quietly. "Can you hear me?" Without turning away from the patient, she said, "Bring some water. Quickly."

I was pleased to have something to do. When I got back Dr Archibald was sitting on the bed. She took the glass from me and tried to get Mum to drink, but the water just dribbled over her lips and chin.

"I've given her an injection, but if she can't drink we might have to take her in and put her on a drip."

"But what's wrong?"

"It's a reaction of some kind. A severe reaction. Can someone stay with her?"

It was Sunday, no trains to catch. "I'll be here."

The doctor had been trying to support Mum's shoulders but now she laid her back on the pillows. Mum's breathing still sounded bad, but maybe not quite so noisy as before, or maybe it was just less scary with the doctor in the room.

"As soon as the swelling goes down, you have to get her to drink."

"She has lots of allergies. Why is this so bad?"

"I'm not sure. Do you know what she's taking?"

"Just what she got from you."

"I need to be sure. Where does she keep medicines?"

We went downstairs and I let her see the bathroom cabinet. There was a fair old assortment in there, but the steroids she'd been taking were by the washbasin.

The doctor picked them up and studied the label. "These are new. She got them last week. I thought they'd be more effective than what she had before."

"Depends what you mean by effective." I felt myself flush.

Dr A said nothing but put the tablets in her pocket. Then, "If she hasn't had any fluids by," she looked at her watch, "one o'clock, ring me." She handed me a card with what I assumed was a direct number. "Otherwise I'll come back tonight."

"Is there anything else I should do?"

The doctor smiled. It was a bit of a shock. "Try not to worry. She's not likely to get worse now. I've given her adrenalin and antihistamine. If she does relapse, ring for an ambulance first then ring me."

Half an hour later Mum did take a drink of water, and I sat with her until she had finished a glassful. Dr Archibald came back at five. She went upstairs by herself and I heard her and Mum talking.

"She'll be fine," the doctor said when she came back down. "Just keep up the fluids."

"What about the longer term?" I was trying to use doctor-speak.

"Your mum just reacted to the steroid I prescribed for her rheumatism. Unfortunate, but these things happen. There shouldn't be any lasting damage."

Yeah, right.

She offered me a crumb of comfort. "You did the right thing, calling me out."

"But what if I hadn't been here? Could she have…"

It was back to the usual frown. "Now now, don't let's get carried away. You were here, weren't you? Just make sure she keeps eating and drinking. I've taken the tablets away. She can come in next week to sort out a new prescription."

As I saw her out, the wind caught her straggly hair and her open jacket. She grabbed the edges of it in one hand, anchoring them where her waist might have been.

"Bye. Thanks for coming," I said, but she was already cramming herself behind the wheel of her car. For a minute I wished she were staying. Her presence had just been starting to feel benevolent.

Friday night and Ian picked me up in the van. More than ever I appreciated his rude health and his solidity. With Ian beside me I could chase away Mum's face, pale and bloated. Ian was a good thing, I was sure of it. He already knew about Mum's turn for the worse. I said she was better, that it was just a reaction.

"Is that what the doctor said?"

"Yeah, she was pretty sure about it."

"Ye'd think they'd have got to the bottom of it by now."

85

"They're still doing tests." But he was right. Why would tests take that long? I pictured Mum creeping around in her half-life, having more days like Sunday, days when she shouldn't be alone.

Ian stretched beside me in the van. "What do you fancy doing? Pictures?"

I shook my head. Through the top of the windscreen the sky was bright and full of stars. I fancied being somewhere else. "Where could we go?"

There was a pause in which Ian adjusted his own horizons for the evening. "How about Limekilns? We could go to the Ship."

Limekilns, where the Forth was just starting to widen into sea, was only a few miles away. But a mile down the road, he pulled off the tarmac and into a gateway surrounded by trees.

"What beer do they have here then?" I was teasing him and he knew it.

He switched off the engine. "Looks like the beer's off," he said.

This was the first time we'd been at close quarters since the party, and the memory of sex was enough to make me want more. I said nothing, but leaned towards him for a kiss. Soon he was unhooking my bra with one hand while the other voyaged under my skirt. I opened my legs, inviting him to carry on, closing my eyes, then opening them to watch the stars through the windscreen, pouting my lips for him to kiss me again, working my tongue around his mouth while his fingers did the same for me. This time I wasn't going to let it go. Even now I was pretty damn close, but Ian's fingers came to rest.

"Let's go in the back."

The van had no back seat, but a glance behind revealed that in the space usually reserved for trays of haddock, there were now two sleeping bags, one plain blue, the other emblazoned with a Spiderman picture. I couldn't imagine where these had come from. But that didn't matter. I clambered over the seat and pulled Ian on top of me.

Soon we were hard at it, our first experience of horizontal sex. As the van swayed and rolled under us, a branch from an overhanging tree tapped a rhythm, keeping time to our beat, like an audience giving a slow handclap. Even with the sleeping bag the floor of the van was hard, but I liked its resistance. I arched under Ian and he came.

"Sorry."

This time I still had him in my grip and off I went again, "a-rockin" and a-rollin".

"Ailsa," he said as he hardened in me again, "you're the fucking best."

I thought he might be right. He leaned back and reached to work me again and I came with a whoop of shock and pleasure that tailed off into a moan. Satisfaction, elation, and just a moment of sadness. So this was it. Over.

We rolled over and I nestled against him, letting him cradle me and stroke my hair. I don't think he knew I was crying.

"Are you cold?"

I sniffed. "A bit."

He made a fuss of getting one of the sleeping bags on top of us and cuddling me warm. Before long, his tongue was in my mouth again. That was fine. It was a comfort, knowing he would always be there when I needed him, offering the hot darkness that drove everything and everybody away.

When we got back in the front, our ardour had condensed on the windscreen and the stars were invisible.

Ian wiped his sleeve across the glass to make a smeary gap. "I never did take you to Largo."

Largo. A muddle of memories now.

"Do you still want to go?"

"Yeh, why not?"

With Ian I was safe from the bad things.

My first day back at uni and Barbara was on the platform. "Hello, stranger." We settled into our favourite carriage with a table between us. The scratchy seats and the smell of half-eaten bacon rolls were reassuringly normal. Barbara was wondering where I'd been and so I told her about Mum. Maybe it was because we only saw each other on the train, but Barbara was easy to talk to. She also spoke her mind, on anything from modern art ("my uncle had a pile of bricks in his lobby, but nobody offered him money for it") to the love-life of our local MSP. She didn't suffer fools gladly, but you always got an honest opinion. I started with the doctor's version of Mum's latest episode.

"Helluva reaction, if you ask me," Barbara said.

"I've been thinking the same," I said, though I'd been trying to avoid thinking anything at all, forcing myself to do some work, struggling to keep up with my reading.

"Do you think she's coming clean?" Barbara said. "I'm no expert, but it doesn't sound like ME to me."

I sighed. "Nobody even agrees on what ME is exactly. What else could it be?"

"Did you say she has a rash?"

"Not always, just sometimes."

"Mum had an auntie, Auntie Jean…" Barbara seemed unsure if she should go on. "She lived in Glasgow so we didn't see much of her. She had this thing that was pretty weird and she had it a long time before anybody knew what it was. And she had a rash, a red mark across her face."

The train had just reached the Bridge, its red girders criss-crossing outside the window in an endlessly repeating puzzle.

"So what was it?"

"It was called lupus."

Lupus. I didn't like the sound of it. Below the Bridge and between its giant pillars, grey boats nudged the waves straining for home, seeking shelter from wayward currents and sudden squalls. "I've never heard of it."

"I think it's quite rare."

"And what is it exactly?"

"I don't really know. She just wasn't well. They thought it started when she had the menopause."

"Well Mum's had it for ages." And as far as I knew, she hadn't had the menopause.

Barbara shrugged it off. "Probably no connection."

We pulled into South Queensferry and the carriage filled up. A commuter sat down next to me without so much as a by-your-leave, an earpiece stuck in his ear.

I thought of things that can trigger disease, like stress, like mental trauma. "So what happened to your Auntie Jean?" I said.

Barbara shifted in her seat. "It might not have been the lupus thing. I just know she died young. I was still at school." The carriage was still chilly but Barbara's face was getting pinker by the minute. "Look, I hardly know anything about it. She might have died of something else. I can ask my mum, if you like."

"It's okay. Don't worry."

We stopped talking and watched as the Jenners' warehouse came into view and the spires and turrets of Stewart's Melville College, a fairy castle dropped in the wrong place. As we pulled into Haymarket, the man next to me got up and headed for the door. I got up too.

"What's wrong?" said Barbara.

"Nothing. I've hardly been out of the house for days. I'm going to walk from here."

"It's raining," she said.

"Rain never hurt anybody," I said. "The exercise'll do me good. See you tomorrow."

I jumped off after iPod man. I'd had a break from running and thought I would enjoy it, but I had too much to carry. My big shoulder bag bumped against my hip and it felt like hard work. Barbara was right. I was soaked by the time I got to the West End and ended up taking a bus.

When you go online you forget what's going on around you. Maybe that was why Mum went on the internet so much, to be free of the stuff that tied her down: her body, the memories of Dad. I was in the uni library, but I could have been anywhere. The web can make a prison of a different kind.

I Googled "lupus" and got sent straight to Wikipedia. *Latin word for wolf.* No wonder it had given me the willies. *"Also the disease lupus."* I hit the link then stopped myself. There had to be better places for medical information.

On the official NHS site I found *"disorder of the autoimmune system"*. Now things were coming together. Immune system. It all made sense. Mum didn't have AIDS, but if her body was still at war with itself, that would explain a lot.

I started a new search and found a UK charity that helped lupus sufferers and found myself reading Mum's life story, and my own. The sunlight thing, the rash on her face, even the joint problems. They were all there and a lot more besides: something to do with "sticky blood" that brought on headaches, something else that affected circulation. For every symptom that could be controlled, there was another that just had to be put up with. The thing also came in fifty-seven varieties, each more complex than the one before. It was hard to diagnose and could be mistaken for a number of things, including ME. It could be triggered by hormonal events, like Auntie Jean, or it could just crop up, unexplained. It could lead to major organs being compromised, particularly if it went undiagnosed. How long exactly had Mum been ill? How much could anybody do?

What really got to me was the statement at the top of the Home Page. *"Lupus is no longer the death sentence it once was."* What kind of a comfort was that? The words "death sentence" could have been in dayglo letters, ten feet tall.

I clicked around to find out about tests for lupus and it sounded like a long, drawn out business. Dr Archibald was on the ball, she must have made a start. What about Mum? Did she already know? She had been upbeat

91

lately. Maybe it wasn't confirmed. Maybe she was waiting, or maybe she just wasn't going to tell me. But thinking about the week I'd just had, I remembered this wasn't someone whose condition had stabilised.

CHAPTER TWELVE

At home I went straight upstairs and found Mum in bed, reading a woman's magazine. My laptop was on the bedside table. That morning she had asked me to leave it because she was getting bored. I wondered how many health sites she might have surfed since I'd been gone.

She flung the magazine aside. "This is rubbish."

"Did you use my laptop?"

"For a wee while. You were right, it gave me a headache. But I'm okay. I'm just getting up."

I removed the laptop and went to the kitchen. We had plenty of eggs so I broke three into a dish, whisked them up and added milk. The knob of butter sizzled in the pan as I poured on the eggs. I liked doing this. I could have stood there forever, smelling the hot butter and stirring the mixture until it went thick and lumpy. Pity it only took a few minutes.

Mum came down to eat. She seemed untroubled. I could only think that the lupus thing hadn't arisen. Knowledge, they say, is power. But would it help her to know she had something that would never go away? Assuming, of course, my guess was right.

"Can't say I'm impressed with your new doctor. She prescribed you something that made you ill."

"I know. But I think it was just bad luck. She's determined to get to the bottom of it."

She was wolfing down the egg. The event, whatever it had been, had clearly passed. I felt the need for more information.

"Mum, when did you actually start having, you know, the allergies? Was it after Dad left?"

Mum was concentrating on keeping the last morsels of egg on the toast.

"No, not really. It got worse then, but I wasn't well. Even before." She drank some tea. "After you were born, I thought it was just, you know, hormones and things, but I found it hard. I got tired easily. I didn't feel like going out. That's why your gran took you to the playgroup and your dancing class. And your dad played with you more than I did. You were always a daddy's girl."

A knot gathered inside me, below my stomach. Daddy's girl was not something I wanted to be. "No I wasn't."

Mum cut the toast into squares. Her face was still distorted by swelling. She gave a sigh. "He was fond of you. In his way."

If she hadn't been ill I would have got angry. Dad was neatly packed away, I didn't need him to be resurrected or rehabilitated. I knew he had been fun, that he had got down on the floor, pretending to be a pony, that he had thrown me up in the air to scare me and caught me on the way down. But the illness wasn't about Dad, not any more. It had started with me. Had I always known it was my fault?

94

"But the rash and everything. You didn't have it then."

"Not at first, no. That came later. That holiday. The one the two of you enjoyed so much. When I couldn't go out."

I thought of the caravan. The holiday at Largo and leaving Mum behind to go to the beach. When we got back, Mum said, "Look at my face?" Dad said, "I said you were off colour." They both laughed.

But this was it, the start of the funny red rash across her forehead and cheeks. I only remembered the stale smell of the van every time Dad took me back. With so much else to do, I'd erased Mum from the picture. While Dad and I were enjoying ourselves, Mum had been harbouring something sinister, the bite of a wolf.

Mum pushed the tray away. She was looking a bit pale.

"Are you okay?"

"I think I might be sick."

I ran to fetch the basin from the kitchen and a towel, but when I got back she said she was okay. I cleared away the remains of the meal. "Leave the basin, just in case." She hobbled over to the armchair. "I think I'll just shut my eyes for a wee while."

Childbirth was a major hormonal event in anybody's book. I was pretty sure Mum had fallen prey to the wolf disease around then. From that point on it was only ever going to be a matter of time.

Ian was as good as his word. On the Sunday we drove down into Lower Largo and parked next to the Crusoe Hotel. In front of us the rocks that protected the harbour were being uncovered by an ebbing tide. These were the rocks I had scrambled over with Nancy.

The harbour itself, fed by a sluggish stream, was tiny. A place for toy boats and fishing nets, where a gang of boys had caught tiddlers and flung them at us for the fun of hearing us scream. Nancy and me. A faded t-shirt, warm sandy fingers that yanked me along the beach, or pulled me to the side of the road as a car trundled past. She was allowed to go places by herself. I was allowed to go with her.

Now, a group of teenagers lounged on the quayside, exchanging fags and God knows what else. What had happened to the boys who dared each other to jump off the pier into the deep water, each one disappearing from view with a flash of white legs and a splash? I reminded myself this was winter. In the summer there would still be diving games and girls to chase.

Ian and I walked along the pier past the hotel's deserted patio to where we could see along the beach. At the water's edge there was a line of stones, then seaweed, then finer shingle that sifted itself into proper soft sand, the kind you sink into as you walk.

"We used to have races," I said. "On the wet sand." That was where your feet could get a grip. Nancy always gave me a start and hung back so that I was ahead until the end. Sometimes she let me win.

"Do you want to go down?" Ian said.

"Yeah, let's."

We walked along the beach, watching the tide dwindle back, revealing the lines of black rock dividing the beach into segments. On our left was the row of houses whose gardens back on to the beach. I remembered how towels and swimsuits had danced on washing lines, ready for the next excursion onto the sands. Today there were no swimsuits. One or two families played football between coats or had races to keep warm. Most people, like us, were just walking, looking towards Elie Point with no intention of going that far. By now we had reached the boat park, a wide entrance between beach and road. I stopped. "There was a café here," I said. "We used to get ice cream."

Where the shop had been there was a window, boarded up. I remembered sitting inside with Dad, out of the wind. He was teaching me to count the boats. *"How many have blue sails? One, two, three."* I couldn't remember getting past three.

Ian and I kept walking until we got to the place where a burn splutters from a pipe in the wall and wends its way in rivulets to the sea. For Nancy and me it had marked the outer limits. *"Don't go past the Temple Burn."*

The spread-out area of wet sand had been our favourite place. So many ways of damming and diverting the stream, continually building cities of sand that we knew would fill with water and disappear as the stream met the rising tide.

"My dad used to help me dam up this burn," Ian said.

"We did too," I said. "Me and Nancy."

"Who's Nancy?"

"Just a girl who was here." Nancy had a big spade. My blue plastic one was no good. "Think how many times its course must have changed."

"Not by much, though. Always finds its way to the sea," Ian said.

"So did you come here for your holidays too?"

97

"Only for odd days. We had a house at Ayr. And then we started going to Majorca."

To Ian, Largo was nothing, a local diversion when nothing more glamorous was on offer.

We climbed up from the beach and walked back along the road past Crusoe's House, where the bearded sailor scans the horizon for destinations way beyond East Lothian. As we passed the boat-park again, I stepped off the pavement to avoid a man with a can of paint. The front door he was painting was right on the street. He looked up and nodded to us and I stopped for a minute to look back at him, at the house with its two storeys and one added on at the side. Wires in my brain jangled. The letters on the nameplate were smaller than on the painting in the Chalmers' living room, but the name was the same.

"Lauder House," I said to Ian, who gave no reaction. "This is the Chalmers' place."

Ian looked from me to the house. "I don't think so."

The man was concentrating on his painting again. From his clothes and his fumbling with the brush, he was the occupier rather than a tradesman.

"Well not now. Obviously. But I bet they had it before. Or came here for holidays. There was a picture of it in their living room."

The great and the good, the Chalmers and the Mackays. Presumably they had divested themselves of their second homes, or in Eddie's case moved up-market to Edinburgh property. But how old exactly were Andy and his brother? Like Nancy and me, they might have been playing on the beach, daring each other to jump in the harbour, teasing the girls.

By now we were back at the hotel. In the burn an old tyre and a shopping trolley had been uncovered by the falling tide. The smell was familiar, sea-weedy and just a bit rank. There were two Largos here and I knew which one I liked. I turned my back on the grimy reminders of the pokey caravan and Mum's unhappiness and made Ian take one more walk along the pier. In the opposite direction to the beach was Lundin Links with its warren of dunes; beyond that Leven and the tall chimney that marked Methill, the place where holidays ended and real life began.

Ian took a last look around the harbour. "It's nothing special, is it?" he said.

I gave him a bit of a push. "I thought it was heaven."

He caught hold of my hand and pulled me against him. "You're a case," he said. He kissed me and I snuggled against him. When we broke apart he kept hold of my hand. "I have something to ask you."

"What?"

"Mum says, will you come for your tea next Sunday? You will come, won't you?"

I squeezed his hand. "Of course I will."

Sunday tea meant high tea, the most formal meal of the week. I pictured myself amongst the capo di monte, my best shoes on the cream carpet where Ian and I had almost made out.

"I'll be on my best behaviour."

He grinned. "Just be yourself. It'll be fine."

Maybe that was the moment when everything was decided.

CHAPTER THIRTEEN

I didn't even hear from Faye until after Christmas. She said she'd been skint and had no credit so she rang me at home, over the landline. I was keen to meet up with her because it would be easier to deliver my news face to face.

"Will we go for a drink?" I suggested.

"Sorry, I'm off back to the flat tomorrow. We're havin' a party for Hogmanay. I have to clean the place up and buy stuff. Hey, you could come. Why don't you?"

The invitation sounded like an afterthought. I let it pass. Anyway, I was expected at the Mackays and it wasn't something I could refuse. Not now.

"What about Wednesday?" I said. "I'm going to the sales." My one and only black number was a bit risqué for a family party. "We could go together."

I was in funds. I could buy her lunch. Before I could hang up she flung in a remark, "How's fat boy?" as if she'd forgotten until then that Ian existed.

"He's fine," I said. "We're engaged."

We met in Rose Street outside the bar she had suggested. By no stretch of the imagination was this a gastro-pub. Faye went prospecting for chairs while I bought drinks and two pies that had seen better days.

For a minute or two we were awkward with each other. I was conscious of my new chinos and a t-shirt I'd bought from Per Una. Faye was wearing jeans that really were distressed and a lacy cotton cardigan whose sleeves covered her wrists so that it looked like she had no hands. Her fingernails were no longer dark green but unvarnished and showed signs of being chewed.

"Come on, let's have a look then."

I proffered my left hand.

"It's lovely," she said. "Really. It's gorgeous." It was her way of saying sorry for slagging Ian off.

"Thanks."

The ring was lovely, a row of stones in a wee bar, dark green emeralds with diamonds sparkling in between like stars on a frosty night. I loved its solid feel on my finger. When I wasn't doing anything much I found myself feeling for it with my thumb, checking it was still there, sending out its winking message to the world. I was spoken for. I was loved. I could afford to apologise too.

"Sorry we can't make your party. I've been invited to his folks. They're having a big bash. Couldn't really get out of it."

It was true – to back out would be to let Ian down. But given the choice, where would I rather be? Having a sedate Gay Gordons in the Mackay lounge and home to a warm bed, or fending off drunks in a student flat?

"Fair enough," Faye accepted my dilemma even if there was none.

She rocked back on her chair. "So, when's the wedding?"

No one had actually mentioned a wedding. "Let's get engaged," Ian had said, and I thought, "Yeah, lets." Not that I didn't want to marry him, but the whole wedding idea just took a bit of getting used to.

"Och, we're not in any hurry."

Faye wasn't having any of it. "Next summer?"

"Oh no, I don't think so."

"After you finish?"

The end of my degree felt too far off to even contemplate. "We haven't decided."

"But you will finish?"

"I expect so."

I was beginning to see that getting engaged could change a lot of things. "I suppose I could just work in the shop."

"The fish shop?"

"Yeah, I like it. I've been there every Saturday since November."

"God, Ailsa, you're off your head, you are." But she was laughing, as if choosing life as a fishmonger was at least a statement of some kind.

I thought she might be right. "Yeah, you never know, I might start going out in the boat." I imagined salt spray on my face. "Can you have a lady fisherman?"

"I don't see why not. You could be Captain bloody Birdseye if you want to."

By "you" she meant people in general. But then that was the difference between her and me.

"Ailsa Robertson," I tried it for size. "Fisherwoman of the year."

"Wouldn't that be Ailsa Mackay?"

"Oh, yeah, Ailsa Mackay. Sound okay, though?"

"Uh-huh. Could be worse."

I was pleased Faye accepted my new situation. I asked her about the flat.

"It's great. We all get on really well. Three of us do nursing or child-care. Then there's Danny. He does Lens Media."

"What's that?"

"Photography and stuff. He came late."

Danny had the place in the house that would have been mine. "So what does he photograph?"

"God knows. He's a bit of a mystery, Danny." There was one of those tiny pauses, the kind that tried to make Danny and his photography into a throwaway remark and failed.

I got up. "Come on," I said. "Help me choose a party frock, something suitable for a respectable Hogmanay."

"No such thing, surely," Faye said, but she followed me out of the pub and towards the shops.

The St James Centre provided slim pickings. We rifled through rails of clothes that looked like they'd had too much rifling already. When I emerged from a changing room in a green velvet bustier with sequins, Faye took hold of my arm.

"Come on, I have a better idea." She steered me though the doors of John Lewis and up to the fashion floor.

Big store stuff was boring and cost the earth. "What are we doing here?" I asked.

Faye ignored me and walked up to an assistant. "We're looking for a wedding dress."

103

I caught her arm. "Are you off your head?" I asked her. "We are not," I said to the assistant, but Faye somehow got in the way. The woman, in her suit and immaculate make-up, looked at us doubtfully, but Faye grabbed my arm and hissed in my ear.

"Have you forgotten how to have a laugh?"

She fixed the woman with an ingratiating smile and said, "Sometime in the spring."

The woman clearly couldn't see me as a candidate for the full meringue but wasn't going to let a sale slip past her. She started pulling things out from different ranges. "These aren't bride's dresses as such, but a lot of girls prefer them."

The third one she came up with had a wide ruffled neck and high waist. I couldn't disguise that I liked it. It certainly wasn't white, or even cream exactly, but it had a watery sheen that caught the light. Sales lady clocked my interest.

"Oyster," she said. "A very flattering colour."

"Go on, try it on," Faye said.

In the changing room I got cold feet. "I feel like a freak," I muttered as Faye warsled the dress and its underskirts over my head.

"Don't be daft. And you never know. When the Mackays are wanting you dressed up like a Barbie doll, you'll need to have a plan."

She finished doing up the screwy zips and catches then pushed me out in front of the big mirror. There were one or two women out there, standing sideways on and drawing in their bellies, but when I came out from behind the curtain they all stood aside, like I had a kind of priority. Faye gave me another shove so that I was right in front of the mirror. My audience let out a collective sigh of admiration, envy or maybe nostalgia.

"You see," Faye said, "I told you it would look good."

She was right. I felt it. I'd never worn a long dress and it made me feel taller, and more elegant, like someone who can be on a man's arm. She stood behind me and drew my hair up on top of my head.

"God," I said, "I look ancient."

"No you don't. You look…"

I knew what she was trying to say. I could feel her fingers against my scalp, willing me on to this new perception of myself. I looked like the future Mrs Mackay. I was back in the changing room pronto.

"That's enough," I said. "Game over. Get me out of this."

I couldn't risk damaging the material. Between us we got the thing off just before the sales woman reappeared with two more dresses on hangers.

"Now," she said, sticking her head around the ballooning lace and tulle. "These are our latest lines."

Faye had caught my urgency. She took me by the hand and yanked me past.

"Sorry," she said to the woman. "Wedding's off. She's dumped. By text, would you believe? Lovely frocks, by the way."

We made a run for it.

Outside the shop Faye took out her phone to check the time. "I said I'd be back. We're going to buy the booze for the party."

We hugged a goodbye. Her body felt thin and the scarf knotted around her neck made a hard lump between us. Her hair smelled of cheap coconut shampoo, her clothes of a student flat or a stuffy lecture hall, of nowhere. I was conscious of the expensive perfume Ian had given me for Christmas giving off its own message. I wondered when we would see each other again.

I also realised I had just missed a train.

I drifted up to the café where I ordered an over-priced latte. Waiting for it to appear, I spotted a leaflet stand for tourist attractions: the Zoo and Greyfriars Bobby rubbed shoulders with an adventure park and the Tartan Museum. Nestling at the back there were some pamphlets in black and white headed *Pioneers of Photography.* On my way to a table I pulled one out.

Under the lettering there was an old photo of a man beside a boat with grainy children huddled at his feet. I wondered how much connection there was between these ancient prints and the digital trickery Faye's Danny might be engaged in. Inside the leaflet there were more photos: women, children, boats. These were the real fishwives.

According to the map on the back, the exhibition was only just round the corner. For a minute I quite fancied going. I had no idea that the pioneers of photography, whoever they were, had connections with the fishing villages of Fife. But it was getting on for four. No point in missing another train. I stuffed the leaflet in my bag and headed for Waverley.

At home I was surprised to see that the lights were on in the Treatment Room. Depilation being a seasonal treat, the run-up to Christmas was hectic, but business tailed off long before the fairy lights were down. As I passed the door I cocked an ear and registered a local accent. I assumed it must be Liz who had turned up for a chat, and headed upstairs. Too late. The door opened and Mum called me back.

"There you are! I thought I heard the door. Come down a minute. We've a visitor."

I turned round, bracing myself for patronising comments on my engagement from some neighbour who'd had a sudden need to see in the New Year with a neat bikini line. But next to Mum was a new customer: Rhona Mackay.

When Ian and I got engaged, I'd expected Mum either to be angry *("What about your education?")* or else gratified that I was going to be around for the foreseeable future. In fact, I got neither a rebuke nor a celebration, just a deep sigh and a "What's the hurry?" And despite several invitations she hadn't shown the least interest in meeting up with the Mackays. But Rhona had taken matters into her own hands. It looked like her presence in our hall was something I'd have to get used to.

"Hiya, Ailsa," she said. "Have you had a good day?"

She was wearing black jeans pressed to a perfect crease and the cashmere jumper Gordon had given her for Christmas. This was her version of casual. The sweater was pale lilac with a v-neck that showed off two gold chains, one bearing a real pearl, which I knew had been a present the year before. Her lipstick toned with the sweater. It has to be said that Rhona's make-up and clothes, despite being deadly dull, were nicely done and as a result she looked, at least from a distance, a good ten years younger than Mum. As she spoke, she wrapped herself in a black poncho and clambered into some ankle boots, which for some reason she'd carried out of the Treatment Room into the hall.

"Yes, fine," I said.

Mum, who could probably see I was struggling for conversation, came to my rescue.

"Rhona and I were just talking about the party," she said, deadpan.

"We're just so pleased you'll both be there," Rhona said.

Mum had refused to join Ian and me for the Hogmanay bash, but maybe she didn't feel she could accept Rhona's business and still decline the invitation. I could see there was more to Rhona than met the eye.

"We have a wee announcement to make." She fixed both of us in her blue gaze. "You won't want to miss it. And Gordon'll get you a taxi home, of course."

As Mum muttered her thanks, Rhona fished in her handbag and came up with a slim mobile which she unflipped expertly. "I'm all done, pet," she said into it. "Can you come and get me?" Then to Mum, "Now, what do I owe you?"

This was a signal for some protracted negotiations.

"No, no," Mum said. "I wouldn't hear of it. It was only half-leg and we had a good natter."

"Och, that won't do." Rhona tucked a twenty-pound note under the plant pot on the hall table. "If you don't take this, I won't be able to come again."

Mum whipped the note out again and tried to force it back into Rhona's hand. "That's far too much."

Eventually honour was saved by Mum accepting a tenner to "cover costs" but offering to treat Rhona free in future, by which time a car had pulled up outside and Rhona had swept out on a "See you on Hogmanay!"

Mum and I were left breathing in the backwash of her perfume.

"What was all that about?" I said.

"Don't ask me. She rang up at dinner time, out of the blue."

"I expect it's her way of welcoming you to the family."

"By offering me a tenner?"

"She offered you twenty. You turned it down. And what's the announcement?"

"It might be about the shop. From what she said, it sounds like Gordon's retiring." She sat down on the edge of the table. "But this party... Do I have to go?"

I sighed. "Why not? It might do you good to get out. I know the Mackays are a bit full-on, but they're all right."

She looked down at her hands, smoothing in some imagined remnant of ointment. "I'm not in that crowd. I suppose the Chalmers will be there, and Irene?"

I remembered how she'd been funny about my trip to Torryburn.

"No idea," I said. "Anyway, who cares?" I linked my arm through hers. "You can be in my crowd."

I needed to catch up on uni work, but instead of rushing up the stairs two at a time, I stepped carefully, feeling the rustle of silk around my ankles. If Gordon was going to retire, it meant Ian would be next in line. I could be a fishwife after all.

CHAPTER FOURTEEN

The Mackays certainly knew how to throw a party.
When the taxi deposited us on the doorstep at nine, it
was already in full swing.

"Oh, come in, come in." Rhona, swathed in dark
blue silk, divested us of our coats and hustled us into
the dining room.

"Here they are!" The assembled company was
hovering next to the buffet, clutching forks and napkins
but apparently not allowed to set to until we had
arrived. I tucked my arm through Mum's, making sure
my ring was showing, just in case anybody didn't know
why we were guests of honour.

Gordon came over and pecked Mum on the cheek.
"Nice to see you, Lorraine. What can I get you to
drink?"

"Thanks, Gordon, just a white wine for me."

I felt Mum relax. The Chalmers were conspicuous
by their absence. I guessed they would be at their own
family do or off in search of winter sun. When we had
shuffled around the table Gordon took Mum off to meet
some other family. I went to join Ian.

At midnight songs were sung and kisses exchanged. Gordon opened champagne and called for a toast to the "young people". I realised this was us, Ian and me. For a second I wondered what other young people might be doing. Andy would be out on the lash in Edinburgh. Faye would be in her student house with countless others, some of them barely known, passing through on their way to other parties. By the following morning only Barbara, keeping her mum company, and me here with Ian, were likely to remember much about the hours between midnight and dawn.

Gordon went round charging the glasses again and held up his hand for silence. He cleared his throat and looked round for Rhona. Finding her right behind him he drew her close.

"You all know how long our family has been in the fish business," Gordon began.

His audience stirred, confused and restless, wondering when they could get back to their real drinking, but I was on the ball. Was he going to give Ian the shop, right here and now? I squeezed Ian's hand, wondering if we were about to be beckoned into a Mackay group hug.

"But the world's a different place these days," Gordon went on. "It's a hard ca' with long hours and not much profit." One or two laughed politely at what sounded like false modesty, but Gordon's face was grave. I grew anxious myself. This hardly sounded like the bestowing of a gift.

"Just yesterday," Gordon gave an audible sigh, as if to signify the difficulty of the decision, "I finalised the sale of Catch of the Day to Scottish Seafoods Limited." This got a reaction, a murmur of surprise and concern.

111

"No, no, don't worry." Gordon was smiling now, confident of approval. "Though I say it myself, I think that I got a pretty good deal!"

Someone shouted, "Do you ever do any other kind, Gordon?" provoking a ripple of relaxation. This was the Gordon they knew and loved. Situation normal. Gordon, meanwhile, gave Rhona a wee hug and she simpered back at him.

"With any luck," Gordon was enjoying himself now, "we'll have a comfortable retirement and should be able to help out these young folk too." He turned a benevolent smile on Ian. "And so I hope you'll all wish me and Rhona all the best."

The toast echoed around the room. "To Gordon and Rhona!"

No wonder he'd had the champagne laid in. But a Mackay without a fish shop. Surely this was unthinkable?

"Did you know about this?" I asked Ian.

"Och, yes," he said. "But I wasn't to say."

I took a gulp of fizz to steady myself. The fish shop had been sold from under me. But if my plans as wife of the owner had just gone out on the tide, I could hardly let on to Ian.

Scottish dance music now filled the room. The table was pushed back and conversation gave way to drinking and laughter punctuated by the thump of unaccustomed feet on the parquet flooring. Half way through a Dashing White Sergeant, Mum whisked past me on someone's arm, hooching with the best of them.

When the music stopped she sidled up to me with a hand on her chest. Her blouse was untucked from her black trousers and her hair was all over the place.

"Well, that's a turn up for the book," she said. "I suppose you knew all along?" Her knowing look made me feel even more stupid for not having seen it coming.

"I had an inkling," I lied. "Makes sense, after all."

By now it was getting on for one o'clock. "Are you okay?" I asked her. "I thought you were getting a taxi."

"It's on its way," she said.

I thought she was looking pretty good for somebody who didn't get out much.

Two hours later Ian said he would walk me home. We were taking a shortcut through the park and I was tottering on high heels. I rounded on him.

"How come you never told me?"

"It was only decided yesterday, for definite," he said, clearly at a loss as to why he was getting it in the neck for his dad's business acumen.

"Well, you might have said."

"Dad wanted it to be a surprise. He's dead chuffed. I can't see what you're so bothered about."

On the Middle Walk, where the lights across the water disappear from view, we crossed paths with a group of New Year revellers who seemed to have got lost between parties. One of them hailed us for directions while the others stumbled through a version of *Flower of Scotland* that could have done killed national unity at one go.

"Ye're on the right road," Ian hailed them back. "Keep on up the hill. Look for the roundabout then straight on again." Good old Ian. You wouldn't catch him drunk in a public park, not these days anyway.

"Thanks, pal, Happy New Year!"

"Happy New Year!" The rest of the gang joined in the chorus, cans and bottles brandished in a friendly salute. We waved back and walked on. I heard the start of *Three Craws sat upon a Wa* from behind us. It provided a better beat for walking and soon the voices diminished on the wind. I clung to Ian's arm, wondering if I was in the wrong camp.

Why had news of the sale of Catch of the Day made me so grouchy? What did I care what Gordon did with his money? Rhona's house was fully stocked with all the stuff she could possibly need, and Gordon himself would be more than happy playing golf and doing good works with the Rotary. But what about Ian?

"When the shop's sold, what are you going to do?"

"I'll soon get another job."

Ian was twenty-two with no work experience that I knew of other than sourcing and selling fish.

"I suppose the new people might keep you on, as a manager?"

"I don't think so. I'd rather have a change." He sounded huffy.

I sighed. "I like you as you are."

"It's only a job. I'll be the same."

Fair point. But whatever future I planned for myself, Ian's place in it was behind the counter of Catch of the Day. That was the deal.

"Dad's done well for us." It was as if he'd been reading my mind.

"I gathered. But you'll still need a job."

"Obviously, but he's said he can help us out."

"What do you mean?"

"He's paid off the house years ago. He says he can give us something for a deposit."

"What deposit?"

"On a house. When we get married. Well, any time really."

I processed the fact that Ian was talking weddings already, and home ownership.

"Don't say I told you. He'll be telling you himself any minute. Said he didn't want to seem like he was showing off." Ian stopped and put his arms around me. "We can have our own place. And you'll be near your mum."

The fact that Ian was taking care of me communicated itself through multiple layers of clothing. Mum had been well since the doctor had given her new drugs. But it could only be a remission.

"Yeah," I said, "that's great."

"Eddie Chalmers has some new houses at Crossgates. What do you think?"

"For us?"

"Maybe. The wee ones aren't so dear."

Me? In a house of my own? I pictured its bare walls and plain carpets, free of any mother's touch – Lorraine's or Rhona's.

We walked on. "You'll still need a job."

"Don't worry. I'll get something."

"Maybe I should get a job too. Then we'd be in clover."

"Och, no, we'll be fine. You don't want to give up at Edinburgh, do you?"

There was something in his voice, like Faye when she mentioned the boy in the flat. With Ian it might have been an innocent question, or hope, or desperation. Did he want to be married to a clever girl at the university, or did he want a wife who worked in the

115

bank or the council offices, one who went out with the girls on a Friday while he went out with the lads?

"I'll see how it goes. If I don't do some work soon, I might be out anyway."

We were at the bottom of the park alongside the railway track that issued from the darkness of the station buildings. The signal light was on green, but nothing was moving tonight. It would be a day or two before the world got back to work, a week until I went back to uni. I didn't like this in-between time, living with Mum, thinking about coursework but not getting on with it. I was beginning to wonder what it was all about.

On the first day of term Barbara didn't turn up. That wasn't unusual. One of her kids was probably ill. But travelling alone gave me too much time to think. If I left uni, my life would be tidy, joined up in a recognisable shape, like the pattern pieces of the frock Gran had once helped me make. But what about the rest of the material, the stuff we cut off and threw away, or the big roll it came from, metres and metres of it? But now I'd agreed to marry Ian, maybe it was too late to throw the pattern away and start again.

I looked in my bag for my mobile, as if there might be some message there to tell me what to do. Underneath it, I found the leaflet for the exhibition I'd picked up the day I met Faye. *Pioneers of Photography* was still on. I looked again at the photo of the man with his boat and his bairns. I wasn't going to make a fishwife after all, but I had nothing better to do than take a look.

I'd expected the National Portrait Gallery to be like the one at the foot of The Mound, all columns and big open spaces. In fact, there was no comparison. From outside it looked like a church, with spires and pointed windows. Inside it could have been the castle of some medieval baron. Around the walls there was a huge frieze in red and green and gold, filled with figures from history, parading like saints in a stained glass window, as if we might forget them if they weren't preserved on the wall. The ceiling was so high it made me feel lonely and in the wrong place.

When I waved my leaflet, the woman behind the desk smiled at me with all of her teeth, relieved me of seven quid and pointed down a corridor. I made a mental note not to get lost. It might be like the doctor's, with only one way out.

I didn't realise the pictures would be so old. Although photography was invented by an Englishman, these had been taken soon after, here in Edinburgh. I wondered if the Englishman had been a bit miffed. By all accounts this photographer had taken it to a new level. I looked more closely at the labels next to the pictures. There were two photographers, Hill and Adamson. Not that I was bothered for who did what and when, I just liked being among the pictures. All sepia and shadowy, they matched my mood.

One in particular caught my eye, a woman alone with a fishing creel. Her clothes were the clothes of a fishwife, a big striped apron, and a kerchief round her neck, but she looked proud, like this was her best outfit. Her name was Elizabeth Johnstone Hall. It made her sound dignified, rich in some way. Her face and hands, dark from wind and weather, or maybe the photographer's skill, looked strong rather than coarse. If she spent her days gutting herring she was unbowed by it. She was looking to one side, away from the camera, but not from shyness. I pictured her own kids playing in a corner while she sat for her portrait. It took a long time in those days to take a picture. What had she thought of the men with their cameras? What had they thought of her?

I was a bit disappointed that the photos weren't taken in Fife but less than a mile away from where I stood. It looked like a good life, but not without its risks. One year, I read, the men rowed north to beyond Aberdeen, where the wooden boats that had served them well for untold years were destroyed in a storm. The design, it turned out, had been wrong all along.

Back in the foyer, along with Scotland's saints and sinners, I remembered that Mum had never asked me to stay at home this year. So why had I? Maybe I'd wanted to have my life planned out for me, my options restricted. I sat down on one of the gallery benches and turned my new ring on my finger, looking at its green winking stones. I liked the feel of it. I liked Ian. Or did I just like the sex, the fish shop, the trips along the coast?

I slipped the ring off my finger. My hands, their nails stripped of varnish, were white and bare. There wasn't even a mark where the ring had been. I put it back on quickly, reminding myself that this was the right thing to do. Only uni was the problem. By choosing Ian, had I ditched my education? And if I had, how much did it matter?

CHAPTER FIFTEEN

Waiting for the train home, I realised the guy next to me on the platform was Andy Chalmers. I hadn't laid eyes on him since the party at Torryburn. He was wearing a black wool overcoat and his canvas bag had a designer label. Despite a stubbly chin he looked more like a businessman than a student.

"Hi," I said. I wasn't sure if he'd be up for conversation. He was staring into space like people do when they are waiting for a train. As I spoke I peered past him, as if he were incidental to the impending arrival of a two-carriage diesel locomotive.

"Hello there!" He was surprised, but in a good way, as if he'd forgotten I existed this side of the water. "I hear it's congratulations."

"Thanks."

"I hope you'll be very happy." Now he was doing the looking down the platform thing. He turned back to me, "You're still at uni then?"

"Och, yes. I still have my brilliant career to attend to."

He grinned. "That's the spirit."

This was enough to establish we were on the same wavelength. When the train rolled in, the carriage was crowded and there were so few seats it would have been stupid not to choose the one next to Andy.

"Do you finish this year?" I asked him.

He shook his head. "Next year, with any luck."

"Then what?"

"Work, money, life."

I noticed marriage didn't figure, but that was probably normal. "Will you stay in Edinburgh?"

"Probably, or Glasgow. More solicitors, bigger firms."

I nodded, as if I was up with the whole career thing.

"I suppose you're staying put, with Ian?" he said.

"We're buying a house in Crossgates, one of your dad's."

He gave a short laugh. "Best of luck! Make sure it has all the guarantees. I wouldn't put it past him to sell you a pup."

I hoped Andy's remark was more to do with family friction than any knowledge of building regulations. I worked out why I'd never seen him on the train. "So what's happened to the car?"

"It's in the garage. Gearbox. I'm working in the town for a couple of weeks. I came over today for a court case."

"Working, like for a lawyer?"

"Yeah, work experience, basic money. Has to be done."

"And you're staying at home?"

"Some of the time. I'm still over here for the course. And for weekends."

There was no company in Torryburn. I thought of the big house, comfortable but empty. "Nice place, though, yer dad's."

"I suppose."

"Listen. I saw a photo. The night of the party. Did your folks have a place at Largo?"

He was surprised but didn't seem bothered I'd been snooping around. "Yeah, we did. We had it for years. Went there every summer, other holidays too. It was a great place. Over the road from the beach."

"Next to the boat park."

"That's the one. And the ice-cream shop." He looked at me with new interest. "Do you know it?"

"Ian and I went there not so long ago. Walked right past it."

Andy was looking out of the window towards the lights of Inverkeithing and Rosyth. I guessed he was seeing a rocky beach and a burn just asking to be dammed.

"The shop's gone," I said. "All boarded up. But the hotel has a patio now, tables out on the pier."

"What? Café society comes to Lower Largo?"

We both laughed at the incongruity.

"That ice-cream shop, though," said Andy, "it was always packed."

"Yeah," I said. "It was."

He got it, that I knew about then as well as now.

"Did you go there, to Largo?" he asked.

"Just the once. I was only wee. Had a great time, though."

"Yeah, it was the best. My brother and sister were always after going somewhere new. But I was the youngest. I loved it."

121

I could see him trying to place me back in those days, on the beach or out on the rocks. The train was pulling out of Rosyth. We'd be at the Lower station in a couple of minutes. I thought of the brother who was married now and living in Glasgow.

"I never knew you had a sister."

The train was pulling into the station and he got up, eager to be off. "Yeah, three of us. Back in the day."

On the platform he was accelerating away from me but looked back over his shoulder.

"Look, here's my number. If you and Ian fancy a drink, give me a ring. I'm in the Glen most nights after work."

He strode off through the ticket office and out to the road, raising his arm in farewell.

I waved back. Meeting Andy had raised my spirits. So what if he and Ian only wanted to talk football? With Largo on the agenda Andy and I had a connection of our own. I turned the ring on my finger three times for luck. There might be more to life than running a fish shop.

Mum jumped when I walked in.

"You're back early." She was on edge. I put it down to the suspicion I had been skiving off lectures.

"Yeh. Got the early train."

In her hand was a long white envelope, another pay-out from the lawyer. I hadn't asked how much longer they would last. Being a student was one thing, but engaged? Married? For now I stepped around the twin minefields presented by my life and Dad's money. I flopped into the nearest chair. "Mum, did you know Andy Chalmers has a sister?"

Her hand was still on the envelope, half in and half out of the pocket of her overall. She went over to the sideboard and tucked it into the drawer.

"Who told you that?"

"Well, he did. I saw him on the train."

She shook her head. "I wouldn't know. I don't know them that well."

But well enough to take an interest when Ian and I went to the house. Well enough to not want to meet them at Rhona and Gordon's party.

"She would have been older," I said. "Older than the brother, I think. A lot older than me. And I know they had a house at Largo. Ian and I passed it when we went there, before Christmas."

Mum's expression was blank. I would like to have shaken her. To me, it was obvious. I'd recognised the house at Largo not just because I'd seen the photo at Andy's, but because it had been Nancy's house too. I had been there, I was sure, in a walled garden where a gnarled tree bore green apples. Nancy gathered them in a pail. "Let's play shops," she had said. "But don't eat them, Ailsa, they'll give you bellyache."

"That girl, Nancy, surely she was…"

Mum got up and walked through to the kitchen. I heard the clatter of pots and utensils.

"For goodness sake, Ailsa, you're nearly nineteen. What's so special about a girl you knew when you were five?"

For whatever reason, Mum wasn't going to tell me Nancy was Andy's sister. But it didn't matter in the slightest. I had worked it out for myself.

Thanks to his unsullied driving licence, Ian was taken on by a parcel delivery service. Within a week he had a brown uniform instead of a white apron, and a van that left him smelling of nicotine and petrol rather than raw haddock. He worked shifts and the money was good. "If I save up I might get a wee car soon."

In the evenings he started to go out with his workmates to a drinking hole of such mythical maleness I wouldn't have dreamed of putting in an appearance. "It's a laugh," he said." You don't mind, do you?"

I didn't mind. I was pleased for him. He'd stepped up to the mark. Even with the shift system the mornings were no earlier than before. Maybe it was better for him than the fish shop. But would it be better for me?

One Monday in March, I had a phone call from Rhona to say Ian had had an accident. She was calling from the West Fife hospital. By the time I got there Ian was lying on a trolley, white faced, with an oxygen mask for the pain. Standing next to him was a burly man I didn't recognise. He gave me a stubbly smile and held out a hand. I caught sight of the tail end of a blue tattoo on his wrist.

"I'm awfu' sorry, hen," he said, as if he'd known me for years. "I'm Dougie. Dougie Shawcross." This was Ian's boss.

"What happened?" I asked.

Some driver had been backing out of the yard and his reverse alarm didn't work. Ian was helping shift a pallet stacked with parcels and didn't even see the van until it had tipped the pallet over and he was on the ground with his leg under it. As Dougie related events, I winced on Ian's behalf and squeezed his damp hand. He gave me a feeble smile in return.

"Ian's had the training," Dougie said. "We have all the certificates. Just an accident, ye ken." I caught the whiff of fear in Dougie's bluster. Ian was technically still on probation, but I guessed there would be no problem with time off or sick pay.

Ian got home next day with his leg in plaster. He was still in pain and could do bugger all for himself, and so Rhona and I worked out a system. For a couple of days a nurse was going to call, but the following week I had a break from lectures. That meant I could be at their house on weekdays, leaving Rhona to help Gordon, who was still in the process of winding up the business. In a way, if there was ever a good time for Ian to have broken his leg, this was it.

Unfortunately, by Monday, when I was in charge of the patient, he wasn't in need of what you might think of as medical care.

Rhona had helped him downstairs and left him in front of the TV. By the time I arrived he was already bored out of his skull. I had brought my laptop to do some work, but he obviously saw the empty house as an opportunity and his predicament as a challenge. As soon as I got within an arm's reach he pulled me onto the sofa beside him and kissed me voraciously. When I pulled away from him he sighed. "Come on, I fancy you something rotten." He then took my hand and pressed it against his erection, which for someone in a plaster cast up to his knee was, I thought, impressive.

Sex with one leg wasn't something I'd anticipated, but I was always ready to be persuaded. Ian's jeans had had most of one leg ripped off. After a few minutes of

125

frantic petting I freed his good leg and swivelled the jeans around to lower myself onto him. It was surprisingly successful. Ian's groans didn't sound like pain, and even the sofa came out of it unscathed. We lay there panting and giggling.

"Some invalid," I told him.

I made him hobble through to the kitchen to eat the sandwich I made. "You need to keep moving," I told him, "or you could get DVT."

He was getting the hang of crutches and afterwards swung himself out to the downstairs loo and back to the sofa. By then I'd set my laptop up on the kitchen table.

"What's this?" Ian called through. "I thought you were looking after me."

When I went into the lounge he wriggled along to make room for me and I laughed. "Blimey, give me a break."

"Anybody'd think you weren't up for it."

I kissed him and let him delve under my jumper but moved out of reach. "I have stuff to do."

I went back to the kitchen from where I heard him rustling the *Scotsman*.

"There's fuck all in here."

"You'll have to get something else to read," I said. I had never seen evidence of Ian reading a novel. I made a mental note to look for a car magazine or something about football.

The next day Rhona said that Dougie and Jim were going to call round and she had left him some dinner, and so I left my visit until later on. When I got there I could smell drink and fags. There were two empty cans of lager on the coffee table. When I went to pick them up Ian made a grab for me and pulled me onto the sofa.

His hands were all over me and I could smell drink on his breath.

"Are you allowed to drink? What about the painkillers?"

"Who cares?"

He carried on feeling me up but I extricated myself and said I was going to make him coffee. Later I made out I was coming on and gave him a hand-job. The truth was I didn't really fancy full-on sex. The smell of the plaster was starting to get to me.

Later, with Ian in the loo, I was tidying the sofa. Under a cushion I found a girlie mag. It was a cheap one with rubbish pictures that were obviously fake. Something told me this had been provided by Dougie or Jim, thinking they were doing Ian a good turn. At this rate he'd be getting hornier every day. I put the magazine back without saying anything.

The novelty of the nurse/patient thing was wearing off. I wondered how long it would be before I could entice Ian out for a drink with Andy Chalmers.

CHAPTER SIXTEEN

At home, Mum's cheerfulness was grating on me almost as much as Ian's one-track mind. The following Wednesday I had an appointment with my tutor. I got up early to find Mum already downstairs cooking porridge.

"What's going on?" I said. She rarely booked customers in before ten in case she wasn't feeling up to it.

"I'm off to the hospital later. Thought I'd get ahead. And you could do with something hot before you go out."

I didn't like the sound of the appointment. "You never said about the hospital."

"I'm seeing a consultant. For the results of those tests. He's a specialist."

I poured too much milk on the porridge so that it started to cool and break up into lumps. "Would you like me to come with you?"

"Don't be daft. You have your tutor to see."

I didn't like to say that what she was about to hear might be worse than any rollicking I got from Gill Patterson.

* * *

I got to Gill's room in good time. With the inter-semester break under way, the university was unnaturally quiet. There was no one else around in the corridor and the even the staff tea room, which I glimpsed in passing, was deserted.

Gill was already in residence. "Ailsa, take a seat," she said.

The room looked more like an office than an academic study. All Gill's files and folders were tucked neatly into a wall cupboard, and her desk was clear except for a laptop and a clear wallet containing a printout of my assignment, handed in the previous afternoon, three days late.

"Now," she said, frowning into her laptop, "is it my imagination or is there a problem here?"

Gill liked to give the impression of being The Next Big Thing in lit. crit. but was better known among the students for her extravagant taste in shoes. I tried to clock them but today they were out of sight behind the desk. The rest of her clothes matched her workspace, a bright pink blouse poked jauntily from under a black jacket. Her earrings were black and white swirls, as big as Liquorice Allsorts. There was nothing of the unkempt professor about Gill. It was as if she were accustomed to addressing business leaders rather than undergraduates. I knew she had just got back from some big academic conference in Chicago, which explained why she hadn't been on my case sooner, but she looked sharp as a tack.

"Sorry," I said. "I got a bit behind over Christmas."

129

On the screen she had a record of everything I had done so far. My last essay had been late too. The curve could only be downwards.

"It happens," she said. "I just need to know it won't happen again. You know the rules."

I nodded. I was only dimly aware of how many times you could miss a deadline before you were booted out, but I suspected anything I said would only make things worse.

"The question is, are you going to catch up?"

I hoped this was a rhetorical question. Despite recent developments, I was no clearer than I had ever been about where my life was heading. In fact, if anything I was more confused. In a year's time would I be throwing myself into the study of war poets in a new semi with my own study, or dividing my time between a husband and a mother with very different demands?

"My mum hasn't been well," I said. "She's waiting for a diagnosis."

"Well…" Gill paused, maybe wondering if she should shift from bollocking mode to sympathetic. I expect she didn't want to lose any more students than was necessary, but she was yet to be convinced I was a cause for concern. "That's a shame. Is it likely to be serious?"

"I'm not sure. It might be."

"Is there anyone else to look after her?"

"Not really. Only me." I inadvertently touched my ring, an action that didn't escape the eagle-eyed Ms Patterson.

"And I see you're engaged?"

I felt myself colour, as if romance shouldn't be a priority for a dedicated scholar. "At New Year," I said. "But we're not getting married just yet."

This seemed to have been the right answer. She frowned down at my assignment. "This needs filling out. I've marked the gaps in your research. Can you get it back to me by Friday?"

"Och, yes. I'm just off to the library. Right now."

She gave me a hard look. "I need to know you're committed, Ailsa."

"I am, really," I said, trying to muster more conviction than I felt.

"And I need your next term electives. Today, if possible." She gave me a form for filling in my new module choices, then rifled in a desk drawer. "And if things at home are difficult," she handed me a glossy leaflet, "I suggest you get in touch with Student Support. They might be able to help out."

"Thanks."

I took the rest of the paperwork from her. Before I left the building I read the list of new modules, ticked three at random and left them in her pigeonhole. It looked like I had got off with a warning. I might not be so lucky next time.

When I got home, the Liz-mobile was parked outside. This struck me as a bad sign. Wednesday was a busy day for waxing. Clearly the news from the consultant had made Mum call Liz and cancel her afternoon appointments.

I wanted to know what had happened without having to discuss it with Liz. I dumped my bag in the hall and flitted through the living room to the kitchen

131

where I kept my antennae working. Not that you needed antennae with Liz around.

"Guess what?" she called through as I boiled the kettle. I could hear a response from Mum, something like "just a minute", or "not yet," but Liz wasn't one to hold back.

"We're celebrating." This was Liz. "Yer mum's cured."

Mum cut in, "Don't be daft. I am not." But there was no anger in her voice.

"As good as," Liz said.

I had to go through. It sounded like they had been drinking, and right enough there was a bottle of white wine open on the table.

"What's all this?" I stood at the kitchen door, hands on hips, like a parent finding kids with booze in the house.

"I saw the consultant today," Mum said. "They know what's wrong. Can you believe it?"

I wasn't quite ready to join the celebration. I wondered if they had pulled the wool over her eyes.

"So what is it then?"

"It's lupus, *Systemic Lupus Erythematosus*." She rolled it around her tongue, savouring it like a luxury chocolate. "SLE for short. I can hardly believe it myself."

She was made up. And she was waiting for me to say something. Liz took one look at me and for once in her life read the signals.

"I'll away," she said. "You two have a lot to talk about."

132

I sat down in the chair she had vacated. Mum was sitting opposite me, her face clear of any rash and with a new placidity.

"Don't look so worried," she said. "It sounds scarier than it is."

She was wrong. It was scarier than it sounded. "Tell me about it then," I said.

"It means 'wolf', because of the rash, like the bite of a wolf. Now they call it a butterfly rash. You know, like I used to get."

I nodded. "You mean the sun thing?"

"Uh-huh. That's it. Sun makes it worse for most people."

"And what about the other stuff?"

"Well, it's different for everybody, but skin problems are most common, and headaches. And the swollen joints. There are eleven indicators, and eleven tests. You have to have four to be confirmed. I have six." She was grinning. She had passed with flying colours.

"How come they didn't tell you before? Have you just got it?"

"Oh no. You know how long I've been like it. But because the symptoms are so varied, it can be hard to diagnose. Look…" She got up and looked in her handbag and gave me a leaflet with a butterfly on the front.

"And you didn't know, until now?"

"Well, I knew that's why they were doing the tests. But we weren't sure. Especially after that bad turn."

"So what was that about?"

"Just bad luck. Turns out one of the steroids that's popular for rheumatism can be really tricky for lupus sufferers. That's what put Helen on to it."

Mum's reaction was spooking me. I knew what was in her leaflet, I knew what she had. But she was radiant. She could have generated enough electricity to light up the street.

"So. They can treat it?"

She came down from her high, forcing herself to be sensible, to be realistic. "Well, no. There isn't a cure, not really. But it can be controlled. I might still have bad days, but I know what to do to make it better. I know *what it is*."

I was beginning to understand. Know your enemy. For years she'd been fighting something she couldn't identify.

"So, will you get worse?"

"What do you mean?"

I suppose it did sound like an odd question, but to give her due, Mum took it on the nose and applied it to what knowledge she had.

"Och, no, I don't think so. It's not *degenerative*." She had all the vocabulary. "Not with the right treatments."

Not with the right mind-set. She was probably just as ill as she'd ever been, it just didn't matter so much any more. She could cope.

"That's good," I told her and gave her a hug. "I'm pleased." I never liked to see her suffer.

"Thanks." She hugged me back with more force than I remembered her ever using before.

I could see why Liz had been congratulating her. It was like she'd just passed a big exam, or got married. She had crossed some big divide.

She sat down in the chair. "You have this wine," she said. "I don't really want it. And it's still not good for me."

She didn't need alcohol. She was on a high of her own making, or one made by her consultant. I took a gulp then wished I hadn't. The acidity hit my empty stomach. All the same, I had another to help it down. I was lost for words, but the silence felt wrong.

"Well," I said, "this is a bit of a turn up."

"We should celebrate," she said.

"How do you mean?"

"Go out for a meal?"

Something in me felt off balance. I pictured going to a restaurant with Mum. It didn't work.

"Sorry, can't do tonight," I lied. "We've got something on. Ian and me." Ian was laid up and didn't have anything on other than me, but Mum had other things to think about.

"That's a shame."

"Phone Liz back," I told her. "You two can go out."

"Och, I'll see her tomorrow."

I sat there, playing with the wine glass. "I'd better go and get ready."

When I stood up I nearly toppled over. Mum grabbed my elbow. "Mind. Maybe you've had enough."

"I'm fine, I just didn't have any dinner."

She clicked her tongue. "Will I make you something?"

"No, no. I'm all right. We're eating. Quite soon."

Upstairs, I fired up the laptop and went back over the stuff I had read about lupus. It was still there, the same as before. But now I read it from a different perspective. From the point of view of somebody who'd suffered for years and never known the cause, somebody who was used to being thought of as a freak, and was actually the victim of a relatively well-understood condition, one that people lived with.

It wasn't nice. It could get nasty. But what they said was true. It wasn't a death sentence. No wonder Mum had new horizons. But where did that leave me?

I changed into a new top and clean jeans. At the door Mum handed me twenty quid.

"You two enjoy yourselves. Have a drink on me."

"Thanks, thanks a lot." I took it from her before she could ask where we were going.

Outside, the fresh air stung my cheeks and I jogged to the corner. If she was looking, I could say I was going for the bus. I'd kept my trainers on, but I didn't want to run alongside the traffic, even at this time of night. I doubled back along Woodmill Terrace then into the park. It was dark and deserted, but it didn't scare me. I liked to be alone and if I needed to I could run. I got into my stride and breathed to the rhythm of my footsteps, up the hill, the route we had walked on New Year's morning.

Just before the swings I had to stop for a breather. I'd been neglecting the bike. As I leaned against the upright of the swings I made a belated New Year's resolution to get back on it. Then I stopped myself. What would be the point, exactly? A train was pulling into the station, on its way to Edinburgh, because that's where trains went. It came from the mining towns of central Fife, the dead end. I could have been out of here, in Edinburgh, and ready to go further. To follow a job or a boy or whatever took my fancy, but I'd cut my coat according to my cloth, Mum's cloth.

I started off again up the hill, the cold air rasping in my throat, my heart banging at my ribcage. I wanted to be angry at her for keeping me here, but I only felt angry at myself.

CHAPTER SEVENTEEN

Ian was on his own. "Are they out?" I asked.

"Yeh. Some Rotary thing. Why don't we go on up?" He meant to his bedroom.

"Okay."

We lay down and he started to caress me. It felt familiar. I liked it, or maybe not. I was still churned up inside.

"What's up?" He knew something was wrong. He was good like that: a nice boy, I reminded myself. We were going to have a house, kids maybe. When they were older we could take them on holidays by the sea. It would be fine.

"Mum's seen a consultant. She's got a disease called lupus."

He kissed the front of my neck, taking Mum's medical bulletins in his stride. "Is it bad?"

"They can treat it. She should be okay. Not a hundred percent, but better."

He started to undo my bra, but I rolled away from him. When he leaned over me again, impatient, I shook him off. There was always a wetness to his mouth. I tried not to think of a dog drooling.

"What's up?" he said again.

"Nothing."

"Thought you were up for it. You usually are."

I tried thinking about the nice wee house at Crossgates, how Ian was my friend, how I couldn't let him down.

He got up off the bed and came back with a magazine.

"Come here and read this," he said. "Just for a laugh."

He handed it to me, open at the letters page. It was, as these things go, quite tasteful. I couldn't be bothered to read, but I didn't want to argue. "Give it to me," I said, and I lay on my side to flick through the pages with Ian behind me. We were fully clothed, but as we looked at the pictures of girls in thongs and keyhole bras he rubbed me through my clothes.

"What if they come back?" Rhona and Gordon probably assumed Ian and I were sleeping together, but coming in and knowing we were up here at it would be different.

"So what if they do?" He breathed into my hair and his hands were moving faster. He took one of mine and put it against his erection. Something felt wrong but I didn't have the energy to reject him. I turned the page and a girl in an old-fashioned gymslip was leaning over a desk, bare bottomed. She had the back of her head to the camera, faceless. It was crude. Behind her there was a blackboard with chalk writing. It said, "Little Miss Naughty".

The wine had formed a vinegar pool in my throat. "I don't like it," I said. "Not this one."

"That's a shame." Ian's voice was hoarse in my ear. "I'm liking it just fine."

I wanted to leave there and then, to run for the door, but if some part of me did leave the scene, the rest was still on the bed, with Ian's hands in my knickers. I turned the page. The same girl was facing the camera now, cross-legged on the desk with one leg half unbent. The pinafore was yanked off one shoulder, the blouse undone so that one luminous breast tumbled out of a black bra. One hand was lifting the hem of her skirt. The other pointed at the camera, demanding attention. Her mouth was in a pout, her eyes wide.

I felt sick with some deep-seated fear, some knowledge best unknown. And there was something worse than knowledge. The picture and Ian's fingers had concocted a magic potion, a witch's brew that had me wanting it like I'd never wanted it before.

"Shit," Ian said into my hair, feeling me respond.

I closed my eyes so I couldn't see the picture, but the girl was still in my head. I couldn't let her go. I gave in to this new fantasy, an older man, one who knew what to do. Now I was the one moaning for it, but Ian had different ideas. His hand slowed and he whispered in my ear.

"So, Miss Roberston. Shall we go on to Lesson Two?"

He made to pull my jeans off but I wasn't so far gone as I thought. I flung myself away from him.

"Fuck off," I said. "Just fuck off." I fumbled to do up my jeans and fix my bra but my fingers were clumsy, my body still pumped up for sex.

Ian sat up. "Jesus Christ. What's got into you?"

I ran to the bathroom where I ran cold water into the basin, submerging my wrists, forcing them under, then splashed it on my face. The cold slap brought me round and I went back into the bedroom.

"I don't want it, pictures and stuff. I can't do it."

He was doing up his flies, defeated. He barked a laugh. "That's no' how it looked to me."

I shook my head. "I'm sorry. I just can't."

The sexual energy had drained away. Ian narrowed his eyes. "What's the big deal?" he said. "How come you have to be different to anybody else?"

"I'm not," I lied.

"Oh yeah? One minute gagging for it, the next Miss High and Mighty. It's just a picture, for fuck's sake. You were liking it well enough."

He was right. That was the trouble. The shock of seeing myself mixed up in a sleazy sex game that had my dad in it, and God knows who else, had worked. Maybe it was just as well tonight had happened. It made me see that whatever I wanted, it wasn't Ian.

"I'm sorry. It's not your fault."

"What are you talking about?"

"I can't do it any more."

"Do what?"

"You know. Being engaged. Getting married."

Ian looked like he'd been hit by another ten-ton truck. "Give it a rest, will ye. We're good. You know we are."

I shook my head. "I'm sorry. I can't explain. It was a mistake."

"Well, thanks a million. I'll put that on my gravestone. Ailsa Robertson's mistake."

"I don't mean it like that."

141

"You can't fool me. I suppose that teacher stuff got to you. You with your clever family."

It was never going to work. Ian didn't have a clue. I'd used him because I had no one else and nowhere else to go.

I ran for home where I went straight upstairs and threw myself onto the bed. There, the first thing I did was to finish what Ian had started. After that I went downstairs and made myself sick, heaving up my wretchedness on a trickle of sour wine.

In the morning, I felt a dull ache. Dumping Ian was the right thing to do, but I certainly wasn't ready to tell the world. I guessed Ian wouldn't be shouting about it either. I had a few days grace to get used to the idea, but my head was all over the place.

An email arrived with links to new course reading, but no way could I concentrate on anything like that. I needed company. I sent a text to Faye and got no reply. It didn't take me long to find Andy Chalmers' number. I couldn't bring myself to speak but I didn't have to. My fingers did the work. "*Up for a drink tonight? Ailsa.*"

At half past five the Glen Tavern was almost empty. Andy sat alone in front of a pie and chips with a newspaper folded by the side of the plate. He hadn't even looked up and I nearly bottled it. I could have ducked outside. I could have rung him and cancelled. The truth, that Ian was out of action, would have been enough. But seeing Andy there, our last conversation rushed back into my head. I reminded myself of the places I wanted to be, the people I wanted to be with. I took my purse out of my handbag to make myself look purposeful, and walked over.

"Hi, can I get you another?"

"Hi, Ailsa." He was looking behind me, expecting Ian. "On yer own?"

The ring was still on my finger. I hadn't been able to abandon it and I had said nothing to Mum. Having it there gave me time to think, to adjust to being just me again. And it meant I didn't have to tell Andy about my new situation. Not yet.

"Ian had an accident. He broke his leg two weeks ago. I thought he'd be okay to come, but he didn't feel like it."

"Poor guy," Andy said. "Still, I bet you make a lovely Florence Nightingale." The implication was obvious, but friendly, not having a go. I took it as a compliment.

"Hope you don't mind. I felt like a change of scenery."

"Sure. Why not?" He was surprised that I'd come alone, but not unduly perturbed.

"Drink?" I reminded him.

"Just a half, thanks. I'm driving later. Promised my mum a lift to see some of her pals."

I wondered if Irene Chalmers' pals included Rhona Mackay, but couldn't be bothered to worry about it. I bought myself a cider and some crisps, thinking I was managing pretty well for a girl who'd never been in a pub on her own.

I sat down opposite Andy and shrugged off my jacket. Andy's eyes strayed briefly past my neck to where beads of sweat were forming in the U of my scoop-necked top.

"Walked fast, did you?"

"Pretty fast. Sometimes I run. I like running."

"What, you mean like training?"

"A bit. I have an exercise bike, though I've been slacking lately. Time I put more effort in." I let him play around with the picture of me on the bike, getting a sweat on. Almost a smile. The idea of flirting with me wasn't too far away.

"I used to go to the gym," he said, "but not really my scene."

"What's your scene then?"

He shrugged. "My brother was in the rugby crowd so I used to hang around with them, but I don't like the game. I sometimes play five-a-side football with guys at Law School. Just for a laugh." He was appraising me again, reminding himself I was Ian's girlfriend. "That your usual running gear?"

"Not exactly. Just felt like some exercise on my way up."

He finished his pint and picked up the half I had bought. "S*lainge.*"

I raised my glass in response. I guessed that as soon as he'd finished his meal he'd be off.

"How's the food?"

"Not bad. Are you eating?"

"No. I'm okay." I'd opened the crisps. Food was pretty low on my priorities right now, but I'd nearly finished my drink. I went to the bar and got myself a vodka.

Andy raised his eyebrows. "Interesting fitness regime."

"All work and no play," I said.

"I had another look at that picture, the photograph," he said.

"You mean the house at Largo?"

144

He nodded. "I'd forgotten it was there. Must have been taken years ago." He put down his knife and fork. "Talking of houses, have you moved in yet?"

"Och, no. We haven't even signed anything." I watched my dream of domestic bliss, forgotten in the events of the previous night, dissolve in the bottom of my glass.

He looked surprised. "I would do it. Soon as. I hear they're selling well." He wiped his mouth on a napkin, a gesture that was oddly fastidious, then drank again from the half-pint.

I steered the conversation away from Ian and domesticity. "So, your sister. How old was she? Is she, I mean."

Andy grimaced at the unexpected question and did some mental calculations. "Four years older than me. I suppose she'd be twenty-eight, twenty-nine. Why?"

When I was five Nancy must have been around twelve or thirteen. That was exactly right. "And was she quite tall with blonde hair?"

"Tallish, I suppose. We all were. My mum's tall. And she was fairer than me, I think."

I played my trump card. "And she was called Nancy." Not even a question, I just knew it.

"She was indeed." He gave me an appraising look, as if I were party to classified information.

"I was there," I said. "She used to look after me on the beach."

That made him sit up. "You're kidding?"

I had him now: surprised, interested – interested in me. "My mum wasn't well. I got to stay with Nancy, sometimes on my own. She was really nice to me. I remember now that she had brothers."

He laughed. "Well, would you credit it?" He turned a few things over in his mind then the smile faded into a frown of forgetfulness, or maybe regret. "She was always off doing stuff on her own. Sometimes she did have other kids in tow."

I tried not to think that I was only one in a line of beach companions to Nancy.

"Well, one of them was me."

He sat back from the table, looking at me with fresh eyes, grinning openly, showing his even, white teeth.

I grinned back. "I bet you went fishing off the pier," I said.

"Too right."

"And flung fish at us."

"And you cried."

I laughed. "Well, I was only five, remember."

"And my sister chased us off. She could be quite scary. I remember that."

"Yeah. Scary, but nice." Andy and I were partners in some long-forgotten adventure. "What happened to her? Where is she now?"

The frown again. "She went away. Boarding school. There was some bother – with a lad I think. Must have been bad. My folks never got over it."

"And now?"

He shrugged, embarrassed at his own ignorance.

"You mean you don't hear from her? She never came back?

He shook his head. "We don't talk about it. She just became… off limits, I suppose. I think my brother might be in touch with her, but she and I were never close."

"That's terrible. Did you never want to know what happened to her?"

It was a rebuke and Andy looked uncomfortable. "Sounds bad, doesn't it? But it's funny how you get used to things. If your questions don't get answered, you stop asking."

I couldn't argue with that. He drained his glass and grabbed his coat from the back of the chair. "Look, I have to go. But I'll be in here next week. What about Thursday? Get Ian up off his arse and we can make a night of it."

Outside the pub, I hugged my new knowledge to myself. Nancy might be off the scene, but Andy was centre stage. I slipped the ring off my finger, put it in the pocket of my bag and pulled the zip across. It was time to cut loose.

CHAPTER EIGHTEEN

I tested my wings by sending Faye a text: *"Latest news. Dumped Ian."*

It was a day before an answer came back and I was surprised at it. *"Sorry to hear. What happened? R u okay?"* She hadn't liked Ian much, but she'd come round to the idea of me and him together.

"I was thinking," Mum said the next night. "Can I use your laptop some time? I'd like to do some research on lupus. Maybe you could give me a hand?" She was too full of her new found status as official lupus sufferer to even notice I'd taken off the ring.

I stomped off upstairs. "Fine," I said. "Whenever you like."

On Saturday morning I showed her the sites I'd already seen myself. By midday she had an email account and was chatting to some lupus person in Glasgow. At one o'clock she called me through.

"I've had enough for one day," she said. "But it's great. I'll have to get one for myself. In fact, if I get clued up, I was thinking I might get a wee job."

"What kind of job?"

"I don't know. Maybe I could be a doctor's receptionist or something?"

"What about Smoothies?"

"I could wind it down. A job would be better money, I think. Or I could even do both."

"Best take it steady for a while, don't you think?"

I closed the lid of the laptop and she noticed my empty finger at last.

"Where's your ring?"

I carried on packing away the laptop. "Ian and I are on a break."

"Why?"

"Just a bit of a disagreement."

"Sounds like more than that to me. Or if it's only a tiff, why on earth break it off? You've only been engaged two minutes."

I shrugged. "His idea, not mine."

This was an out-and-out lie, but it had the desired effect of shutting Mum up.

The following week, I went to Edinburgh every day but didn't go to lectures. I worried about bumping into Gill Patterson, still waiting for the essay. I worried about the essay, but failed to do anything about it. Mum didn't seem to need my care any more and Ian was in the past. There was nothing to stop me making a go of English literature. But was it still what I wanted to do?

On the Thursday I met Barbara on the train. "What happened to you? Patterson's after your blood."

I sighed. "Yeh. She's been sending me emails." By now I'd had one from the head of department. "I split up with Ian. I needed to sort my head out."

149

"No!" Barbara was scandalised. "What happened? I thought you were all fixed up?"

"So did I, but I came to my senses. Think it's a bit too soon to settle down."

"Well…" Barbara was still gobsmacked. I'd really sold her the idea of me as a wee wifey. "Still, better now than later," she conceded. "Maybe they'll give you an extension for the essay."

"Hope so," I said.

To keep Barbara happy, I went to the lecture, but I sneaked out before the end. Walking back over George IV Bridge I saw the big public library and went in. I couldn't see my academic career lasting much longer. But I didn't know what else I might do. In the echoing reading room I was at least anonymous and didn't feel I had to hide. I wandered up and down the bookshelves, thinking of futures I might have had and what might be left. There were no books that I could find on being a fishmonger, but there were quite a few about fish.

I took a few off the shelves and gazed for a while at tropical oceans and coral reefs. But this wasn't the sea I knew. I went back and found another. *Scotland's Coastal Waters*. This was a less glamorous kind of ocean, the marine life that teemed below the waves more workaday, but just as fascinating.

I thought back to Largo. Me, plowtering with Dad in a rock pool. Dad looking in my bucket. "Ye've a wee crab in there, look." The big girl appearing, curious and unabashed. "Hiya, what have you found? Can I see?" We made room for her and she hunkered down. "I found a starfish yesterday," she said. But in the book there were more creatures than Nancy and I had ever seen as we dipped and raised our buckets at low tide.

A text arriving made me jump. It was Andy.

"Sorry. Can't make pub 2nite. In Ebrough."

Andy's Edinburgh and mine had always been separate entities. But it didn't have to be that way, not any more.

"Me too. Where r u?"

He replied with the name of a pub on the Royal Mile, not ten minutes from where I stood. I took it as an invitation.

As far as the legal community was concerned, it looked like Thursday lunch-time was the start of the weekend. The pub was cramped and filled with people, not couples but gangs, men, women, or both, all intent on getting bevvied up.

Andy was at the bar with two mates. They had their elbows on the counter, staking a claim on their territory. When he saw me, he didn't acknowledge me but turned back to his pals and finished his drink. I reminded myself I had as much right to be there as anybody. There were still some tables free, so I bought myself a cider and sat down. I took my phone out and sent a text to Faye, just to make it look as if I had somebody to talk to.

A few minutes later Andy came over, followed by a gust of muted laughter from his cronies. In slouchy jeans and a t-shirt bearing the name of a heavy rock band, he looked scruffier than usual.

"I wasn't expecting to see you," he said.

I thought he'd had a few already. "You said where you were. I was only round the corner."

"No lectures?"

I shrugged. "I'm not really in the mood. Ian and I broke up."

151

"So I heard."

Ian had spilled the beans. I was looking at my hand without its ring. I was getting used to it. I preferred it.

"Why did you?" Andy said.

"What?"

"Why did you break up?"

He was a lot less affable than the last night we'd met. I put it down to his already having had a bit to drink. To catch up, I knocked back more of my own.

"Irreconcilable differences."

He leaned back in his chair, looking at me. I couldn't see a problem so I looked back at him and smiled.

He watched me drinking. "So is this a celebration? Or drowning your sorrows?"

I dodged the question. "So what else is new?" I asked him. "How's work?"

"S'all right. Same old."

I made a face. "Yeah. Know what you mean. I'm pretty much in the doodoo right now."

Somebody at the bar hailed Andy. "Your round, man. Get them in. Leave that lassie alone."

"Okay, in a minute," he called back. Then to me, "Maybe you should be catching up. Getting back on track."

"Give me a break," I said. "You sound like my tutor. Anyway, you were going to tell me about your sister. We could go somewhere else," I said. "If you fancy a chat."

"I don't think so," he said. "Here'll be fine. But I need to get the drinks. Same again?"

He went to the bar and a wad of money changed hands. When he came back he had a long glass in his hand. The drink was blue and had a plastic umbrella floating on the top with a pineapple chunk.

I'd had cocktails before but this one had a hell of a kick. "What's this?" I said.

"It's called Sex on the Beach. Like it?"

It was taking my head off, but I wasn't going to let him know. "It's okay. A bit strong for dinner time."

"Yeah, well. It's a big bad world. Maybe you shouldn't be out in it alone."

I could see he wasn't pleased. Surely he wasn't miffed at his dad losing a house sale?

"Look, Ian and me, it wouldn't have worked."

He shrugged.

"I liked your sister," I said. "We got on. I was wondering if I could get in touch with her."

"I don't think so. Like I said, I'm not really in touch with her myself."

"But you could get me an address, or a number?"

Andy got up. "It's probably best if you finish that drink and go home."

I'd gone too far, or hit a raw nerve. If I hadn't had the drink I might have done as he said. But he was the one who had bought it for me. I couldn't decipher the messages. He was moving away but I got up and went after him, catching at his elbow.

"What's wrong?" I said to him. "We've only just started."

Andy took my arm off his. I caught the words of a song being sung at the bar, not loud and raucous, but in the undertone of a joke shared between friends. "*The girl can't help it, the girl can't help it.*" Nudge, nudge, wink, wink.

Andy came back towards the table, but we couldn't sit down because another couple had pounced on it. "Started what?"

"Having a drink. Talking."

"And now we've stopped."

"But what happened to Nancy? Where is she now? Why won't you tell me about her?" I said. In a pause in the conversation around the bar I heard my own voice, strident and needy.

This time Andy took my elbow and steered me into a corner.

"For God's sake, just leave it," he said. "You're making a scene." His voice was quiet, like a teacher trying to calm down a class of rowdy kids. "Look, I shouldn't have bought you the drink. The guys wanted to see you get drunk. I shouldn't even be the one telling you this."

The drink made my head swim. Luckily I was lodged in the corner between two walls. Otherwise I wouldn't have fancied my chances.

"Telling me what?"

He ran his hand over his hair. I remembered him doing this before, maybe that night at Torryburn, when I had kissed him for no reason. You could do that kind of thing when you were with someone. Freedom was more difficult to manage.

"All right," he said. "Have it your own way. My sister Nancy. She was only thirteen or fourteen when she got into trouble. My mum wouldn't have her in the house. She got sent away. She didn't even come home in the holidays."

"That's awful."

"I know, but that's how it was."

154

"What kind of trouble? With the police?"

"No. Not that kind of trouble."

I blushed, realising I sounded naïve. There was trouble and there was trouble. "She was pregnant?"

"I don't actually know. But let's say we're in the right area."

My befuddled brain sensed that girls "got into trouble" all the time. What made it different was the lad, or maybe not a lad. "A man then, an older man?"

Andy nodded.

"And she was only thirteen?" I was thinking of Zoe Lawson who'd had to leave school when she got up the duff. But she had been older, fifteen at least. What men does a thirteen-year-old know, I asked myself.

The words tumbled out. "Someone in the family?" That would explain why the parents had flipped. Never to see her again. That was terrible.

Andy was looking at the wall over my head. "No, not family."

"Who then?"

"If you must know, a married man, a teacher. Someone she knew from school."

His eyes flicked down to me and away again, but it was enough.

That night with Faye in the East Port. *"My brother went to the High School."* Before she'd been sent away, Nancy had been at the High too. Dad left the year after we went to Largo. The girl had been thirteen.

I heard an awful groan and realised it had come from me. I clamped my mouth shut against the sound of it.

Andy stood back next to me, leaning against the wall, talking to the air.

155

"I only knew she'd been in trouble with a man. Then last week I told Dad I'd had a drink with you. That you were a laugh. He said best to keep away, did I not know that your dad was a teacher, *the* teacher? That's when I realised. Until tonight I thought you must have known too."

I shook my head. My dad. And her. Nancy. Andy's sister. Oh God. I was crying so much I couldn't speak. The kind of crying that isn't tears but comes up from your guts in big gusts.

"I'm sorry," Andy said, pulling himself together, still not looking at me. The boys at the bar had lost interest. At least we were in Edinburgh. I somehow knew that if we'd been in the East Port Bar his mates would have known. Known I was the daughter of that teacher, the one who had to leave.

"I wouldn't have told you," Andy said, "but you were getting on my tits. Practically making a pass at me. You want to watch that, drinking too much. Never a good thing in a woman."

If Andy had more to say I never heard it. There's that instant between feeling like you're going to throw up and actually doing it, when your stomach heaves even if it's empty and anything your body can throw out is on its way, hot, sour and unstoppable.

I made it to the loo just in time.

CHAPTER NINETEEN

By the time I emerged, Andy had disappeared and conversation in the bar had reasserted itself. I was forgotten; just another lassie that couldn't take a drink. I headed for the street where the thin sun of early spring felt too bright on my face. I was in a cold sweat. I could see her now – Nancy on the beach, long brown legs and a faded t-shirt, looking over my head, scanning the foreshore. "Look Ailsa, they have a big sandcastle over there, let's go and help."

When she knelt by the rock pool was he looking at her then, where her legs disappeared under the frayed denim of the cut-off shorts, wondering what the t-shirt concealed? Or had it taken longer, seeing her again at school, inviting her to his classroom after hours, Little Miss Naughty. I steadied myself against a wall, no way could I be sick again.

I managed to get to the station and onto a train where I slumped against the window, cringing at how I had behaved. I'd been a prat to make a play for Andy. I'd stepped in their family shit, but then how was I to know? No one had ever told me. By the Bridge, the rhythm of the train had calmed me down. The nausea had passed, and some of the guilt. That left only anger.

At home, Mum was settled in front of a TV detective series. When she saw me, she looked twice.

"What happened to you?"

"I was sick."

In the last few days her buoyant mood had subsided, but she still looked happy and at ease with herself. I thought of all the years I'd taken care of her. Years when she had known full well what Dad had done – and the girl he had violated.

"Where were you sick?" she said. "At the university?"

"No. In a pub."

"Are you not well?"

"I'm fine. I was just drunk."

"At this time of day? What were you thinking of?"

I was still in the doorway, afraid that if I sat down some of the anger might go out of me.

"Is this about Ian?" Mum said. "He's such a nice boy. It'll be a shame if you split up."

Trust Mum to wait until it was all over to voice her approval.

"I thought you didn't like him."

"That's not true. I just wondered if it was a bit quick, the engagement. So why does he want to break it off?"

"He doesn't. It's me. I want to be a free woman." I held my hand out in front of me, checking that the ring hadn't magically reappeared. "So now I am."

Having said my piece, I decided to sit down after all. On TV, the detective hissed annoyance at his plodding side-kick. I leaned back in the chair and stuck my legs in front of me, turning up the toes of my trainers in defiance. "Yeah. I'm back on the market."

"Don't talk like that."

I leaned down and rolled up one leg of my jeans. When I stroked my bare shin I found a satisfactory growth of stubble. "I think it's time I smartened up."

"Or sobered up, more like. I think you need a good night's sleep."

I submitted the other leg to inspection. "Students, eh? No money for beauty treatments. But you could give me one. You always said shaving was a mistake."

"Well, I can if you want me to."

"Yeah, I think I do." I sat up. "Come on then."

"What, now?"

"Why not? You wouldn't want me going about with hairy legs. What kind of an advert is that?"

If she was thinking it had never bothered me before, she was too stunned to say so.

The Treatment Room was as it had always been: a spruced-up kitchen cupboard with a diary on top, a trolley with bottles and jars jostling for space, the TV in its corner, waiting to be brought to life. Without any sun coming in, the room was soft and welcoming. Mum left the main light off and switched on a spotlight that fell on the table, leaving the rest of the room in shadow. I was glad of the semi-darkness; it might take the edge off what was to come.

Mum delved in her cupboard for some sugar paste, put a chunk in the heater and switched it on. Her movements were practised and economical. Unlike me, she was at home here. I stood inhaling the warmth of the melting sugar, waiting to be told what to do.

159

She looked round at me. "Changed your mind?"

"No."

"Go on then."

I stepped out of my jeans, hung them over a chair and got up on the narrow bench. I was the patient on the table. No chance of etherisation.

"What do you want me to do?" Mum asked.

"Just my legs."

She was still assembling her tools. "I'll just do half. It's usually a bit sore the first time. Next time I could do the rest."

"No, I want it all. Whole leg. No point in hanging about."

She looked at me again, laid out on her couch. "If it's just legs, you don't have to lie down." A pause. "Don't blame me when it hurts."

I half sat up, leaning on my elbows, and she slapped a wodge of sugar paste on my leg. It was searingly hot, but I liked it that way. Then, before I knew it, she had ripped off the sticky paste and taken what felt like half my leg with it. I yelped. "Ow!" Tears welled up.

Mum said nothing, but put her hand over the place she had assaulted.

"Okay?"

"Yeh." I sniffed and gripped the edge of the bed, ready for the next one.

"Yer skin's quite fair," she explained, as she must have done to countless unlucky customers. I wondered why they put themselves through this. Or did they all have something to beat themselves up about?

After a few more goes, I got used to the rhythm. Stroke, *rip*, press, stroke, *rip*, press. This is what I had wanted. I deserved it for the way I had treated Ian, for liking the pictures in the magazine, for dumping him, for flirting with Andy – Andy whose sister Dad had… The pain brought welcome catharsis. Maybe Aristotle knew about hot wax.

"Turn over a minute and I'll do the back." She grasped my ankle so that the muscles were taut, and started again. I was used to it now, and able to talk through the seconds when the hair came off.

"I know about Dad."

I couldn't see her face, but felt her concentration on the task in hand. A professional, she didn't want to get distracted.

"So are you going to tell me? What it is you know, or think you know?"

"Well I've known for ages he was done for rape. A schoolgirl."

Her voice didn't change its tone. The rhythm stayed the same. "Who told you that?"

"Not exactly a secret, when it's in the *Press*."

"It would have been a secret if you hadn't gone looking."

"Well, what did you expect me to do? Stay in the dark all my life?"

"You could have asked me."

But it was like Andy had said, some things you don't ask. You know they're off limits.

"The charges were withdrawn," she said. "He wasn't found guilty."

"But he was guilty, wasn't he?"

She had finished the back of my leg and so I rolled over. She looked back at me. She had given up her fight to hold on to the truth.

161

"I don't know. I never did know what to believe. I was angry with him, all right. Just for being there, for letting it happen, whether he started it or not."

"She was only thirteen. Of course he started it."

That was a mistake, reminding her. She set about my other leg, working faster, not taking so much care. It bloody hurt.

"Why now?" she said. "Why can't you just let it lie?"

"Because I know who she was. Nancy, the girl on the beach."

"And does that make a difference?"

"Of course it bloody does. I knew her. I liked her." I didn't add, "She's the sister of the boy I've been chatting up", no need to confuse the issue. "I liked her a lot."

Mum stopped what she was doing. She wiped her forehead, using the back of her hand so as not to make it sticky.

"I wasn't to know you would get so hung up on her. It's years ago."

"I spent half the week with her. She was my friend. You must have seen it."

"On holiday? I didn't spend much time on the beach, if that's what you mean."

She didn't say it but it hung in the air, the thought that her illness might have contributed. As I thought about it I did remember, suddenly, how one afternoon she came along the beach to join us, with sunglasses on and a hat. I pointed and laughed. "Here's Mum. She looks really funny." Dad looked up but kept on shovelling sand from the moat of our sandcastle. Nancy appeared with a bucket and poured in the sea water. It

162

swirled around the trench and disappeared to leave a scum of foam. "Look," I said to her, "my mum's coming." But when I'd next looked up, Nancy had gone.

"Well, maybe it was better then that you didn't know," Mum said, "if she was so special. Who told you? Was it Ian?"

"No, not Ian," I shouted in exasperation. Outside in the street, footsteps went past. The neighbours had always had suspicions about our house and our family, about what happened in the Treatment Room.

More surprise from Mum. She remembered I had asked about Andy. "I suppose you've been seeing the Chalmers boy." As if that had been an obvious mistake.

"I went to his party, for God's sake. I was buying his father's fucking house."

Mum was wiping my legs with something cold and moist. "I did wonder, when you started off with Ian. But I didn't think Rhona would say. She's okay, despite her airs and graces. There was no need for anybody to say, for anybody to even think about it."

"Well, it doesn't matter any more. I won't be seeing any of them."

The cold stuff had dried on me and now she was rubbing lotion onto my legs with a firm stroke. This must be what women came for, the relief after the pain. But I wasn't ready for relief.

"You just let me go on making a fool of myself."

"What do you mean?"

"Other people always knew. Knew about Dad. Knew who I was. It was only Ian who was okay."

"Maybe you should have stuck with him then." Mum wiped her hands and took off the thin latex gloves

163

she'd been wearing. "It's a shame she was the one. But it could have been anybody. Anybody young and silly enough."

I couldn't believe she was doing this, dismantling my dream, shredding my memories like so much dead skin, while she closed bottles and wiped surfaces. I sat up, oblivious to my newly naked legs.

"Are you saying it was her fault?"

"No, I'm not saying that. But some things we'll likely never know. Not now."

"What things?"

"Like if she led him on, even without meaning to. And if it really was…" Even Mum stumbled over the word *rape*. "Like I say, he wasn't charged."

I'd heard enough. I got up off the bed and hauled my jeans back on as fast as I could. "I bet you didn't say that at the time," I said, fumbling with the fastenings. "You never wanted him back. I heard you say it."

She gave a half smile. "Well, of course I said it. And I meant it. But looking back, he wasn't all bad. He was a good father to you. Maybe I should have stood by him."

"A bit bloody late for that," I said.

What had brought this on? Mum speaking up for Dad. It didn't make sense. But I knew she might be right about some things. If Nancy had given Dad any encouragement that would explain why she had left in disgrace. Otherwise the family would have stood by her and looked after her, not cut her off for good. Or had there been a baby after all? Whatever had happened in the Chalmers' household, Andy had been kept out of it too.

Mum ran the back of her hand across her forehead again. She looked exhausted. "Look, there's something else you need to know."

Oh great. What else could there possibly be? But I'd been asking for the truth. I couldn't stop her now.

"Well, go on then. Spit it out."

"Your father won't be bothering us again. A letter came, the end of last week. He died, more than a month ago."

CHAPTER TWENTY

"What do you mean, died?"

Under my jeans my legs felt clammy from unabsorbed moisturiser. Mum went through to the back room and came back with an envelope. This must be the letter I had seen before. The one that had put her on edge.

"Open it," she said. "See for yourself."

I took out the single sheet which unfolded in my hand under its own weight.

"*We regret to inform you that following the death of the account holder, and in the absence of any provision in his estate, payments to account 12759 will cease forthwith.*"

My legs, already stripped and smarting, gave way under me. I sat down on the floor with my back to the wall. Mum stood leaning against the treatment bench. Of all the things I'd thought about Dad, I'd never imagined him gone.

"So when was it? When did he die?"

"I don't know. Nobody told me."

"So did you contact these people?"

"No. But I'm guessing it would be some time ago. This is just winding up the estate, or whatever he had to wind up."

"Why didn't you say?"

"I haven't seen much of you. And you were in a state. This thing with Ian. Running upstairs every night."

She held out her hand for the letter and I gave it back. I guessed she'd needed to process this news and work out what it meant for her. I remembered the idea of a job.

"Will you be short of money?"

"I don't think so. Not really. The maintenance would have finished when you left uni anyway."

I felt a weight lifting. My dad, hero or villain? Like Mum had said, I would probably never know. I could see it was for the best.

Mum came over and gave me a hand up off the floor. "Think about it. This is good for you, Ailsa. You can forget about Tom, and that girl, for good. Put your mind to your studying, get back with Ian. Everything will be fine."

As soon as I was on my feet I let go of her hand. What she had said about not finding time to tell me just wasn't true. We'd spent most of Saturday together. Was she only telling me now because she thought she could keep me here? I could have cried, but instead I laughed.

"Oh, Mum, you don't get it, do you? I don't want Ian. I don't even think I want uni."

She looked, not angry exactly, but hurt and confused. "But surely—"

"Why do you think I didn't go to Edinburgh in the first place? Why do you think I went out with Ian? I

167

was scared of meeting other people. I was scared of Dad somehow coming back to mess things up. Well, I'm not scared any more." I was so pumped up I could have gone there and then. "I'll be off," I said. "In the morning."

"Och, Ailsa, no. You need to calm down. We're both tired. We'll talk properly. Tomorrow. I only want what's best for you."

I picked up my shoes and socks and left her down there in the empty room, the letter still in her hand.

Upstairs, I tried to recapture the momentary elation I had felt when I realised nothing bound me to Mum and to home any longer, but it had been replaced by a creeping sense of emptiness and cold. Now even the good stuff had gone, the memories of a nice Dad ruined by what had happened after the days on the beach. Whatever he had been, now I could never get him back.

I reached for my phone and sent a text to Faye: *"Need somewhere 2 stay few nights. Can we meet 2moro?"* I fell asleep with the phone in my hand, still waiting for a reply.

It arrived next morning. Faye said she'd be out all day but that Danny would be in. He knew I was coming.

I had imagined student houses to be up closes in the old town or overlooking the Meadows, stone built with high ceilings. If Scottstoun Gardens was anything to go by, Napier students inhabited run-down semis on estates that been reclaimed from the council or simply gone out of fashion. Even "Gardens" was a misnomer. The outside space had been paved over for extra parking, a cracked flowerpot outside number sixteen, where I was headed, contained only two dog-ends and a ring pull.

When I rang the bell, the door was opened by a boy whose mousey-blond hair fell across his face on a sharp diagonal. In the half of his face that I could see, there was one greenish eye, the corner of a mouth and a fair-skinned cheek with pale freckles visible under the surface.

"Hi," I said to the one eye. "I'm Ailsa. Faye said I could come."

"Yeah."

I followed him in.

We went to the end of the hall towards the kitchen, passing an open door on the left where I saw a sofa in patterned green velour that might have been thrown out by Rhona Mackay ten years earlier. I reminded myself that the sofa might be the only thing between me and the mean streets. The colour hardly mattered.

Danny padded ahead of me on black socks worn thin on the heel. In the kitchen, he opened a cupboard and surveyed the meagre offerings. With his narrow eyes and silent footsteps, he reminded me of a cat.

"Tea? Bovril? I think Faye's goin' for some messages."

"I'm okay," I said. "Wouldn't mind some water."

The sink was full of dirty dishes. He picked a glass off the draining board, inspected it for dregs, then rinsed it under the tap. The water splashed off the mucky crockery onto his sweatshirt. "Shit," he said, shook the fabric dry, then filled the glass and gave it to me.

"Thanks."

The water was lukewarm because he hadn't run the tap for long enough. The kitchen, the whole house, smelled of something cooked yesterday mixed with something else, leaking gas or a damp carpet.

169

He opened a tin and offered me the contents, half a packet of cream crackers. I shook my head.

"You're a student then?" he said.

I nodded. "Could be past tense. I'm about to get chucked out."

He grimaced. It happened.

"Faye said I could crash here for tonight," I said. "When is she back?"

He shrugged. "Some time this afternoon. She said to make yourself at home."

"Okay."

We stood there, neither of us knowing how this could actually be achieved.

"There's a TV," he said, "in the front."

Danny disappeared upstairs. I sat on the green sofa with my holdall beside me and watched a presenter rummage through household junk in the hope of finding antiques. I remembered I had bought a newspaper and started looking through the jobs pages. There was nothing that looked suitable for a first-year uni drop-out with experience of selling fish. I wished it was Christmas or even the summer holidays, then there would have been more casual work.

After half an hour I needed to pee, badly. There was one other door off the hallway at the front of the house, but it was closed and had a Yale lock on it, probably a bedroom. A look in the kitchen confirmed there was no downstairs loo and so I braved the narrow staircase, clumping up as loud as I could so that Danny, wherever he was, didn't think I was prowling. It had the desired effect. His voice came through a half-open door.

"The bog's second door on the right."

"Thanks."

170

Inside, the fittings were muddy green, except for a new-looking shower jammed into the corner between the bath and the door. The shower tray was white and carpet next to it a darker colour than the rest. Scented candles cluttered the ledge behind the bath. I picked one up to test its fragrance and uncovered a cracked tile. I wondered what Danny made of the bras and thongs that hung on the edge of the bath. Did he hang his washing here too?

As I emerged onto the landing I could see into Danny's room. He was sitting on the floor next to the bed, with a book and a notepad balanced on his knee, having abandoned the laptop open on a desk under the window. He wrote left-handed and curled his arm around to get the writing in the right direction. With most people it looked awkward, but with him there was a kind of gracefulness about it. On the floor beside him there was another book. I recognised the woman on the cover straight away.

"Elizabeth Johnstone Hall." My reaction was spontaneous and it covered that moment of embarrassment when Danny looked up and saw me looking in at him for no good reason.

"Sorry?" With his head tilted upwards towards me I could see two green cat's eyes.

I nodded towards the book and the sepia fisherwoman in her striped frock. "I saw that photo. In an exhibition."

He nodded. "Portrait Gallery. Keep meaning to go."

"You should. It's really good."

"No time," he said. "Essay's due Monday. Anyway it's all in the book."

"Can I have a look?"

He said nothing but I went in, lifted the book from the floor and retired to the doorway. Close lines of text surrounded photographs and line-drawings, all on the heavy gloss paper favoured by art books. I flicked through some of the plates: the Scott Monument half-built, rearing up from its surroundings like a broken tooth, portraits of Victorian women in stiff-bowed bonnets, or younger girls, dreamy in muslin and ringlets.

"Do you know much about this stuff?" I said. "I mean, what is a calotype exactly?"

Danny kept writing and frowned, probably wondering why he should give me the time of day.

"It's the earliest kind of photographic print on paper," he said. "Up to then they had the daguerreotype, just one picture, created on metal, beautiful but unique. The calotype produced a negative image and from it you could make as many prints as you liked."

He was frowning at me but thinking of something else, probably how what he had told me would fit into the essay. "The trouble was," he was still thinking aloud, "they hadn't perfected the process. The chemicals were unstable and the exposure time was ridiculous. The sitters," he indicated the book in my hand, "had to keep still for over a minute."

I looked again at some of the pictures and was doubly impressed. "I thought you did modern stuff, film and digital."

"I do. This is the history option. I kind of like it, to be honest."

I made to put the book back on the floor.

"Take it if you like," he said, back at his note-taking. "I won't need it for a while."

172

I went downstairs with the book. I liked its weight in my arms. I thought I could feel at home here.

"Ailsa Robertson. Look at you!"

I woke with Faye standing over me. I had no recollection of falling asleep and felt groggy and cold. The green sofa had turned out to be surprisingly firm and I rubbed my stiff shoulder. Behind Faye there was a girl with red hair. Red as in the colour of an overripe raspberry, eyes so blacked out with make-up you could hardly guess her expression. I wasn't sure it was friendly.

"Mo, this is my mate, Ailsa."

We nodded silently and Mo, having viewed the new arrival, disappeared.

"You look like shite," Faye said.

"I feel it."

"No Ian?"

"Nope."

"No uni?"

"Nope."

My phone buzzed with a text. I glanced at it. Mum. Again. I switched it off. "I can't stay at home, not any more."

"God, Ailsa. You don't do things by half, do you?"

She sat beside me and looked straight ahead. Despite our years of friendship and shared confidences, neither of us was quite prepared for this, a real crisis. I was grateful for her silence. If she had asked me for an explanation, I wouldn't have had the first idea where to start. With Andy, with Ian, with my mum? As for Dad, Faye didn't even know the beginning of the story.

Eventually she did put an arm around my shoulder and I leaned against her. "Thanks," I said. "I will explain. Some time."

"No rush," Faye said.

Mo walked in on us and picked up the remote. "Do you mind?" she said and changed the channel before either of us could reply. Not long after another girl came in. She and Mo went off together. Faye said she was Sadie. She and Mo shared the front room, the one with the lock on.

"Don't worry," I said to Faye. "I'll get a job and find some place else."

"It's no problem," Faye said. "Stay here as long as you like." She got up. "You'd better come and see my humble abode. Bring your bag. If you have one."

Upstairs the door to Danny's room was closed. Faye's was along the landing, next to the bathroom. She said I could unpack some stuff but there wasn't much room. I left my bag on the floor, kicking it into a corner.

Faye was outside again, banging on Danny's door. "Fancy a pizza, McLure? Or are you still in the sack?"

"Fat chance." Danny's reply was just audible through the closed door.

I went on downstairs as they completed their negotiations and heard the door bang as Danny went on his way.

Faye came into the lounge. "He won't be long. I got some milk and eggs but I'm just famished. Bet you are too."

"Yeh, sure." I had no say here. I would do as I was told and eat what was provided. Luckily I had withdrawn some cash on my way over so could make a contribution. I was more interested in how things lay between Faye and Danny.

"Are you and Danny… you know?"

"Naw."

"But you'd like to?"

She shrugged. "Dunno really. We get on. I like him."

I nodded. "He's okay. I can see you together."

"You reckon?"

I had said what she wanted to hear. After all, she was helping me out big time. And I could see them together, in a way. But something about him didn't quite fit.

"How old is he?" I asked.

Faye picked at her sleeve. "He's a year younger. He skipped sixth year. He already had the grades."

That was it. Faye had always gone after older boys; it was usually older boys who fancied her.

"So what?" I said. "He's nice. I like him."

CHAPTER TWENTY-ONE

The girls had gone out for the night. With Danny on the
pizza run the flat was empty; I knew I would have to tell
Faye something.

"Last summer I found out the real reason Dad did a
bunk."

We were both on the green sofa, our feet on a low
coffee table patterned with overlapping ring marks. On
TV a soap opera was trundling through the fallout of a
family feud.

Faye uncrossed her ankles and stretched her toes.
"You never said."

"I'm sorry. I was going to, but you were already
over here, in the house. Once I knew, I didn't really
want to talk about it."

Faye shifted in the seat but her gaze didn't move
from the TV. I wondered if she was actually watching
the show. "So, do you want to talk about it now?"

"Not really. But I feel bad that I didn't tell you. He
raped a girl in his class at school."

Faye tensed and drew away to look me in the eye.
"Oh God. Really? Are you sure?"

"It was in the papers and everything. The charges were dropped, so he didn't go down. But something must have been going on."

Faye was shaken. She had never met Dad, she had never had much to say for him, but even she had never envisaged this.

"But this was in September?"

"Yeh. That's partly why I plumped to stay at home. It kind of shook me up."

"What did your mum have to say about it?"

"I never said. I guessed that her illness was all part of it. No point stirring things up. Then later on – just last week – I discovered the girl, the victim, was somebody I knew. It was the summer before Dad left. We were on holiday at Largo. I'd palled up with her on the beach. I idolised her."

"And was that when your dad... on holiday? With you—" Faye's eyes were wide now, her voice failing to conceal that this news wasn't just horrific but sensational too, more sensational than any soap opera.

I cut her off. "No. I don't think so. It must have been later. But she was my friend. And my mum had never told me anything about it. That's why we had the row. Well, other stuff as well, but mainly that."

We heard the front door open and Danny arrived back, the flat box he bore in his arms giving off a stronger version of the aroma that already permeated the ground floor of the house. He laid the pizza on the coffee table. "Get stuck in," he said.

I moved away and sat cross-legged on the floor so that he could sit next to Faye. I hadn't got to the end of my story, but it didn't matter. Dad had always been out of the picture. In that respect not much had changed.

"What are you doing at uni?" Danny asked me as we divvied up the Neapolitan.

"I was doing English."

"Sorry, sorry. I forgot," he said. "Just wondered why you were into Hill and Adamson."

Faye looked between us. "Am I missing something here?"

"Danny and I were talking earlier, about his essay." Faye raised her eyebrows. "I went to an exhibition last month," I continued. "It was after that day I met you."

Danny detached a string of cheese that was binding a wedge of pizza to the one next to it. "I gave her the run-down on early photography."

The book had slid off the sofa during my nap and was still on the floor. I reached for it and handed it to Faye.

Faye took the book from me and studied the cover. "Who's this?

"A woman from Newhaven," Danny said. "It was a fishing village then. There's a whole series of pictures. Documentary photography they would call it now."

"Oh God," Faye rolled her eyes. "Not the fish fixation."

Danny looked at me from under the floppy fringe then back down at the remains of his pizza. His smile had changed to a grin, directed at Faye.

"No worse than some other fixations I could mention," he said.

There was a scuffle as Faye aimed a kick at him under the table.

"Pay no attention," Faye said. "Private joke." Then, "So, what will you do?"

"Give her a break," Danny said. "She's only just got here."

My status of crash victim at least guaranteed me time to draw breath. "No, it's okay. I'm going to get some place to stay. And a job."

Faye chewed through a portion of crust. "Doing what, exactly?"

That was the problem. A shop would be easiest. Somewhere to lick my wounds and think about what I might really want to do. I could go down Princes Street and see what turned up. I dug out the newspaper, still folded, from my bag. I'd circled a small ad, though I wasn't sure why.

I handed it to Faye. "I wondered about this. Though I'm not that good with computers."

Faye read it out. *"Girl Friday required by art dealer. Edinburgh based. Some travelling. Reilly Reprints and Reproductions."* She looked at me. "Hmm. Sounds well dodgy. It's only a mobile number. Could be anybody."

Danny leaned across and took the paper from her and studied the small print. "I know him."

Faye didn't seem as surprised as I was. "And?" she asked him.

Danny gave a Dannyish shrug, shoulders making new shapes under his thin jumper. "Bit of a wheeler dealer. He comes in the Dean with a laptop and mobile."

Now I was the one confused.

"Danny works for the National Galleries. Mostly the Dean."

"It's meant to be work experience," he said.

179

"That's bollocks," Faye said. "He works in the café."

I had never heard of the Dean, but that didn't matter. "So what about this Reilly outfit? What do they do? Buy stuff for the galleries?"

"Och, no. It's to do with the shop. He sells them mugs or ashtrays or whatever. Sometimes he gets them to release copyright of artworks so he can get things made, but usually he just sells standard souvenirs you can buy anywhere. Van Gogh or Monet or…" Danny tailed off through lack of interest.

Gift shops and copies. Not high art, just a business proposition. I thought I could cope with that. And it might be more fun than standing at a counter in BHS waiting for somebody to come in and recognise me. Someone like Liz. *"Och, Ailsa, so this is where you've been hiding?"*

Faye got up and stretched. It was only ten, but she had a laptop and a TV in her room. "I'm knackered," she said. "Bags first in the loo." Danny followed not long after.

I got into the musty sleeping bag that had been unearthed from Faye's wardrobe. Upstairs, doors opened and closed. I left it ten minutes then went up to the bathroom. I couldn't help noticing there were lights on under Danny's and Faye's doors, so it looked like Faye was telling the truth. They weren't making out, not yet. But I thought they would be soon. As long as I didn't get in the way.

CHAPTER TWENTY-TWO

Next day, I'd raised myself from the sofa and was making coffee when Danny came downstairs.

"Do you fancy coming with me to the Dean?" he said. "See what it's like. In case you go for that job."

I had no other plans. The thought of another day on the green sofa didn't have much to recommend it. I opened my mouth to accept then hesitated. Danny seemed to know why.

"Faye won't be bothered," he said. "You can be back in a couple of hours, sooner if you like."

Danny started at eleven. On the bus he explained that he usually worked Saturday and Sunday afternoon. Occasionally he got drafted to other galleries or did extra hours when they needed catering for special events like exhibition previews.

The Dean Gallery, an off-shoot, as Danny explained, of the Scottish National Gallery of Modern Art, was a stone building blackened by age, not huge exactly but imposing, set next to a green lawn. The entrance was spacious and formal, but inside we were in a narrow corridor. At the other end I could see the gift shop, flashing gaudy scarves and jewellery at me.

"How much is it to get in?" I asked Danny. Tourist attractions didn't figure in my current budget.

"It's free. Except for really big exhibitions."

Danny disappeared in the direction of the Terrace Restaurant and I went for a wander round. I didn't take much in at first. Paintings didn't mean a lot to me at the best of times, but the place had a good feel; the rooms were high but there were no big open spaces. It was more homely than institutional. I found a card that said the building had started life as a children's home. I hoped children had been happy here.

I found sculpture, pottery and a mock-up of some artist's workshop. Then I found a huge robot, half man-half machine. It took up two floors and the room had been built around it. The robot turned out to be Vulcan, a Roman god. They had given him his own personal kingdom. Quite right, too. He filled the space with his muscular presence. I wondered if he could be cranked or sparked into motion, and where his lithe and lumbering legs might choose to take him.

"Excuse me." Another visitor was trying to get a view of the giant.

I apologised and stepped aside. I'd been miles away. Was this the point of art? To take you out of yourself?

I drifted back to the restaurant, another narrow room with dark wood panelling. Black bentwood chairs with cane seats made squeaky grunts as they moved on the polished floorboards. It was a bit old-fashioned, a bit gloomy, but it looked and felt right. I envied Danny his job in civilised surroundings.

At one end there was a long bar of polished wood with an Italian coffee machine behind it. A girl in a black t-shirt and apron was dispensing hot drinks. A few tables were occupied. A couple clad in walking boots and anoraks, temporarily strayed from the main tourist trail, were working their way through two guide books and a plate of scones. A family looking for diversion on a dreich day were having trouble keeping the troops in order. "Sit down, Michael, we'll go to the park later," the frazzled mother addressed a boy kicking at a chair in frustration, while the father peered into a pushchair parked alongside. Despite them, the place had an air of calm.

Danny appeared from a door to the kitchen, said something to the girl then nodded an acknowledgement to me, his hair flopping back and forward, like it did. I hadn't realised the black jeans and t-shirt he'd worn on the way were uniform. He had a long apron too, tied round his non-existent waist, reaching halfway down his calves.

I stood by the bar and picked up a menu in a black plastic cover. Danny came over.

"I'll just get you some water if you like." He was mindful of my lack of funds.

"It's okay. I could do with a drink."

"Tell you what," he said. "I can do you a *citron pressé*. No charge. We don't sell that many. They'll never notice."

I wasn't going to turn down a free drink. He disappeared behind the counter where he was partly concealed by some contraption with a long handle. He pulled the handle slowly, his head bent over in concentration, like pulling a pint but more technical. It was a lemon squeezer.

Danny looked as at home here as he did everywhere else. It was an effort to look the other way. But even if he couldn't see me watching, I didn't want the other waitress to notice. He brought me the drink and sat beside me.

"Tea break?" I asked.

He shrugged. "It'll be busy soon. No sitting down then."

The lemon came in a glass with three sachets of sugar. I poured one in and watched it dissolve in a white cloud.

"Try it," he said, so I took a sip then screwed up my face. My mouth was pulled tight by the acid. Danny was grinning at me, one eye twinkling with glee.

"That's mean," I said.

In the warmth of the restaurant his face had more colour than in the flat. The freckles had deepened to a warm brown.

"You didn't pay, did you?" he said.

"Didn't ask to have my stomach raked either."

He grinned his feline grin. I added the rest of the sugar and sipped slowly.

"Think of it as detox," he said.

Good call. Detox was just what I needed, to be cleansed of everything that had gone before.

"Any jobs going here?" I said.

"I don't think so. Maybe in the summer. Or you could put your name down for temporary stuff. Sometimes there are events."

Temporary stuff meant temporary money.

"Does Faye have a job?" I pictured her in a black apron, next to Danny, serving canapés in a line.

"There's a pub up the road from the flat. She sometimes does Friday nights."

So they weren't joined at the hip, Danny and Faye.

"This Reilly. What do you reckon?"

"Ring him," Danny said, no hesitation.

"It's Saturday."

"Ring him anyway. Shows you're keen."

I was keen, keen to be out of the flat and away from Danny and his cat's eyes.

When I rang Shane Reilly, he suggested we met at the Modern Art Gallery, just across the road from the Dean. Danny called it "the big house."

"Do you want me to come?" Faye asked. "In case he gets funny?"

"How do you mean, funny?"

"You know, trying anything on."

"I applied for a job," I said. "And it's a public place."

"Well, just watch yourself."

I typed out a new CV and Danny printed it for me. I was thinking a job would need a reference. I didn't have much to offer, other than a tutor who'd chucked me off the course and a fishmonger whose son hated my guts. I sent a wheedling letter to Mrs Reedie at the garage, hoping no one had been in dishing the dirt.

Like the Dean, the Gallery of Modern Art was set in lawns, with the addition of a land sculpture, a swirly shape of grass and water that I felt was reminiscent of something I couldn't put a name to. On a cold spring Sunday most people were hurrying into the wide-columned arms of the portico, but two figures were navigating the curved terraces of the water feature. I recognised the couple I'd seen the previous day in the Dean café. They stopped from time to time to take in their surroundings, admiring the shape from different angles. The guidebook was still in the man's hand; they had a plan and they were sticking to it. When they got home they would say they had done Edinburgh, all of it.

Despite my bravado with Faye, my mouth was dry with nerves. A man I didn't know and a job I couldn't begin to imagine. I reminded myself that my options were limited. On the gravel drive, with visitors pushing on past me, I felt exposed against the grey sky.

My phone rang and I took it from my bag. It was Reilly's number.

"I'm in front of the main entrance, where are you?" said the voice in my ear. Looking around I saw a man in a leather jacket standing not ten yards from me, talking but looking the other way. Now I could see him I was less afraid.

"I'm right behind you," I said to the phone. He spun round and I guessed that he didn't like being watched, but he came towards me, smiling and holding up a hand in greeting. It made me feel better that I had seen him first.

The way his leather jacket hung around his shoulders and the downbeat way he said, "How you doing?" marked Shane Reilly as one of those borderline types. Think of an aging rock-star, one who wasn't exactly mega even in his heyday; the bass player eclipsed by the vocalist, the drummer whose name nobody remembers. Shane Reilly had the looks to get out of the gutter, but hadn't quite made the stars. His dark wavy hair was half an inch longer than it should have been for this century but it went with the sallow complexion and the shadows under the dark brown eyes. His mouth was mobile and expressive, giving things away his eyes would have liked to hide.

186

But he was no slouch. Under the jacket he wore a plain white shirt, convincingly white, and a black stringy tie, half undone. His complexion was swarthy but not stubbly, suggesting a recent shave. He had the air of someone who knew what impression he was trying to make, someone who didn't worry too much about the truth as long as he got the desired outcome. But that needn't matter to me. We could get to know each other just as much as we needed or wanted to. We might be well matched. The butterflies in my gut subsided as he led me down to the café.

Unlike the Dean, this restaurant had gone for the modernity of plastic and chrome. We sat under harsh lights as Shane (was it even his real name?) explained that he worked on the move, networking, doing deals. He had no office, but he needed an assistant.

"To do what exactly?"

"Extra research. Checking upcoming sales and exhibitions, a bit of correspondence. Sometimes I go abroad. You'd arrange flights and book hotels." His fingernails were bitten and his hands fidgeted with his cup, his phone or anything else that fell in their path. I thought he might be fancying a fag.

"You're an art student?" he asked.

"No. I was doing English." If money was going to be involved it seemed best to come clean.

He noticed the past tense. "Flunked it?"

"Problems at home." I had a moment of unlikely inspiration. "But my father was an artist."

A spark of interest. "Professional artist?"

Damn. I couldn't back up my claim. As far as I knew, Dad had never made the leap from teacher to artist and I had never thought of him in that way. In the living room we had a bland print of a waterfall in the Borders that had been in Gran's house. On the stairs we had some Monet prints from a Sunday supplement special offer. There was nothing at home that Dad had painted or drawn or sculpted. I suddenly wished that he had, and found myself imagining lively and colourful paintings being thrown out with the rubbish by his bitter and twisted wife after he left. But I knew this was just a fabrication to make me believe I could be useful to Shane Reilly, who was asking me harder questions now.

"Just a teacher, mainly. My parents split up. We lost touch. But it's given me an interest."

"How much do you know about contemporary art?" He stressed the "contemporary", like everyone knew about the rest.

"Not as much as I'd like to. I'd need a bit of time to get clued up."

His features subsided into their accustomed languor. "I could probably cope with that. As long as you want to learn."

Oh yes, I was hungry for knowledge, hungry for something. "I left home in a hurry. My references are on the way."

He laughed. "Do you have a National Insurance number?" I nodded. "Have you been in jail?" I shook my head. "No, I didn't think so. Work with me for a week," he said. "A trial period. Then we'll decide."

I kept the questions about who was on trial and for what to myself.

"Ever been to the Burrell?"

I shook my head but at least I had heard of the big art gallery near Glasgow.

"I have an appointment there tomorrow. I'll take you. It'll be good background."

I guessed he'd had no other takers for the job. Either that or he fancied me. Which for somebody in need of board and lodgings might be a good thing. Faye needn't have worried that Shane would get the wrong idea. Now that I'd set eyes on him, I had ideas of my own.

When Shane picked me up, he called me Isla. I didn't bother to correct him. It was a novelty to feel like another person. In the car he handed me an electronic organiser and a mobile. "You can make notes and appointments for me. Then we can synchronise with my laptop." Apparently I wasn't to get my hands on the laptop itself.

"Where will I work?"

"You'll have to be like me. On the hoof. There are plenty of cafés and bars where businessmen work. I'll pay for coffee and snacks if you keep the receipts. Just make it reasonable."

"Do you live in Edinburgh?"

"I rent a flat. Dean Park."

This was the area close to the galleries where we'd met. He could play host in any one he chose.

When we got to the Burrell he dropped me off. "I have a meeting. It's only a mile away. I'll pick you up later."

"Don't you want me to…" I still wasn't sure what my help might entail.

"Next time, maybe. I have to close a deal. And there's plenty for you to see here."

Clearly my art education was to be one of self-study. But that was okay. The spring sunlight flooded in from the gardens outside. I could stand in the middle of a room, bathing in the warmth, and still have a good view of what was around me.

I could have stayed there a long time, walking around in a warm haze, absorbing art by osmosis, but at two o'clock my new mobile rang. Shane said he was in the café and would a cappuccino be okay.

"Did your meeting go well?" I asked him, grateful for the caffeine hit and wondering if I could suggest a croissant.

He nodded and got out some papers. "Look. This is a contract for reproduction rights."

"How do you mean?"

"An artist owns the copyright to his pictures. But he can sell the rights to reproduce them. Paintings, photographs or whatever."

"You mean in an art book?"

"Not just books. Posters, greetings cards, prints. Sometimes the contract specifies, say, framed prints only. Other times you get free reign: t-shirts, mugs, calendars. If the image takes off, it will increase the value of the original." He tapped the papers under his hand. "This painter is a commercial artist. His work will never sell through a gallery, but it has big appeal to the greetings card industry."

Shane was a middle-man, that figured.

"So what did you buy from him?"

He opened the laptop and started a slideshow. The images were of a girl picking roses, her flimsy clothes suggested a naked body underneath without revealing it. They were neither overtly sexy nor entirely innocent. I wouldn't have called it art.

"Eighteenth birthday card?" I said. "Or a cheesy Valentine?"

Shane indulged me with a grin that showed off strong teeth, almost white. "Good girl. You're getting the hang of it. But look at these."

These were in a different class: cityscapes in blocks of colour. I wasn't sure if they were photos or paintings of some kind. I could see them hanging in black frames on white walls.

"This guy's still an art student. One day he might make a name for himself."

"Because you bought the rights?"

"I might do. Then his original will be worth a packet. Meanwhile, we share the profits."

It felt like an upside down way of getting famous. From popular to exclusive, rather than vice versa.

"Where did you find him?"

"Degree show. Glasgow. I go to them all."

"But you don't deal with big galleries?"

"The artists there are mostly out of copyright. They deal direct with printers and publishers. They make a mint from the repro side. But sometimes they take stuff from me. Anything for a fast buck."

I saw that the art world was not as simple as I had thought. It had areas of light and shade and fuzzy bits round the edge, the edge occupied by Shane Reilly.

When we left, Shane threw his laptop and briefcase in the boot of the aging saloon where more cases and packing boxes jostled for space. He was like a snail, carrying his home around with him. The land sculpture at the big gallery where we'd met, that's what it had made me think of – a snail or an ammonite, curled in on itself. As we got in the car Shane handed me a heavy brochure printed on glossy paper.

"Take a look. This is the publisher I deal with most."

The catalogue weighed a ton. It had hundreds of pages covered in thumbnail prints of works of art, arranged by periods and styles.

"Look in 'contemporary figurative'," he said. "When it comes to repro, figurative is the name of the game."

Figurative seemed to mean that it was a picture of something: not abstract or puzzlingly surreal. It had an attraction, that was for sure, but there wasn't much in there I recognised. I remembered Vi's collection of calendars and tea-towels with scenes that recalled old Hollywood films. I was desperate to show Shane some kind of interest.

"Do you do Vettriano?" I asked.

Shane laughed a humourless laugh. "Fat chance. There's a London gallery owns all of it. They've made a killing, as well as him."

It galled Shane that London was making the money. Vettriano came from Fife. The location for his Hollywood scenes was the beach at Leven. I thought of the Leven I'd seen from the pier at Largo, a town of chimneys and factories. Vettriano had made it a place of fantasy.

"Tell me about your father," Shane said.

"Nothing much to tell. He died not long ago. I hadn't seen him since I was wee." I guessed that unless I seriously fluffed during the next few days, the job was mine, and so I resisted any temptation to embroider.

192

Shane didn't pursue it. He was thinking over his day, weighing up what he'd got out of his deal. We sat out the rest of the journey in silence. Maybe he'd been hoping my dad was an undiscovered genius, or the friend of somebody famous.

By now we were in the outskirts of the city.

"Same place?" He meant to drop me off. I preferred to keep him well away from the flat.

"Yeah, wherever suits you."

"I'm famished," he said. "We could go to the flat. And I could show you what's there. Fill you in on the job?"

If he'd hinted at anything more than lunch and a chat, I would have lost my nerve. If he'd as much as turned to me and smiled, I would have been off. But he looked straight ahead without meeting my eye.

And I agreed.

CHAPTER TWENTY-THREE

Dean Park has some narrow cobbled streets, but
Shane's first floor flat was off a wide main road. It
looked fine from the outside, but the interior was grim,
not scruffy like the student house, just way out of date.
The small hallway and the main room were done out in
co-ordinating wallpaper of broad stripes below a
wooden rail and blowsy roses above. The front
windows looked out on the grey buildings opposite and
there was an audible grumble of passing traffic. From
the living room another door led through to a kitchen.
There was no sign of a computer and everything had a
temporary feel.

"How long have you been here?" I ask him.

"Six months," he said with a shrug, as if the
surroundings were of no consequence. He slung his
jacket onto a sofa, squat and shiny, but probably not
leather. "Can I get you a drink?"

We'd been driving for more than an hour. I was
thirsty and followed him into the kitchen. It was fitted
with mismatched cupboards and appliances that jutted
out of the spaces they'd been allocated. The effect was
both bare and cluttered.

Shane reached up to a wall cupboard. His hips were narrow. The shirt hung over his belt but there was no paunch underneath it. "Tea? Coffee?"

I was considering the reasons he might have brought me here, including those not entirely connected to the offer of a job. As if reading my mind, he turned round and added to the drinks menu.

"There might be some cans in the fridge. What do you think? I could order some food in."

He was perfectly at ease in this unlikely place with a girl he'd barely met. He handed me the can of lager and I pulled the ring. It opened with the familiar snap and soft hiss of air. I liked that he hadn't offered me a glass. *Take it or leave it,* he seemed to say, and we raised the cans together, the taste of metal swamped by the cool flow of alcohol.

"Come on," he said, "I'd better show you the rest."

In what looked like a spare room, the bed was pushed back under the window. The main wall was occupied by a tall shelving unit with a built-in computer desk, all in white melamine. Around it red fleur-de-lys danced on a yellow background.

"God, this wallpaper," I said. "How do you stand it?"

He ignored me, intent on booting up the PC. He probably didn't spend much time here at all. The lounge lacked any personal touches, the kitchen cupboards contained what you'd need for a quick breakfast and a drink when you got home at night. There was a stale smell that signified lack of use as much as lack of care.

But nothing awful had happened. My initial revulsion at the place was wearing off. The lager on an empty stomach was conjuring up a warm elation, helped

195

by the presence of Shane, a man with a decent body and, unlike his living accommodation, a very good smell.

Having fired up the PC, he sat down in front of it. "Come and have a look."

The chair was cheap like the units, basic black vinyl with a swivel action. Shane perched on it with his legs tucked underneath. If he was aware of me behind him, I couldn't tell. He'd been on the internet, checking some gallery pages, but now he switched to a spreadsheet.

"This is a list of shows and exhibitions. I update it all the time. I check art schools and galleries. You could do it for me." He flipped to another worksheet. "These are auctions houses and my contacts there."

It looked like he had fingers in lots of pies. Maybe he bought originals with the profits from his repro business. That would explain the travelling. He went through more lists and spreadsheets. Some of them had prices and payments, but I couldn't make any guess as to profits.

I was looking over the top of his head. From here I was fascinated by the tightness of the curls and the way that grey ran through them in almost equal measure to the black. I wanted to know how it felt; if it was soft to the touch or wiry, or if each colour had its own texture. I caught a whiff of shampoo, a zesty cleanliness that balanced the warm and woody notes of the aftershave that had already made its presence felt.

He swivelled in his chair to face me. "What do you think?"

I was wrong-footed, looking at him too closely as he turned to me, his tie removed since we had come in, the open neck of his shirt throwing the line of his jaw into sharp relief. I'd forgotten what we might be discussing. "Sorry, what did you say?"

He didn't smile but he kept looking at me, his head tipped back to keep me in his eye line and I couldn't look away.

"The job. Is it what you're looking for?"

I dragged myself back to the practicalities. "How will I get paid?"

"Cheque. End of the month. Need an advance?"

"I thought it was a week's trial."

Another upward movement of his chin. "I'm happy if you are." He wasn't interested in paperwork. Neither of us moved, but I had the feeling of things rushing by me faster than I could process them.

He held out his hand to shake on the deal. I don't know if he pulled me towards him or if I just let myself think that he did. But in a movement that felt almost graceful, I was on his knee, with his face only a few inches from mine. Shocked at the ease with which I'd straddled him on the flimsy chair, I steadied my legs and tried to lean away from him, inadvertently throwing my hips forward in a pose that was more provocative still.

He gripped my hand harder to stop me falling off and his eyes widened in a smile of acceptance. If he'd been expecting this kind of a gift, its early arrival made it all the better. He raised his eyebrows and his hands went round my waist to steady me.

"Oh dear," he said. "I wonder how that happened?"

He drew me towards him and I reached both hands out to touch his hair. It wasn't wiry but soft and dry. He pulled me closer for a long exploratory kiss.

197

On the photo in the school magazine my dad had looked clean-cut and innocent, but when he touched Nancy and got inside her knickers, he might have had the gently wasted look of Shane Reilly, whose finger was now slipping expertly into my own thong. I closed my eyes.

"Nice," he said, stirring me into liquid warmth, "very nice." He eased my breast from its balcony bra as Dad might have lifted Nancy's from her white school blouse, and weighed it in his hand, tested my nipple with his tongue until it rose in response. I touched my finger to his lips then leaned down and gave him the full tongue. When I paused Shane said, "Oh baby. What a lovely girl you are."

Whatever happened now I had asked for it. I was that kind of a girl.

I started to undo his flies, high on my power to give him what he wanted. He slid his jeans off and climbed back on the chair, where he leaned back and closed his eyes. I eased myself down on his erection and he guided my breast to his mouth, sucking like a baby.

He was a practised lover. After he had come, he rested, then took me on the floor and screwed me again, keeping me on the edge until I let out a long cry of gratitude.

He was laughing. "And here's me thinking I only wanted help with the paperwork." He touched the sodden parts of me and put the same finger to his lips then to mine. I tasted what he offered me.

"I think you got more than you bargained for," I said, pretending that I was in control.

"Oh, I don't know about that," he said.

The next day Shane went out early. I wanted to show willing in the work department and so I surfed the net, trying to continue my art education. I also went through all the files on the PC. A few needed a password which I didn't have, but those I saw corresponded with what he had told me earlier.

He was back by late afternoon and we went straight to bed. Afterwards he rolled me a joint. It was only the second I had ever had, but he didn't need to know that. I wondered what I would say if he offered me hard drugs, but soon I was too woozy to care and we fucked some more. He said I had a talent for it, and I believed him.

When he fell asleep on top of the bedclothes I pulled the covers over him, got up and made myself tea. On my phone there was a message from Faye: *"Where r u? worried."*

I thought of it from Faye's point of view. Now Shane had got me into bed maybe he'd changed his mind about taking me on. Maybe the job had only ever been a smokescreen. I hoped not. Being an easy lay was one thing, but I wanted a job that would last longer than a few shags.

I lay down beside him again and woke him by kissing his neck and his chest. He ran his hands over my hair and sighed with sleepy pleasure.

"Bit of a problem," I said. I felt him tense, anticipating some unexpected demand from me, or maybe the arrival of an irate parent. "I've been bunking with mates, but it was a favour. They don't really have the space." His body relaxed again and I let my hand stray between his legs. "Do you think you could put up with a lodger? Until I get something sorted?"

199

He pulled me onto him and kneaded my buttocks so that we were aroused all over again. "A lodger? Is that all?"

I put the tip of my tongue in his mouth and worked my hips, wondering who was fooling who.

An hour later we got dressed. He threw me a key. "Have to see a man about a dog." He mentioned a private gallery in Charlotte Square. "Can you find it?" I nodded. "I'll meet you there later."

I took advantage of Shane's absence to retrieve my bag from the student house. Only Sadie was around. I doubted she would even bother to tell the others.

At the gallery, Shane smarmed the owners and introduced me as Isla. That night we went to a pub and drank with another dealer. When Shane described me as his Girl Friday, the guy gave him a lecherous wink and asked Shane if he had a lassie for every day of the week.

"No need," I said. "I'm available twenty-four seven."

Shane laughed and the guy just raised his eyebrows. There were no more jokes, not to my face, anyway.

After that first time in the pub, Shane and I didn't socialise together. I suppose he needed to look respectable and there was some unspoken agreement that whatever we did for each other, this was not about being a couple. At meetings and exhibitions I scurried after him with a new netbook but stayed in the background. People we met in work situations gave me a look of curiosity, but we just let them wonder.

Back at the flat, sex got more frantic and more necessary. I started to have a dream that I was in a darkened gallery with a video playing. Lights flashed rhythmically on a dark background that could have been a starless sky. There was a soundtrack of words that fell from my mouth as Shane raked the depths of me. They were words I'd never said before, words I didn't know I knew.

After that particular nightmare I found it harder to swan around art galleries in search of enlightenment. The more intimate places in Morningside or the New Town were fine, but the nationals with their big clean spaces left me feeling exposed. Even though it was close to the flat, I particularly avoided going anywhere near the Dean Gallery. I knew that if I were to bump into Danny he would see right through me. He would know I was sleeping with Shane and doing a whole lot more besides. No amount of *citron pressé* could wash away how that would make me feel.

By now I had an account on Facebook. I knew Ian wasn't into it, but I kept an eye on Faye and sometimes Barbara, just to see if they were doing okay without me, which as far as I could see, they were. I didn't make any posts. My own status wasn't something I wanted to publicise.

I eventually told Shane that his must be the only business in Scotland without a website and I started teaching myself how to make one. I still dealt with bits of accounting and opened the post, but apart from the times he asked me along to an appointment, I became a creature of the twilight zone, peering at strings of code, lurking in internet forums, finding fixes for pages that failed to load.

One morning there was a chirruping from the bottom of my holdall. It was my old mobile telling me

201

the battery had run down. I could have just thrown it away, but the one I was using belonged to Shane. I had better hang on to my own for the day when he tired of me, or I of him.

When I plugged the phone into the charger there were messages on it, mostly from Ian: *"Please call, please call, please call."* That was why I had switched it off in the first place. There were some from Faye too but, like Ian's, they had soon petered out. Friendships needed feeding. I had let them go hungry.

I was still looking through the messages when the thing rang in my hand. I didn't recognise the number, but curiosity got the better of me and I took the call.

"Ailsa! Is that you?"

It was Mum.

CHAPTER TWENTY-FOUR

If I'd seen the landline number, I would never have answered. But here we were, Mum and me, having a conversation.

"I'd nearly given up trying to get you." Mum was clearly as surprised to be talking to me as I was to her.

"Yeh, it's me. You have a mobile then?"

"Uh-huh. It's Liz's old one. I've had it for a week or two. How are you?"

"I'm fine." My response was automatic, defensive even, and it was true. I was fine. But it was oddly reassuring that someone cared enough to ask. I let her carry on.

"The university keep writing," she said. "I rang Vi, but she said Faye didn't know where you were."

"Don't worry about the letters," I said. "I'm not going back."

A pause as she considered her reply. "Well, as long as you're sure."

I had expected her to tell me off. "I'm sure. I have a job."

"That's good." She was still in placatory mood. "What kind of job?"

"I work for an art dealer. Like a PA."

"And where are you living?"

"I have digs."

I was surprised how easy it was to put a positive spin on my precarious situation, on how I spent my days waiting for the hours of darkness and another dose of the gratification that was somehow getting harder to find.

"Have you heard from Ian?" Mum paused, probably thinking, like me, that there was no point in picking at a scab that might heal over if left alone. "I did ring Rhona last week. Just to say I didn't think you would be back for a while. She said that Ian wasn't too bad. That he'd get over it."

Yes, I had thought that he would. But so soon?

"And what about you?" I asked. If she was ready to parley I supposed I could go along with it. "How are you keeping?"

The next pause was one of surprise. She didn't think I cared. Her voice rose in recognition of my interest. "I'm good. Most days. The consultant's still monitoring me. Adjusting the medication. And I've joined a group. Lupus Aware. The meetings are in Edinburgh."

She left it hanging in the air, the idea that we might meet up. The anger I'd been harbouring since I left home seemed to have fizzled out over the phone connection, but if we were face to face it might rise to the surface, like a disease in remission that suddenly gets a new hold.

She asked me more about the job and I gave her a sanitised version.

"Can I ring you again?"

"I'm not using this phone. I'll send you my other number."

"Okay. Take care then."

"You too."

As I turned off the phone I caught sight of myself in the bedroom mirror and saw myself through Mum's eyes. Where my face used to be rounded out there were hollows. My hair was lank and I hadn't got around to putting on make-up. Shane still hadn't offered me anything more than a spliff, but he brought home bottles of vodka on a regular basis and I was beginning to feel like I had a permanent hangover. From a mother's point of view, I looked like I could do with a square meal and a good night's sleep.

But as the phone bleeped its farewell I was flooded with a new a sense of power. I might send Mum my new number or I might not. I might arrange to see her some time, or I might not. I was in charge now. It was up to me. The face that looked back at me from the mirror might be in need of a bit of TLC, but it was no longer the face of a schoolgirl.

About three weeks later, Shane got up early. He was packing a bag and it looked like more than a day trip.

"What's up?" "Where are you going?"

"Only to Glasgow," he said. "I'm looking up a mate. I'll crash at his place." He was checking the contents of his wallet. "I told you about it the other day."

He hadn't, but I let that pass. "How long are you away for?"

He shrugged without looking at me. "Are you okay for cash?"

As he left he threw a twenty pound note onto the bed.

I heard the outside door slam shut. Either he wasn't going for long or he didn't think much of me. Or both of these might be true.

There was nothing in his Outlook calendar. I considered that he might have another girl, a woman, in Glasgow or somewhere else. It wasn't that I had ever expected Shane to be permanent, but I'd got used to my regular fixes of sexual satisfaction and I didn't have anywhere else to go. More troubling was the fact that he hadn't paid me. He had paid *for* me, to live and to eat, but given me nothing that could be classed as a wage.

In the wild wallpaper room I picked up the big catalogue he'd shown me when we went to Glasgow and flicked through the sections. I was surprised how much of it was familiar, scenes absorbed subliminally even by someone with no real interest in art. One page caught my eye: bright seascapes next to dark scenes in bars. The pictures were small and the details of the originals printed underneath were in tiny print. For a minute I thought they might be Vettriano, but I checked the top of the page – USA. The artist was Edward Hopper. I made a mental note to check him on Google.

I looked through the nineteenth century bit for photographs by Hill and Adamson, but there were none. I supposed their appeal was limited, curios rather than wall art. I turned to the back where Shane had the stuff he referred to as his own: "Scottish contemporary painters". There was nothing that looked to me like it would be of iconic status in a few years time, just some colourful abstracts that meant nothing, and some landscapes that were pleasing enough but could have been anywhere: swathes of straw-like grass punctuated by massive grey boulders. I held the catalogue up at arms' length, trying to gauge the effect. What kind of place did these represent? The grass looked like sand dunes, but the stones were too threatening for a beach. They didn't look like any place I had been, but all the same, I knew I'd seen the pictures before.

In my head I retraced the wanderings that had been my art education – the Dean, the Burrell, before that the Portrait Gallery. I tried to imagine the pictures bigger and on a bare wall but still couldn't place them, even in any of the private collections Shane frequented. I tried websites too, but decided I hadn't seen these on a screen.

I closed my eyes and thought hard. I was in a darkened room with leather seats and music playing. My eyes flew open. These pictures had been in Andy Chalmers' lounge, signed by his mother Irene.

For a minute I was distracted by the memory of the innocent humping Ian and I had enjoyed compared with the excitement of being with Shane. I took my tea and stood at the bedroom door, absorbing the smell of sex. With Shane I would always come; with Shane I would always want more.

I walked around the room to clear my head. I went back to the lounge, staring out at the non-view of the houses opposite. The need for sex ebbed away, like waves receding over flat sand.

Irene Chalmers, although I had never met her, seemed an unlikely candidate for a serious painter, a successful one even. I went back to the catalogue and studied the small print. It didn't take long to solve the puzzle. Irene Chalmers wasn't the artist.

I'd read the initials on the painting at Torryburn as "I.C.", a curly "I' like the one on Ian's hankie, but if the catalogue was right, it had been a "J". J for Jenni. The artist given here was Jenni Carstairs.

The same Jenny who had taught me art at the High School. The Jenny that Faye and I had suspected of having it off with my dad, back in the day, before I discovered he preferred jailbait. The Jenny who for some inexplicable reason had always been nice to me. Too nice. Something here didn't add up, but I was still too surprised at Jenni-with-an-i's sudden arrival in the unlikely surroundings of Shane's shabby flat to work out what was bothering me.

By teatime, I was rattling around in the flat and couldn't stand the thought of sitting there all night with only my thoughts for company. It would be light until nearly eight and so when I knew other people would be settling in front of the TV, I dragged my holdall from under the bed in the spare room and got out my running shoes. I let myself out and sniffed the air of Dean Park, like an animal that's been in hibernation. I had only the vaguest notion of local geography but ran down the wide main road that I knew led away from the city centre. I was out of practice and knew I wouldn't last long, but I got a rhythm going. As I passed the local Co-op, a lone shopper emerged with an evening paper and a plastic milk container, otherwise the wide pavements were empty.

I was running north, parallel to Queensferry Road and wondered how long I would have to run to reach the Forth. The mental exercise kept me going and I notched my body up to a high that had nothing to do with sex or skunk until I had to stop, wheezing like a geriatric, leaning over the railings of a drab front garden. I was so puggled I had to walk most of the way back, and realised I'd gone no distance at all, but I felt better and planned to do it again the next night and the night after that.

Shane was only away for two nights – nowhere near long enough for me to get him out of my head. When I took some washing to the local launderette, I unpacked it under the neon lights and found myself getting off on the smell of his aftershave. When the sly-faced woman in charge saw me with my face in his grubby shirt, I stuffed it into the machine. I didn't care what she thought, but she had no right to my fantasies. When the clothes came out I folded them carefully, breathing in the freshness, telling myself I preferred it. Afterwards, I went for another run, trying to cleanse my blood of alcohol and sex, but as soon as I heard his key in the lock I was stepping out of my clothes. I made it a special homecoming, pretending my ravenous self-indulgence was for him.

When we had finished and dealt with the concomitant damage to the shiny settee, he picked up the catalogue, still lying open at the page with Jenni Carstairs' paintings.

"What's this?" Shane asked. "Been doing your homework?"

I was pulling my clothes back on. "I have to do something when you leave me all alone."

He caught my arm and spoke in my ear, "Not complaining already, are we?" He nuzzled my neck but my arm was still hurting. For a minute I thought there might be another side to him. I turned to him for a kiss

209

but when his grip loosened I wriggled away. I took the catalogue from him, wanting to change the subject and the atmosphere. I put Jenni's paintings under his nose. I guessed he would like to play the expert.

"I wanted to ask you about these. She used to be at my school. I didn't know she was famous."

His frown showed he was distracted from whatever had made him grip my arm. "What school?"

"Dunfermline High. I had her in my second year."

Shane laughed out loud. "Jenni was your teacher! That's a good one."

"You know her then?"

"Yeah, I know her all right. Or I did." He walked away from me, searching through his jacket pockets for his fags. Seeing them on the coffee table I picked them up and gave them to him. "Very friendly she was for a while. Especially when she wanted a favour. Very friendly *indeed*."

I watched him sort through his memories and consider giving them an airing. "Not that these," he waved at the catalogue as if the contents gave off a bad smell, "ever did anything. They probably never will."

"I've seen them before," I said. "In a private house."

Shane took a drag and grunted. "Wonders will never cease. I'm pretty damn sure I never got any commission off them."

"But she's a professional artist?" I'd never thought of how successful or otherwise Jenni might have become, or how exactly she made a living. Only now I had a clearer view of the world she inhabited.

"Och, yes, our Jenni's doing pretty well for herself, thank you very much. She's given up sand and rock and got her teeth into something more saleable, thanks to yours truly. Not that I'd hang them in my living room, the things she does now, but the social conscience crowd are all over her." He glared at me as if I were to blame. "Stupid bitch."

Somewhere in this tirade, Shane became more sorry for himself than angry, so that the final insult came out with something like affection. The corners of his mouth turned down, his eyes took on the look of a spaniel skelped for chewing a slipper. I had to try hard not to laugh.

I put my arms around his neck, playing along. "Aw, don't cry," I said to him. "Isla's here to cheer you up."

"Well, so she is," he said, pushing a new and impressive hard-on against my leg. "Maybe I'll get over it, if she's really nice to me." He reached to undo the bra I had just done up. "Really, really nice."

I was eager to please. He knew things, and knew people. He might have been Jenni Carstairs' lover. I thought that compared to me, she would have been a dry old thing, an artist who gave and took away on a whim, not a girl who was always available, who made love just because she could. With my arms around Shane's neck I lifted one leg onto the arm of the sofa, like a flamingo, so that he could reach the places he already knew so well.

By the time an invitation came in the post, inviting Shane to Jenni's latest exhibition, we were settled back into our routine of afternoon sex of increasing frequency and athleticism. I had no worries about him leaving me for an aging ex. I was also curious to see what Jenni was up to, and so I propped it on the mantelpiece.

211

"Will you go?" I asked him.

Shane gave the card with its geometric border and angular typeface one of his world-weary stares.

"Time I looked up the old whore," he said. "Ring up and say yes."

CHAPTER TWENTY-FIVE

The show had some sponsorship from the council. Shane said that's why it was in the City Art Gallery, a place between Waverley and the Royal Mile. I'd been there only once, to see a previous show where Shane had turned down the rights to some ugly abstract scribbles.

The preview started at six, to catch business people before they went home for their tea or started on a full night out. When we arrived we were ushered into a reception room with tables along one wall that were covered in white cloths that reached the floor and rows of glasses waiting to be filled. Double-doors led into what looked like a proper exhibition space where a blonde girl wearing a navy suit checked our invitations. She wore a name badge that read "Gallery Administrator". She handed Shane a catalogue.

"Evening, Mr Reilly," she said, barely looking up from the card file on the table in front of her.

I detected some hostility between them. I'd never heard anyone call him Mr Reilly. Maybe she was a henchwoman of Jenni Carstairs. I was more concerned that, of the waiters and waitresses in white shirts and long black pinnies lined up behind the drinks tables, the tallest and skinniest was Danny. It had never crossed my mind he might be here.

There was no chance of taking cover. Shane, hailed by another early arrival, grabbed a glass and disappeared into the next room. With a flick of his fringe Danny beckoned me over.

"Red or white, Madam?"

"Whatever you've got most of," I said.

He poured me a glass of red that went well beyond the white line drawn on the side and I knew he was smiling. Here, in the halogen glare of an early evening soirée with the voices of polite Edinburgh building up around us, he was clearly an ally. I wondered why I'd been avoiding him.

"Sorry I took off a bit quick," I said.

"Easy come, easy go." Danny continued filling glasses in advance of new arrivals, this time measuring the exact amount.

"Was Faye pissed off with me?"

"For a day or two." He raised his head and flicked his hair back off his face. "She said you probably had your reasons."

I wasn't sure that whatever had made me sit astride Shane and stick my tongue down his throat could be called reason, but I was grateful that Faye wasn't still mad at me.

The room was filling up now and a small queue was forming of men and women in business clothes, all desperate for a drink before getting to grips with art show small talk.

"It'll die down in a wee while," Danny said, "if you fancy a refill."

214

"I might hold you to that," I said and went off after Shane.

I didn't particularly want to attract Jenni's attention, but I was curious about the woman who had bedded Shane Reilly on her way to a better life. In the exhibition room I couldn't see her but I heard her, surrounded by an admiring clique, holding forth in an accent that still bore a strong trace of Fife. Rather than join the fan club I drifted over to look at the paintings, although as I drew closer, something in the subject matter made me take a step back.

Jenni had certainly moved on from what Shane had taken to calling her haystack period. These pictures were all of people, but unlike the demure portraits of folk in their best clothes who stared down from the walls of the portrait gallery, these were real life people, their emotions nakedly on display. One, *Waiting for Baby*, was a roomful of pregnant women lying on the floor, doing relaxation exercises. Their faces were doughy with tiredness or pain. Another, called *Dole Queue*, showed a line of men with expressions between bored and angry. One or two were portraits but without personal names: *Lorry Driver at Grangemouth*, or *Postman on Strike*.

Shane came up beside me and took my arm. "Come and meet the artist," he said. The group around the star of the show had temporarily dispersed, leaving Shane and me face to face with Jenni herself.

I remembered Jenny with a "y" as a strong featured woman in a paint-stained overall, who habitually stroked her heavy bob behind one ear as she contemplated the artistic output of thirty reluctant second-years. If I hadn't known it was the same woman

215

in front of me now, I would never have recognised her. Instead of the mid-length hair that had softened her square jaw, her head had a covering of short red fur, leaving her face as raw-boned and nakedly on show as the subjects of her portraits. The even pelt was enlivened by two asymmetrical white splodges, giving the effect of a piebald squirrel. Not that she hadn't taken care over her appearance. Blusher had been blended into good quality foundation to highlight her cheekbones and she wore lipstick that matched her hair. Her frock was plain but stylish with a dipping hemline worn over thick tights and emerald boots. She wore glasses with green wrap-round frames, a brave style statement in the face of optical necessity. She spoke in a friendly undertone but her body language had none of the polite social engagement going on around us.

"Well, Shane, you old bugger, what brings you here?"

Shane grinned at her over his glass. "I think you'll find you invited me."

"Well, that was a slip-up. I'll have to have a word with my secretary." Her eyes flicked to the door, then back to me. Her copper coloured lips pursed and I saw the fine lines around her mouth that make-up couldn't conceal. "So who's the new... assistant?"

"This is Isla," Shane said, "and she's shaping up very well."

There was little chance Jenni would have recognised me as the shy daughter of Tom Roberston, but it was handy that Shane persisted in calling me by the wrong name.

Jenni was purring, "I'm sure she is." Then the claws came out. She fixed me with a look. "Watch your back, dear. Shane might be out to shaft you in more ways than one. Especially if you have any talent."

With Jenni spitting venom, I was ready to cut and run, but Shane was enjoying her reaction. "Och, Isla's just doing the office work," he said. "Helping me cope with all the new business." He raised his glass to her. "Congratulations. I'm glad your angry phase is still proving profitable."

"Don't flatter yourself," she said to him. "I have a lot more to inspire me than a dealer in second-rate kitsch."

Who knows how long they would have stood there trading insults if the girl from the front desk hadn't wafted towards us.

"Jenni, there's somebody here from *Scotland Now*. They only have five minutes."

"Right you are," Jenni said. "Can't keep the public waiting." Near the entrance I could see a reporter and a cameraman sorting out their kit. Jenni turned to Shane. "What a shame," she said, "when we had so much to catch up on."

As she left, Shane drained his glass. "Hell hath no fury," he said. I wondered if the boot might not have been on the other foot. He motioned to the canvases that surrounded us. "What do you think?"

"Well, they're eye-catching," I said, hoping this wasn't a test of my critical flair, "but I didn't think they'd be your kind of thing." It would be an odd kind of greetings card that had one of these on it.

"Got it in one," Shane said. "But we fell out over something different. I'll tell you about it some time. Do you want to eat? Dave and I are going to for a curry."

Dave would be the guy he'd been talking to earlier. I weighed up my options. I'd still had no actual payment from Shane other than my bed and board. If I turned him down it would be back to a cold flat and a slice of toast. But however much I belonged in Shane's bed or at his PC, I wasn't sure I fitted into his social life, or that I wanted to.

Over his shoulder I caught sight of Danny carrying a tray of glasses into a back room. I liked the way he moved. I wasn't particularly hungry.

"I think I'll give it a miss" I said. "I wouldn't mind staying here a bit longer."

When I reported back to the drinks table, Danny was leaning against the wall, surveying the room and talking in an undertone to another waiter. Seeing me, he stepped forward, picked up each wine box in turn and shook it.

"Sorry," he said, chucking the one in his hand into a bin behind him. "Only orange juice now. They don't half knock it back when it's free."

"When do you finish?" I said.

He looked at his watch. "We have to clear up at the end. Around nine." He turned to his mate who heaved himself off the wall and shrugged his clothes into place. "Craig, do you mind if I take five?"

"Yeah, but don't be long. I need a fag."

In the foyer we sat down on the floor with our backs to the wall of the room we'd just left. Danny tipped his head back. "I'm knackered."

"Long day?"

"I have a deadline for tomorrow."

I pictured him back at the flat in the pool of light formed by his desk lamp, clicking and frowning at his laptop through the night. In some respects, I had it easy.

"I was going to have that room, in the flat. The one you got."

"Yeah, Faye said. Your mum was ill. That was bad luck. Is she better?"

"Pretty much. We had a big row but we're on speaking terms. Just."

"If you'd been here, I would have been at home rowing with my mum."

"Where are you from?"

"Outside Kirkcaldy. Windygates."

That meant he would have gone to Kirkcaldy High, our school's nearest neighbour and rival. I thought about hockey matches and a trip to the Links Market, an annual fair that stretches all the way along the esplanade. I wondered if Danny had been there when Faye and I threw up after too many goes on the waltzer. I would have been fifteen then, Faye sixteen. If he had, we would have ignored a bunch of fourteen-year-olds.

A couple came out of the exhibition and stepped over our legs. All we needed was a dog on a lead and we could have been drop-outs. Danny's long fingers were laid on his black pinnie and his eyes were closed. I would have liked to lean against his shoulder, just for a rest.

I tucked my legs up under me. Some things were easier to ask on neutral ground. "You and Faye," I asked, "are you actually an item?"

He said nothing but he bent his knees up too, and clasped his hands around them. "Yeah, if you like." He shrugged. It was an odd answer, but it wasn't "no." I felt the gaze of his one visible eye on me.

"And what about you, you and Reilly?"

Like Danny, I didn't feel like giving too much away about my relationships. "Shane's all right. Just a bit of… an outsider, I suppose. I think he had a thing with Jenni. Years ago."

"Jenni who?"

"Jenni Carstairs, you dummy, the artist holding forth through there in front of her paintings?"

Danny shoved me in the shoulder. "Don't you dummy me!"

I shoved him back, harder than I meant to. "Dummy yourself."

By the time he'd clouted me back I was on the floor, laughing and struggling to right myself.

Danny got up and pulled me after him. He dusted down his waiter's gear. "Got to get back," he said, "or Craig'll grass me up."

Someone had left the outside door open and a mean draught was blowing in from outside. I would have liked to have followed Danny in and helped him clear up, but I had no reason to. "Yeah, time I was off."

Danny turned to me as he went back inside. "Watch yourself, Ailsa."

"You too," I called after him. But even I knew my problems were bigger than his.

In the morning Shane was beside me, comatose. Apart from his trip to Glasgow it was the first time we'd gone to bed separately. When he woke he reached for his fags on the bedside table.

"Fuck," he said as he knocked them onto the floor.

"Heavy night?"

He retrieved the packet and lit up. Even with a hangover his face had an elegance about it. He blew smoke out and lay back on the pillow. "You could have come along."

I had no regrets about turning down Shane's invitation the previous evening. Even if Dave had a wife or girlfriend in tow, she would have been ten years older than me, a different generation. Danny was more my idea of company.

Shane went to the loo and I got up to put on the kettle. I was wearing a t-shirt that stopped just below my bum. He came into the kitchen wearing only boxers and wrapped his arms around me from behind. I was ready for him to bend me over or to lift the hem of my makeshift nightie and feel for the places he knew so well, but he leaned against the worktop, waiting for me to make the tea.

"Cheers, babe." We stood side by side with our mugs. Maybe he was having his own doubts about where I belonged in his life. If my time was running out, there were things I had to say.

"Look," I said. "I don't like to mention, but..."

He looked at me over his mug. "Let me guess. I owe you money." He could easily have changed the subject or distracted me, but he put his mug down, businesslike. "I'll sort it out. Next week. Really, I will. It's just that cash flow's not all it might be."

"Okay, thanks."

He went to put on a shirt and came back to the kitchen. I stuck some bread in the toaster. What did we have to talk about, Shane and me, over what seemed to have become breakfast?

"So, tell me about Jenni," I said. "What's the angry phase all about?"

We took our plates into the lounge and sat in front of the coffee table. He chewed his toast and stuck his bare legs out in front of him.

"She contacted me when she first came to Edinburgh. I took those landscapes because I was new to the game and thought she might come up with something better. But she didn't. I got tired of her asking. She got tired of me saying no. Then she took me to see this picture that was totally different. It had won a competition years before. She thought it would be up my street. And in a way it was. A life study, amateurish, but something that would sell. It had a good feel to it."

"You didn't want it?"

"I did, but she was asking too much, silly bitch. I was the one taking the risk. I wouldn't give her much up front. Then I said why didn't she give up the rocks and haystacks, that this had more selling power. She took offence at that. Went off in a huff. Eventually found what she was good at. People, right enough, but not the kind that interest me."

"So what was it, this painting?"

"Just a girl. A girl on a beach. Not old enough to be sexy, but it was…," he sought for a word to convey the picture's particular appeal. "Sensitive."

The incongruity of this coming from Shane shocked me into an echo. "Sensitive?"

He grunted into his tea. "Okay. No. I dunno. Affecting, maybe. Of course I didn't know then that Jenni's tastes ran in that direction."

"You mean girls?"

I tried not to look shocked. If Jenni was gay, I'd missed it. But clearly Shane had missed it too, until, that was, she knocked him back. That would account for the personal nature of their feud.

"So what happened to the picture? Did she sell it? Did it make any money?"

"Not that I heard. At that time it was still being held by the body that ran the competition, some arts charity. It was in a storeroom in the Dean. I suppose she might have asked for it back. Or it might still be there for all I know."

I picked up our mugs and plates and took them back to the kitchen. Shane followed me. As I leaned over the sink his hand between my legs was warm from holding the mug. He had caught me unawares. I let out a gasp and turned to face him as he knelt down in front of me. I sank my fingers in his hair, relishing his piebald curls between my fingers as his tongue did its familiar business. This was more like the Shane I knew.

CHAPTER TWENTY-SIX

As soon as Shane had left for the day, I rang Mum. I wasn't planning moving out just yet, but if I needed a temporary bolthole, I thought I should gauge the welcome I might get. I was also starting to make a list of questions she might be able to answer. I suggested meeting in Edinburgh, but Mum had other ideas.

"Well, look, I've got these tickets. To Deep Sea World. The new place? The offer was in last week's *Press*. And you always did like stuff about the sea. We could go today."

I'd heard of the new attraction in North Queensferry, Mum's side of the Bridge. It sounded like a bit of a trek.

She sensed my hesitation. "I'll check the buses. I'm sure there's one for both of us."

I gave in. If she could make the effort so could I.

We'd arranged to meet at eleven. When I got there, Mum was standing outside wearing dark glasses and one of those swing coats that were all the rage. I had showered and put on make-up. If she saw any change in me, the glasses masked her reaction. I was relieved that she didn't try to touch me.

"This is a change," I said, meaning the location.

"I'm making up for lost time," she said.

Through the turnstiles we found ourselves in an outdoor area where a seal pool gave off the reek of raw fish as its occupants wheeled up to the surface and rolled away again. It was a weekday and inside the barriers a party of schoolchildren were being handed clipboards and worksheets. As they set off, the teacher and two helpers scurried alongside, chivvying them to slow down one minute, keep up the next. Spring sunshine warmed the concrete patios and the kids were asking to take off their winter coats, so that they struggled with armfuls of clothing as well as pencils and boards.

Lost time. I thought Mum had meant her own lost time, time spent indoors when she could have been out and about, but maybe it was the things we'd missed together. I'd gone to the zoo with friends, ferried in unfamiliar cars for birthday treats, or on trips organised by school, where we gawped at the sea lions and penguins. I thought of all the other country parks and kids attractions I'd done without her. Maybe she was right. Without Dad coming between us, we needed to start again, to fill in some of the gaps.

Inside, we peered over into a manicured pool where signs informed us we could spot several species of amphibian.

"There," I said, as a yellow frog darted out from under a leaf and plunged into the water. "Can you see?"

Mum was wearing her dark glasses. "Och, yes. I can see fine."

Polystyrene pools weren't my idea of sea life. Soon we found the shark tunnel, one of those where you walk through an arch with the fish all around. I caught the

225

beady eye of one of the occupants as it glided past, showing me his pale flank and mean mouth. *Catch me if you can.* But he was the one caught in his giant goldfish bowl. Had he been unlucky to get here or just plain stupid? I read the information sheet. Apparently the glass made the fish look smaller than they actually were. Did that mean they had more or less space in which to loll and glide? Did they know they were always patrolling the same watery room?

"It's pity they don't have other fish. Species you'd find around here," I said.

"I expect they do. Somewhere."

Kids ran around pressing their noses to the glass, but we walked on and found a seat next to a luminous tank where a swarm of jellyfish rose and fell in a filmy cascade. We sat in silence for a while, drinking in the mysterious world of water.

"I saw one of these before," I said. Another trip without Mum, the Sea Life Centre at St Andrews, Faye and I running about and moaning to go to the shop. Had I not seen how beautiful it all was? I made a mental note to tell Shane. There must be a way to make these into art.

I took a breath, as if going under water. "Mum," I said. "Do you remember Jenni Carstairs, the art teacher?"

Mum barely paused. "She left the town, didn't she?"

"Yeh. She did, years ago. She's a full-on artist now. I saw her at an exhibition. Just last week."

"Did you speak to her?"

"Not really. I was with Shane, my boss. She didn't recognise me. She and Shane have some kind of feud."

"And what did you make of her?"

226

I shrugged. "I dunno. She was just a bit weird. Artistic. Full of herself."

The school kids straggled past us again with a new chorus of pleas. "Can we go to the shop, Miss? Miss, I need the toilet."

I could have left it there, but maybe too many things had been left unsaid. "The funny thing is, she was always nice to me at school, too nice really. It got on my nerves. Do you know if she and Dad were… pally?" It was the first time he had been mentioned between us in months. I tried to keep my tone neutral, not wanting to stir up an argument, or get Mum on the defensive.

Mum frowned, as if she couldn't see the connection. "Oh, I see what you mean." She paused, recalling a time she had always avoided thinking about. "He never talked about her much, except as 'the boss.' But I suppose they must have been on good terms. She offered to testify for him. If it went to court."

"How do you mean?"

"I don't know. A character witness, I suppose." Mum was frowning, as if there was something she hadn't considered before.

"Shane says she's a lesbian," I went on, but if I had thought this would prompt a reaction, I was wrong. Mum showed no sign of shock, laughter or even disbelief. She still seemed to be in some train of thought brought on by my comments about school.

She got up from the bench. "I'm wearied now. Time I was off."

We walked through the shop and out of the aquarium complex.

"I got that job," she said. "It's good."

227

I had to rake around in my memory for what she'd told me on the phone. "What is it you have to do again?"

"I've been sending out leaflets, to every doctor's surgery in Fife." The penny dropped. Charity work, to do with lupus. "That's taken me a couple of weeks. My number's on there as the Fife contact. I've already had one or two enquiries." I tried to visualise Mum at the centre of some self-help group. It wasn't as hard as it would once have been. "I've just had a meeting with the people at Lupus Aware. Somebody else has come forward who wants to help. They're going to put me in touch."

Our bus stops were on opposite sides of the road.

"Look after yourself," she said.

I gave her arm a squeeze. "You too."

She hesitated as she turned to go. "Jenni Carstairs," she said. "Are you likely to bump into her again?"

"I wouldn't have thought so. Why?"

"Well, I thought myself it was odd that she offered to speak for your dad. You did know that she's Irene Chalmers' sister?"

Mum walked off leaving my thoughts jumping around like popcorn in a pan. If Jenni was Irene's sister, it made her auntie to Andy and Nancy. It certainly explained why the Chalmers had Jenni's paintings in the house. The puzzle was that this connection had never cropped up until now.

At the bus stop I was flanked by two mothers each with a toddler in tow. They discussed the price of Deep Sea World over my head as I tried to untangle the knots in my thinking. It was Ian who had suggested the artist was Irene, but he'd be the first to admit he wasn't close to any of the family. I thought back to the party. I'd asked Andy about the picture of the house at Largo, but not about the "real" art up on the wall of his front room. In the conversations I'd had with him since, I'd only been interested in Nancy.

The bus arrived and as it rumbled back over the Bridge, my brain was going ten times faster. Through Barnton and Blackhall I re-jigged everything I already knew. Jenni would surely have had an insider's view of what happened between Nancy and my dad. But she'd also been willing to speak up for him. Why would that be? Surely she would have taken the side of the family. And if she and Tom already had something going before Nancy came into his sights, wouldn't that make it even worse?

I jogged back to the flat, adding Shane to the mix. He had tried to buy the picture, painted by Jenni, showing a girl on a beach. Knowing Shane's tastes, it wouldn't have been a child. The picture was sure to have a sensual element. Was the picture of Nancy? And what about his suggestion that Jenni was a lesbian?

I paused at the entrance to the flat, drawing breath and collecting my thoughts. Jenni was Nancy's auntie and had most likely painted her picture. Whatever her sexual preferences, she wasn't going to letch after her niece. Dad was still the one in the wrong. But what about Nancy, my friend of the rock pools and the sweetie shop? Dad might be dead but Nancy was out there somewhere, living with the truth. Jenni Carstairs almost certainly knew the truth too, but before I jumped to too many conclusions, I wanted to see that picture, to know if it was the girl I was looking for.

Back in the flat, I Googled "Jenni Carstairs artist". There was only a modest number of sites to visit. She had won plenty of prizes, but they were all recent. I tried again, using Jenny with a "y" and found she had been runner-up in the McKechnie Award of 1997. The Arts Council Scotland had sponsored the prize, which was worth a couple of thousand quid and, presumably, a fair amount of kudos. This could be what had prompted her to give up teaching. The painting wasn't displayed, but it was described as a landscape called *Fields Lie Fallow*. This must be a contender for the haystack phase. I couldn't see it as being a girl on a beach.

Out of curiosity, I clicked on earlier years. On the page for 1996, I found that a picture called *Line in the Sand*, submitted by J. Carstairs, had been shortlisted. *Line in the Sand* sounded more like a beach scene. As far as I could see there was no prize. Jenni might well have wanted to find a way of making some money from it. Hence her approach to Shane.

It was no good, I was going to have to go and see this bloody picture. It might not be Nancy, but if I saw it I would at least know. Then I could decide what on earth it all meant.

Not wanting to stir up old wounds between Shane and Jenni, I rang Faye.

"I need to ask Danny something. When is he next at the Dean?"

"Hi, Ailsa. I'm fine, since you asked. How about yourself?"

"Sorry. Yeh, I should have rung."

A sigh. "Danny said he met you the other night. That you were okay."

"Yeh, I am."

I sifted through my recent life to find some nugget of interest to share with Faye other than a sudden interest in her boyfriend, but my head was in too much of a mess.

"Things are fine, really. It's just that something's come up."

"Like what?"

I could have said it was about Dad, but I assumed that Faye had kept my family secrets to herself. I didn't know that I was ready for her to share them with Danny, not just yet. This left me with nothing to say at all. Faye sighed again into the emptiness of our non-conversation and said Danny would be working on Sunday. Maybe she trusted him. I wasn't sure that she trusted me.

CHAPTER TWENTY-SEVEN

I left my visit to the Dean until late in the day, thinking Danny would be nearly finished his shift, but when I went to the café counter to speak to him, it looked like the worst time.

"Can you wait?" he said, wiping the counter while dealing with an argumentative customer. The other girl on duty shot me a filthy look.

I left and waited outside on the stone steps until he came up behind me.

"Sorry," I said. "I should have come earlier."

He sat down beside me as the rest of the staff drifted past on their way home. "Doesn't matter. What's it about?"

They were locking up the door behind us.

"Do we have to get out of here?" I asked.

"Only the building. The grounds stay open until later. If you fancy a walk, I can show you something."

I was grateful he wasn't in a hurry. Being with Danny always felt like space to breathe.

He took me down a path beyond the gallery that led through a gate into a cemetery, a big one. Some of the monuments close to the gate were like complete buildings, decked out with statues and polished marble inscriptions. Beyond them, rows of smaller graves were criss-crossed by a grid of paths.

"Like postal districts, packed like squares of wheat," I said.

"What?"

"Did you not do him at school, Larkin?"

He shrugged. If he had, he'd forgotten.

I thought of how these lines were meant to convey fertility. There wasn't much of that around here.

Danny was leading me down one of the main paths, obviously in search of one particular dead person.

"What would you rather have?" Danny said. "Burial or cremation?"

I said I didn't much like the sound of either.

"My dad died last year," Danny said. "He was cremated."

"I'm sorry. What happened?" I didn't say my dad had died too; I was embarrassed not to know where his grave was or if he even had one.

"Heart attack. Really sudden. He wasn't that old."

I pictured Danny's house with people crying and dressed in black. Any mourning we'd done for Dad had been a long time ago, when I was still only six. On the day he left home.

"That's why I was late starting uni," Danny said.

"Do you have brothers or sisters?"

"My sister, she's younger. Doing Standards this year."

I read the names on some of the graves. They were professors, writers, businessmen. Despite the gloss on the stone, they were mostly a hundred years old or more.

233

"Look," Danny said, 'do you recognise this?"

It was, as you might say, in the middle of the range, a marble plinth with a sculpted head on it. I checked the inscription: *David Octavius Hill, 1802–1870*.

"Oh cool," I said. "The Newhaven photographer." I did a quick calculation. "He wasn't that old either, not really."

Danny was not consoled. "They all died younger then."

The head had been sculpted by Hill's wife. The man's face had a proud and leonine look. If it hadn't been for the hollow eyes, I thought he could have been handsome.

"How did you know this was here?"

"Just found it one day, on a break."

There were park benches dotted along the path and I sat down on one.

"What did your dad do?"

"He taught geography. I hated it, and having him for a teacher."

"He was at Kirkcaldy High?" I didn't even try to imagine how it would have felt to have Dad teaching me art.

"Yeah. Were you at Dunfermline, like Faye?" I nodded. "He started there. But he said moving to Kirkcaldy was the best thing he had ever done."

"My dad taught art. I hated that too."

"But you like it now," Danny said.

I hadn't thought of it that way, but it was true, I hadn't been able to keep away. And it was the reason I had asked to see Danny.

"Look, I don't know if you can help," I said, "but Shane told me about a picture. By Jenni Carstairs. She tried to sell it to him."

"Would that be Jenni the artist?"

He made to elbow me in the ribs but I wriggled sideways. "Yeah, one and the same. It won a competition, yonks ago. Do you know if it could be at the Dean? That's where Shane saw it. I think it might be in a store, or something."

"There's no real storage here. Anything not on display is kept at Granton."

Granton is Edinburgh's industrial port, an unlikely place for an art gallery. Danny seemed to read my mind.

"It's a kind of repository for all the things that aren't on view in the galleries. Just a big purpose-built store room."

"Is there a way of knowing what's there?" I asked.

"Must be, I suppose."

I told Danny all I knew about *Line in the Sand*. He said he'd ask around and get back to me.

"Why the interest in Jenni Carstairs? What's Reilly up to?"

"It's not Shane, it's me. I think the painting is of a girl I know – or used to know."

"Oh, that's cool."

"Well… it might be seriously uncool," I said. "But I think I'm up for it." After all, how many people wanted to see a picture of a father's rape victim?

Danny rang me two days later to say that *Line in the Sand* was at Granton. He had filled out a form so that I could go to see it on Friday afternoon. Except he was coming too. "It's quite near Newhaven," he said. "We could make a day of it. See where Hill took his photos. If you can get away."

It was only fair to humour Danny since I'd asked him the favour.

"Yeh. Why not."

"Faye's coming too."

Faye, still wondering why I wanted to meet her boyfriend after work. So that would be three of us looking at a picture of the girl whose life my dad had ruined.

We met at the bus station. Faye and I greeted each other, trying to ignore the gap that was between us, a gap of three months that felt like several lifetimes. When the bus came she and Danny sat together and I sat in front.

"How's your mum?" Faye asked.

Danny and I answered simultaneously. "Fine."

"That's the single parents sorted then," Faye said.

When we got off the bus, we were standing in a cobbled square of low houses, overshadowed by a tall apartment block of concrete and steel. The grey monolith dominated the square where we stood, puncturing any period feel.

"Platinum Point," Faye said, with a nod to the tower block. "Places there cost an absolute packet."

"There's a big sports centre too," Danny said. "A kid at my school used to play tennis there. I went with him once. Saw Andy Murray practising."

"Ye're kidding," Faye said.

Even I was impressed at this meagre connection with superstardom. I remembered that the tennis star came from Dunblane, like Faye, except his family hadn't been touched, not directly.

We instinctively walked away from the new development towards a harbour filled with powerboats and sailing dinghies, a symptom of the gentrified neighbourhood. Like everywhere else, the fishing had come to a halt.

Danny had a camera with him and was lining up pictures without taking any. I remembered that with conventional photos, you couldn't just keep clicking away.

"You're not going to see any fishwives," I said to Danny.

"Were we looking for any?" asked Faye.

Danny was frowning into his lens.

"Why don't you do digital?"

"There's a dark room at college," Danny said. "I like the developing."

While Danny mooched around the harbour, Faye and I walked out along the pier. Over the water, Fife was nudged by the green shoulder of the Ochil Hills.

"Come on then, Ails, what gives? Dan says you're on some mission to do with a painting?"

It was hard to know where to start, but it looked like I would have to.

"You know the girl, the one my dad…"

"The one who you knew on holiday?" Faye was cautious, wondering why this needed to be raked up.

"Yeh. Her name was Nancy and she was Andy Chalmers' sister."

At the mention of Andy, Faye grimaced. "That wanker? I never knew he had a sister."

"Well, he did. Does. Before I left home I... bumped into him a few times. That's when we got talking, about Nancy, about the holiday. Andy was the one who told me Dad had... interfered with her."

Faye wasn't stupid, she could guess that something had been going on between me and Andy, even if it had come to nothing. She let it pass.

"Okay. But what's the connection with Jenni Carstairs?"

"She's their auntie, Irene Chalmers' sister. And I have a theory this painting she did is of Nancy."

"And that matters why exactly?"

"I just feel like I need to know. Maybe then I'll contact Jenni and ask what happened to Nancy."

"But she's not your problem, is she?"

"No, but... Maybe I'd just like to know that she's okay."

"You're not still seeing Andy Chalmers then?"

"No way, José."

Faye clearly regarded this as good news. "Look, Ails, don't go thinking you can make up for stuff your dad has done. If you're that bothered, you should get in touch with him. I bet you could if you really tried."

"That's the other thing. My dad died. Not that long ago."

There was a pause as we watched Danny pick his way over the cobbles towards us. Faye was stuck for a response.

"Well... Sorry, Ails. It's just all really crap, isn't it?"

"Yeh. Pretty much," I said. "I should have told you. But I'm fine with it. For the best, you might say. And

238

now that he's gone, things are getting a bit easier with Mum. It's like we're starting again."

Danny caught up with us and took a photo of Faye and me against the sea. I was glad he was there, just for the distraction.

On the wharf there was a museum. The notices on the outside said that it contained reconstructions of the harbour and fishing scenes from the past, but the place was closed for refurbishment. I peered through the glass doors and sighed. "Typical."

Despite the lack of fishing boats there was a fish market, also closed. I wondered if it was just for show. Next to it there was a fish restaurant, part of a chain.

"They probably get their fish from Thailand," I said, "or Canada."

Danny was walking with Faye, one arm slung around her shoulder. From time to time he detached himself to take pictures of the original buildings. There was nobody around. I guessed that at night the restaurants got busy. Now it felt dead, an anachronism, clinging on by its fingertips and the signs that marked it out as a conservation area.

"Shouldn't you two be at uni?" I asked them.

"Day off," Faye said.

"Can't be arsed," Danny said.

"He's thinking of giving up," Faye explained. "Doesn't like the course."

"Why not?"

"Too much about graphics and digital media. I just like taking photos, the old way."

I thought Danny might be an anachronism too. He wandered off again, leaving me and Faye together. I couldn't work it out, her and Danny.

239

"Is he okay?"

"He's been worrying about his mum. Some money thing."

As we walked towards Granton, the old houses petered out. On the corner of a busy road a chip shop threw out the temptation of hot fat laced with vinegar. Shane had stumped up two month's wages.

"Come on," I said, "my treat."

We ate inside, leaning against a tiled wall. Faye had a fish she was sharing with Danny, breaking off segments and transferring them onto his tray of chips. When one lump threatened to disintegrate she stuck it straight into his mouth, like a bird feeding its baby. They were both laughing. I'd never thought of Faye as maternal. Then I thought again of Dunblane and something clicked: James, her younger brother. Was that why she had fallen for Danny, two years younger?

The art centre was further than we thought. We trudged for miles along ugly new roads that cut across building sites. The wind got up and blew concrete dust around us, and the sea, only a few hundred yards away, was invisible. Danny stuck the camera inside his jacket and his hands in his pocket. When we came to another main road we all crossed separately, dodging cars and lorries, then found ourselves marooned in some new business park with empty streets, and windows covered in posters advertising office space. We convened on a windy corner between two high-rise blocks.

"What a place to put an art centre," Faye said.

We eventually found the right building. Inside there were signs advertising guided tours, but it was hard to imagine they got many takers. It was hardly the

National Gallery. Who would queue up to see what looked like a gigantic office?

The place was curiously silent and the air, now that we'd lost the dust and debris of the outside world, had a sterile quality: dehumidified and drained, not just of moisture and odour, but other things too – history, culture, emotion.

The guy with thick glasses and a comb-over on reception gave us a stony look. By now we all looked like something the cat had brought in and probably smelled like it too. He said Danny would have to leave his camera at the desk. Danny didn't want to let go of it.

"It belongs to my college," he said.

"It's the rules," said comb-over man and handed him a stub of paper as a receipt.

When Danny glowered at him I got the impression that it added to the guy's enjoyment. He directed us to a side room where he said "our request" could be viewed. As we turned away from the desk, Danny spoke under his breath, "Reminds me of a crematorium."

When we got to the right room I hesitated. Who or what exactly had I come to see? And so it was Danny who pushed open the door.

The painting had been placed on an easel in the middle of the room. The girl in it was sitting on the sand with her bare legs to one side, leaning on her left arm, her t-shirt flopping off her shoulder to show the strap of a red swimsuit, blonde hair scrambled by the wind. In her right hand she held a toy spade which she had used to scrape a casual semi-circle around her, the line in the sand that gave the picture its name. But she wasn't looking at the spade or the circle she had drawn. Her eyes were raised to challenge the onlooker who had caught her unawares, interrupting her daydream by the sea. *"Ailsa,"* she seemed to say, *"what are you doing here?"*

I heard my own voice, "Nancy!" I was as surprised as she was. And finding her here, no older than the day I had last seen her, I felt I was five all over again.

Faye was behind me. "It's her then?"

"Yes," I said, "and that's my spade!"

Nancy's spade had been red with a sharp metal blade. She had always made fun of my blue plastic one. But it had somehow made its way into the painting, the link between then and now, her and me.

Aware of Faye and Danny beside me, I dragged myself back to the present, and an age when the ownership of spades no longer mattered.

"Sorry", I said. "It's just the shock."

I took in the rest of the picture. Nancy was sitting on a rocky foreshore in yellow, blue and black that also suggested seaweed and pooling water. Behind her there was long, tussocky grass. It didn't look like Largo, not the main beach, but it might have been Lundin Links, beyond the rocks, where the sand dunes start.

The style was, I supposed, realistic, or figurative, as Shane would have said. I think I'd been expecting something bigger, something larger than life, like Jenni's angry phase, but it wasn't like that. It was just a medium-sized picture in a plain frame. I asked Danny what kind of paint had been used.

"Acrylics, probably. Brighter than watercolours, lighter than oils."

I could see why Shane had liked it, why anyone would like it. It was neither sexy nor sexless. It was just right. Even in this lifeless room, it added something, a

242

feeling of vitality, a sense of something about to happen. I shivered, remembering that what had happened had been the arrival of my dad, the end for the Nancy in this picture.

"So," Faye said. "What now?"

My plan had been to ask Jenni what she knew about Dad and Nancy, but whatever had happened, Nancy was a long way now from the girl looking back at me here. Perhaps Faye was right to tell me I should let sleeping dogs lie.

Danny, as ever, was on the prowl, looking at the painting from different angles.

"Funny she didn't sign it," he said.

He was right. All of Jenni's pictures I'd seen up to now bore the same black initials I had spotted on the seascapes at Torryburn, the black and curvy J.C. that I had mistaken for I.C. *Line in the Sand* was different. There were no initials, nothing at all on the painting to identify the artist.

"Well," Faye said, "before she was famous she might not have bothered signing things. And this was just a family thing."

"Still," Danny said, "she entered it for a competition."

Danny was scouting around the back. "There's something here," he said. "You'd better come and see."

We went round to join him. Taped to the back there was a typed label. "*Line in the Sand*, submitted by Jenni Carstairs, artist T. Robertson. November 1995."

CHAPTER TWENTY-EIGHT

"Fuck me," Faye said, "it's your dad."

I turned away and headed for the door. I had been captivated by the picture. It took me right back to the Nancy I had known. But Dad had entered the scene and ruined it, just like always. The others came after me, pausing only long enough for Danny to reclaim his camera. On the sparse strip of newly laid turf that separated the art centre from the road, I sat apart, trying not to blub.

Faye moved across and put her arm around me. "I'm sorry, Ailsa. I really am."

"It's not your fault," I said. She had always told me Dad was a shit. Time after time, events had proved her right.

The grass under my hands was dry and coarse. I fished up my sleeve for a tissue and dried my eyes. It wasn't just Dad's painting that was upsetting me. "My father the artist" had been a figment of my imagination, conjured up for the sake of Shane Reilly, whom I guessed would take more interest in someone who had a foot in the art world. But my stab in the dark had turned out to be true. I had inadvertently found a bit of Dad I had never known existed.

I sniffed and scrunched the tissue up for good. "I wonder why Mum never let on he could paint, properly I mean. Do you think this is the only thing he ever did?"

"You mean like a one-hit wonder? Could be, I suppose. And your mum might never have known about this one."

A painting of the girl he went on to rape. Not something that he would have bragged about.

"That could be it," I said. "And why it was entered under Jenni's name."

"His name was on it," Danny reminded us. "I guess the website you found just got it wrong."

"Or maybe she had to, like, sponsor him or something, if he wasn't a well-known artist." Faye suggested.

I shuffled back so that we were a threesome again.

"You know," Faye said, "I don't suppose it helps, but I think the painting's really good, really nice. I mean, did it look to you that this was a girl he was about to… you know?"

I shook my head, not in denial but in confusion. I didn't know how the picture ranked as a work of art, but we had all been struck by its innocence – innocence we assumed had been imparted by a doting aunt, not by a predatory teacher. My revulsion was not for the painting, just the knowledge of what happened afterwards.

I thought back to those lessons in the art room I had hated so much, with Jenni as I had first known her. When she had said Dad would have been proud of me, she was encouraging me to take after my dad, because

245

he'd been a real artist. And this picture proved it. It was the part of him that she admired. The seed of some new knowledge had settled in a corner of my brain. It wanted to put down roots and gain a foothold but I ignored it. I couldn't afford to let it grow.

Danny was lying on his stomach, picking at stubby stalks of grass. "That girl," he said, "the one in the picture. She's familiar somehow. Where did you say she lived?"

"In Fife, a village near Kincardine. The father's a local builder."

"She reminds me of somebody I know. Just can't think who."

I stood up. "It's time I got back." I needed time to think.

"You okay?" Faye said, and I caught the note of concern that used to be the trademark of our friendship.

"Yeah, just need some space."

We dusted ourselves down. We could catch buses straight back from here without the long walk back to Newhaven. The first one that came went to Colinton. I said I'd wait for another. As the bus slid away I watched them sit down inside. Danny had the camera safely round his neck and his jacket over one shoulder. His other hand was in Faye's.

When they had disappeared around the corner I leaned against the bus shelter and watched a plastic bottle rolling around, clattering insistently against the metal frame. Dad's unexpected reappearance had left a sour taste. I had a sudden desire to be with Shane, burning up in the easy darkness where lights flashed in my head and words came from nowhere.

246

There was no sound as I unlocked the outside door. Five was usually a good time to get Shane at home and, as often as not in bed, ready for what he called afternoon delight. Afterwards we'd watch soaps then DVDs to the early hours, or drive down to the Indian restaurant in Leith. But putting my head around the bedroom door I found only rumpled sheets and a smell of stale tobacco. The phone had nothing to tell me; no messages, no texts. The calendar had nothing flagged up for today. I rang his number but the phone was switched off.

I was too restless for TV, and no sex was on offer. I took the glass that had become a makeshift ashtray from the side of the bed and emptied it. In the kitchen I wiped toast crumbs off the kitchen worktop. I had run out of options, so I changed into an old vest and hoiked the running shoes out from under the bed.

Instead of sticking to the residential streets around the flat, I turned north and east to Queen Street and ran with high buildings on my right punctuated by the wide cobbled streets that led up and over to Princes Street. It felt good to be running here in the New Town, with its tidy doors and respectability. On my left were the railings of the gardens where occasional dog-walkers emerged and stood back to let me pass. I measured my progress by counting off the roads I knew better from the Princes Street side: Castle Street, Frederic Street, Hanover Street.

As my trainers walloped the pavement, I turned over the mulch of fact and guesswork I had assembled about Nancy. The painting was a portrait done for the family. Why had it been entered in a competition? When the stuff about Nancy came out, Tom Robertson, the artist, would never have wanted it to be shown, nor, surely, would Ted or Irene Chalmers.

I stopped for a rest. I was at the Portrait Gallery. Ahead of me was St Andrews Square and the St James Centre where Faye and I had shopped. I was boxed in a corner. Ahead I could just see the grassy summit of Calton Hill with its jumble of half-finished monuments. In between lay a swathe of cars jostling for position on the main road. I was in the mood for somewhere new, for a view I hadn't seen before.

Beating the traffic, I started up a path that soon turned into a gruelling flight of steps. Descending tourists swerved to avoid me, reminding me this wasn't somewhere to go at night and alone, but I could hardly stop now, halfway up. As I concentrated on breathing, my thoughts detached themselves and floated free in the air above my head.

At the time of the court case, Nancy needed to be protected, not to have press or public or even a gallery-owner chasing her up. But Jenni had rated the picture enough to enter it for a prize. Jenni had rated my dad, even though Nancy was her sister's daughter. Would she have felt this way towards a rapist?

The green shoot I'd been trying to ignore was struggling towards the light, waving a tendril of hope that things might not be as they seemed. As a member of the family, Jenni had inside information. It didn't make sense for her to have sponsored or even approved of *Line in the Sand* unless she disbelieved the story of the rape. And if she didn't believe it, maybe she was right. Maybe it wasn't true.

I ran to where the path levelled out, and stopped next to the round monument that's on all the postcards.

248

Beyond the bulk of the North British Hotel and the jagged spike of the Scott Monument, the sunset was just pinking the sky. Edinburgh lay before me in all its glory, from the castle right down past the dark fold of the railway to the mellow stone of the New Town and in the distance, the streak of silver that marked the River Forth.

I thought of Danny and his camera and where he might be now, snuggled up with Faye or hunched over the college work he no longer wanted to do. To the north I could just see the island of Inchkeith with its white crown, pointing the way home. But with Ian learning not to care and Mum busy finding herself, I didn't think they were ready to have me back.

So what now? Running away had worked for a while. But I hadn't escaped from Dad. If anything I had got closer, moving in circles where he might have moved if his life had gone differently: if Nancy hadn't fallen across his path. A mangy dog trotted up and relieved itself against the blackened stonework. Climbing the hill had given me no understanding of where to go next, but I still had a mystery to solve: of how Jenni and Nancy and my dad were linked together, and why Jenni had tried to sell my dad's painting to Shane.

There was a shout from somewhere on the other side of the hill and the dog ran off, obedient to the call. I jogged down the hill back towards the flat. I reminded myself if things went badly it wouldn't be the first time I'd stuck my nose in and regretted it. But surely there could be nothing worse to uncover about Dad. And if there was something better, something that would make the case against him less damning, I ought to find out.

Jenni was the key, and Jenni was here, in Edinburgh. Her details must be somewhere in the files that cluttered Shane's spare room.

If Shane had been at home that night, my plan might have gone no further. With Shane, I could have let go of paintings and families and given in to the heady oblivion of sex. But with the flat still deserted, there was no escape. I showered and sat down at the PC.

Finding nothing that looked like a number or an address for Jenni Carstairs, I logged off and opened the filing cabinet huddled in the corner of the room. When that proved equally fruitless, I sat on the corner of the bed and applied my mind to the situation. I could ask Shane when he got back, but I would have to give him a reason. I imagined his reaction if I told him that *Line in the Sand* had been painted by Dad. Shane's eyes would light up at the thought that it might be mine. Then he'd be after more than a leisurely fumble or an energetic screw. But if I did have any claim to the picture, I wouldn't want Shane to take if from me. And after the way Shane had gripped my arm that night, I didn't relish being on the receiving end of his temper.

I kicked myself. Shane might not have any social contact with Jenni, but we had been to her exhibition. Neither of us was exactly keen in matters of tidying up or taking out rubbish. Unless he had handed back the invitation on the night, it might not have gone very far. I ransacked two waste paper bins and was back in the bedroom rifling the pockets of his jackets when I heard the front door open. My hands closed around a stiff piece of card. Before turning round I extracted it and tucked it into my shorts.

"Hi!" I tried to look casual as I turned. "Where've you been?"

A woman stood in the doorway. Early forties, at a guess, with a hard mouth and her hair scraped into a high ponytail tied round with a black polka-dot scarf. She had hoop earrings that would have graced the barmaid in a soap opera, but I didn't feel like laughing. What really freaked me was that she had walked straight in. She must have a key.

"I see we're skipping the introductions," she said, with that Glasgow accent that lends itself to sarcasm.

"And who are you?" I tried to feel like I had a right to be there and she didn't, but she walked past me into the room, surveying the contents of the still-open wardrobe like a detective at the scene of a crime. Her eyes swivelled back to me, the prime suspect.

"So where is he?"

"If you mean Shane, he's out on business."

She barked a laugh. "I bet he is. I suppose telling him I was coming was a bit of a mistake."

I cursed Shane for landing me in it. "Can I help?" I said. I was still pretending to myself that this might be a difficult customer looking for her money back, but it was pretty damned obvious that Shane's visitor had business of a personal kind.

"Well, that depends on who you might be exactly."

"I'm Isla, his… personal assistant." My voice tailed off. She wasn't born yesterday and no doubt had a pretty accurate picture of the range of personal services I'd been providing.

She sighed. "I don't doubt it. I dare say he might even have paid you, but I'm his wife and the party's over. Just tell me where I can get hold of him and you can pack up and move on."

I had never quizzed Shane on his trips to Glasgow and the other appointments he failed to put in the diary. It was hardly a surprise that he had associations elsewhere. Mrs Reilly, in her false nails and stilettos, was a scary sight all right, but considering how little I knew about Shane, it was almost a relief to know she was no more than a wife looking for vengeance.

"I really don't know where he is," I said. "I've had a day off. I've been trying to get hold of him myself."

She raised her eyebrows. "Looks like you have a lot to learn. You need to keep tabs on our Shane. You never know when he might do a moonlight flit."

She marched out of the bedroom into the spare room, where she took out a mobile phone and spoke into it, adopting a cooingly maternal tone. "Kylie, pet, it's Mum. I'm in Edinburgh but I'll be back after eight. I'll pick up a Chinese. Tell Ryan there's extra pocket money if he does his homework. Take care now. Love ya."

Mrs R put the phone away and started disentangling the cables of the PC and printer in a way that suggested years of practice. "Just tell him," she said, reverting to hard-bitten grown-up speak, "that if he wants this baby back he'd better get in touch. The wife and bairns could do with him and his unsteady income." She stood balancing the cumbersome processing unit in her arms and fixed me with a look. "This flat belongs to me," she said.

If she'd added *"Capisce?"* I wouldn't have been surprised.

Mrs Reilly took her leave. I found myself reluctantly impressed by her combination of ruthless wife and doting mother. But even if she wasn't part of some Glasgow mafia, I didn't relish crossing her path again. I cursed Shane. Why hadn't he warned me she was coming? He had clearly known she was on the war path.

Why indeed? My legs gave out under me and I sank down on the edge of the unmade bed, cursing my own naivety. Shane was no fool. Too much of a coward to give me the push, he'd gambled on his wife finding me here and doing his dirty work for him. Anger galvanised my legs back into life and I looked around for something to smash, but the aging monitor didn't have much life in it and the printer, unhooked from its moorings, looked as helpless as me. Mrs Reilly had the bit that mattered. Or did she? I had a sudden recollection of Shane hooking up his new laptop to the PC a couple of nights before, copying data across. What if he had deleted the original files? The box hauled off in triumph by Mrs Reilly was probably useless.

With rage still boiling inside me, I turned to the wardrobe and yanked everything out, throwing shoes at the wall, ripping out the sleeves from shirts and the linings from jackets. If he came back for this lot he'd be in for a surprise. I surveyed the mangled remains, looking for his particular favourites, the pale blue stripe, the plain burgundy silk. Bastard. Prick. Arsehole. Like all of his best stuff, his leather jacket, his Armani suit, they had gone. I ran to the kitchen for scissors, slashing at what was left, making a pile of tawdry ribbons on the duvet. Then I came to the black jacket where I'd found Jenni's invitation, still folded in my pocket. Shane could go fuck himself. I had everything I needed.

The wardrobe and its rickety shelves now held only my own meagre possessions. Those that I'd acquired during my time with Shane I flung onto the heap. I shoved the rest – the jeans and t-shirts I'd brought from home – into my holdall, filling the remaining corners with the things I really needed: shoes, make-up, hair straighteners.

Before I let myself out I went back to the bedroom and poured a bottle of loo-cleaner over the bed and everything piled on it. The smell of disinfectant followed me downstairs like the reek from a public lav.

CHAPTER TWENTY-NINE

It was coming up to seven o'clock. The nearest pub was open but deserted. I sat in a corner seat with a cider and took a minute or two to collect myself, then called the mobile number on the invitation card. I assumed it was a business number with an answerphone. But on the fifth ring I was transferred to another line. The call was picked up straight away. The "Hello there" was casual, the greeting of a woman having a night off, not expecting calls from strangers.

"Is that Jenni Carstairs?" There was an immediate change in the silence at the other end.

"Yes," she said. "And who might this be?"

"We met last week," I told her. I had to get her attention before she hung up on me. "I was with Shane Reilly. I'm his PA. He introduced me as Isla but my name's Ailsa. Ailsa Robertson. Tom Robertson was my dad." I paused to gauge her reaction.

"Ailsa." She spoke my name thoughtfully, working out if what I had said made sense. In the background I could hear an early evening TV show come to its blaring end and the announcer's voice bigging up the schedule for the rest of the night. She was poised between me and the next episode of *Eastenders*. I didn't want Albert Square to win.

"I'd like to ask you about him, about my dad."

"This had better not be some kind of a joke," Jenni said.

"It's not a joke. Shane's not here. He doesn't know I'm ringing you. He doesn't know… who I am." This was the best I could do to prove to Jenni I was acting on my own behalf.

"All right. I suppose you'd better come round. Can you come tonight?"

She gave me an address that sounded familiar.

"Thanks. I'll be there."

I rang off and allowed myself a moment of relief, spiced with a foretaste of triumph. I could do this.

The address Jenni gave me was Western Harbour Drive, the development of apartment blocks that had overshadowed our visit to Newhaven. So much for the working class hero. I entered through a revolving glass door that led into an empty cube of a room with one other door. There was a security camera trained on it. On the touch pad I pressed the numbers she'd given me and the intercom crackled.

"Come up."

Inside the door there was a lift. I took it to the ninth floor and found myself in a corridor with no windows and dim security lighting. If I had had this kind of money, I thought I would have chosen somewhere with a bit more life.

The door to the flat was like a hotel door with a card reader on it. When I knocked I heard footsteps. Before I could change my mind, Jenni opened the door, turned

256

and walked ahead of me into a wide room, entirely dominated by the view from the windows that stretched from wall to wall.

I guessed this was what they meant by a penthouse. Jenni stepped back and let me go closer to the window, where I suppose all her guests gravitated. In the fading light I could see the harbour below, the tangle of newness towards Granton and a vista beyond that stretched up the Forth amid acres of cloudy sky.

Even at this hour the room was flooded with light. I imagined her being here from dawn to dusk, capturing tricks of sky and sea on the canvases propped against the far wall, but they were turned inwards, and an easel in the corner had nothing on it. I wondered if she was still in her angry phase.

Close to where I'd come in, there was a lot less of the penthouse effect. An elderly armchair faced a TV that was far too small for the rest of the room. On the back of the chair was a rumpled throw that suggested Jenni liked to keep down the heating bills. Next to it on the floor there was a rough pottery mug of the sort found in the pricier craft shops.

Jenni switched off the TV and picked up the mug.

"Have a seat," she said, and motioned to a leather sofa in the middle of the room, facing the view. "Can I get you something to drink? Tea? Coffee?"

I shook my head but she disappeared through a door on the right. When I heard the rattle of crockery and the gush of the tap I slipped back into the hall and left my holdall near the front door. Jenni might have noticed it already but I didn't feel like advertising my homeless state. She soon reappeared with a mug that smelled of herbs for herself and a jug of water and a glass for me.

She set it all on the black glass coffee table in front of the sofa, where I now sat clutching my scruffy handbag like an interview candidate who almost certainly was more likely to get a lecture than a job offer.

Jenni was dressed down. Her chunky cardigan with an appliqué flower on each pocket was cosy rather than chic, likewise the long t-shirt and shapeless jeans. Black velvet slippers embellished with gold and pink embroidery, maybe from a foreign trip, made a garish contrast. The funky green specs were not in evidence but on the coffee table, next to a newspaper, I spotted a pair of reading glasses.

She was made up but with only a layer of foundation and none of the care I had seen before. She looked older and more homely, but when she spoke to me I remembered she had been a teacher and I felt like a pupil who was proving to be a problem.

"So. How did you fall in with Shane?"

What had it been: Desperation? Stupidity? "I was looking for a job."

Her face softened, or maybe it was the fading of the light from the big windows. "I did think you looked familiar," she said, "when you came in with him. But my mind was on other things." She sat down in the corner of the sofa, turning to face me. "You do know he has a wife? And two kiddies?"

I nodded. "I do now."

"I take it you've met Gillian then."

"Today. She came looking for him."

"I dare say that was for the best," Jenni said.

She was testing me, to see how much I'd been taken in by him. To see how much I cared.

"I suppose," I said, dropping my eyes and running my toe over the stripped wood floor which emitted a low squeak of protest. In fact, it wasn't Shane's duplicity that had surprised me so much as his ordinary other life. It was hard to think of him as a family man. "I've moved out."

She nodded. "Good girl. I suggest you leave it that way. Sooner or later she'll come after him and he'll run, in one direction or another. It's no life to be following after."

"I went to see the picture," I said. *"Line in the Sand."* Jenni clearly hadn't been expecting this, but she said nothing. "Did my dad really paint it, or was it you?"

"Oh no, Tom was the artist. I just entered it for the prize. I suppose it's still at Granton?"

I nodded. "And the girl. I knew her once. Nancy."

She nodded, but to herself, turning over some thoughts of her own, then a wry smile. "He said you would remember her."

"He did?" It felt like a step forward, to have me and Nancy, our brief joint existence, acknowledged. "When? When did he say that?"

"When he showed me the painting. It was one of the reasons he didn't want to keep it. Said it would just remind him of the whole sorry mess."

Apart from the purr of an air-con unit and the tick of an electric clock, the room was silent. I relished the sense of peace. There was none of the rancour of Shane's wife, or the demands of Shane himself. The muddle that I had made of Dad's story coalesced into something simple: a middle-aged man, and a schoolgirl. Only chance had made Nancy someone I had thought of

259

as a friend, a symbol of the time before things went wrong, when in fact she had been the cause of it. Energy drained out of me and I felt my mouth tremble, ready to give in to tears. I gripped the edge of the sofa to steady myself. Tears might evoke sympathy, but I wanted the facts. I gulped some water and tried to look in control of myself. I guessed that Jenni wasn't fooled, but she carried on.

"So," said Jenni. "What do you know? What did they tell you?"

"My mum didn't say much. Only that he'd gone. But then I found out for myself that there had been a girl, a schoolgirl. It was only recently I discovered she was Nancy. I met her when we were on holiday. I was only five. She looked after me." I felt railroaded. I was supposed to be asking the questions. "I don't understand," I said, "why you had the picture and why you showed it to Shane."

Jenni was giving me a long look. "How about that coffee?"

I nodded. "Yeah. Thanks."

She brought me coffee in a mug like hers. It had too much milk in, just how my gran used to make it.

"Just remind me," she said, "how old are you?" Jenni had changed from headmistress to school nurse, one of those that lets you sit in the medical room for an hour pretending to have a headache.

"Nineteen," I said. "Nearly twenty."

"Yes," she said, "I thought so. Time you knew what went on between your father and my family. Lucky that you've come to somebody who knows."

Outside, lights were bobbing up on the water and along the double spine of a dual carriageway that curved away in the distance. Jenni's lounge was a capsule suspended between day and night. As she spoke, her body sagged into the folds of the sofa and her face relaxed into lines that the glare of publicity had ironed out at our first meeting. She stopped being an artist or a teacher. She could almost have been my mum.

"You probably know that Nancy is my niece. Her mother, Irene, is my sister."

I was suddenly aware of Nancy's presence in the room, lurking in the shadows, or was she hiding in a cupboard, waiting for a time when Jenni felt it would be safe to release her into the world? If so, maybe her time had come.

"When things fell apart, I was the one who took care of Nancy. I still do. I tried to take care of Tom too, or at least to help him out, but he didn't really give me the chance.

"When Tom came back that September, when he'd met the family at Largo, he said what a bonny girl she was. It was the first time he'd felt like painting a portrait, capturing somebody on the canvas. I liked Tom and I could see he wasn't happy at home. I thought it would be good for him to have some other interest. He did some sketches that showed promise, and I got Eddie and Irene to invite him to a drinks do and they were fine with the idea. It was to be a simple portrait. I expect they were flattered that he admired their daughter enough to paint her. A painting's a bit more upmarket than a studio photo.

"As soon as Tom told me, I had to bring it up, the whole sexual thing. She was my niece, after all, and you know how men are. But he just laughed. 'Come on

261

Jenni, she's young enough to be my daughter. That's not my scene,' he'd said. So I'm not saying he didn't feel an attraction, but I accepted what he said. I trusted him not to fall prey to anything like that. He had Lorraine, even if she was a handful, and he had you. But he didn't tell Lorraine about the portrait job. I knew that was a mistake. He said she would only get upset, that things were bad enough without giving her things to worry about. I should have insisted.

"What I didn't spot, and neither did Eddie, was that Nancy wasn't the problem: Irene was. I suppose she was making cow eyes at Tom at the party, but she made cow eyes at a lot of men and I paid no attention. Eddie, as usual, was only interested in the money side: what they would pay Tom and how long it would take."

Jenni heaved herself out of the chair, went through to the kitchen and came back with a whisky bottle. I let her splosh a slug of tawny liquid into my mug.

"Have you met my sister?" she said.

I shook my head. "I don't think so." Certainly not on the beach at Largo where adult introductions were the last thing on Nancy's mind. Since then I'd partied in Irene's kitchen, made eyes at her son, got engaged to a family friend, but still we'd avoided one another. I imagined her as Rhona on a bigger scale, with style and opinions to match her husband's status. What Jenni said next suggested I was right.

"Irene always did cut quite a figure, especially back then. I just never suspected that Tom had been taken in. Even then it might not have mattered. They would have tired of each other, or someone would have got wise and put a stop to it. But no one thought about Nancy and what it would do to her."

Jenni got up again and walked towards the window. If she was looking for escape, the view had gone. The darkness now reflected the room back at her, the coffee table, the sofa with me on it.

"Tom had done some sketches from memory, but Nancy was expected to sit for him. She was flattered by the attention. For Irene, it was an excuse to have him to the house, not too often, just on nights when Eddie was otherwise engaged. When Nancy had been packed off upstairs, she could have Tom to herself.

"It wouldn't have taken Irene long to show her hand, and I guess Tom was tiring of your mother's ailments as excuses for…"

Jenni clearly baulked at mentioning my parents' sex life, or lack of, to me. She waited for my reaction, but when she didn't get one she carried on.

"Then she and Tom were too involved with one another to notice that Nancy was in the flush of a first crush, imagining romantic scenes between her and the teacher who wanted to paint her picture. She didn't know she was only the decoy.

"Needless to say, she eventually worked out that Tom was staying on in the house when the sitting was finished, and decided to gatecrash his cosy evening chat with her mother. Except by then there wasn't much chatting going on. They were in the front room with the lights off and curtains closed. They didn't hear Nancy creeping down and opening the door. Well, they wouldn't, would they?"

I thought of Ian and myself in that same room, stopped only by the beam of a headlight. And Irene had been on home ground, determined to get her share of a man who could offer a lot more excitement than her affluent but bumptious husband. Then I remembered how Nancy had become part of this scene.

"Poor girl," Jenni went on. "Think of the state she was in. In her mind she and Tom were an item. She was just waiting for the night he would finish the picture and declare undying love. Then she found him shagging her mother."

Jenni's words caught the brutality of it. I thought of myself with Ian and later with Shane. I was as much the prick-tease as Irene Chalmers, both of us out for our own satisfaction.

"By the time Eddie arrived home, Irene had gone upstairs, oblivious to Nancy having seen her with Tom. But Nancy was in the kitchen with her clothes ripped and big scratches on her arms. She told him Tom had raped her."

A schoolgirl defiled by an older man who had wormed his way in to the family to get close to her. The idea still sickened me as it would have sickened her father. I pictured her in the big family kitchen, her face greyed out with shock, her arms streaked with blood. It was a minute before I hit on the truth, the truth that had been shouting for attention from the minute I saw the painting.

"But he didn't do it."

Jenni shook her head. "No." Some of the weight in her face and her body dissolved. She had waited as long to say this as I had to hear it.

"The scratches. She did them herself?"

"Yes. But as far as Eddie was concerned, his only daughter had been molested by her teacher. After all, Tom had had ample opportunity. He called the police."

I was shaking my head to rid it of the thought that had been there so long, of Nancy as Dad's victim. I had to say it again. "My dad didn't do it." The tables had been turned.

"No. He never laid a finger on her. But he had no real defence unless Irene spilled the beans to Eddie, and she wouldn't. She thought he might throw her out and she liked it all too much: the house and the money and, I suppose," Jenni's mouth softened momentarily, "her boys." Andy and his brother, both younger than Nancy, kept in the dark like everyone else.

"Eddie went straight to the school and had Tom suspended. Of course there was no way that rape could be proved, because it hadn't happened. But Nancy made it sound like he had at the very least been guilty of serious sexual assault.

"Eventually she broke down under questioning. She admitted she had lied and told the police about Irene and Tom. Eddie had to drop charges, but Irene already had her as the villain of the piece, wrecking her cosy arrangement with Tom. Eddie was furious with both of them. He thought he'd been made a fool of twice over.

"By the time I saw Nancy, there wasn't much I could do except get her out of there. The awful thing was that they never did anything to kill the rumours. Later on, when she'd calmed down, I think Irene wanted to, but Eddie wouldn't have it."

"You mean he let people think his daughter had been molested?"

Jenni nodded. "Rather than letting it be known that his wife had been unfaithful. Maybe it was some kind of revenge on Tom for having… had Irene".

It was shocking. I told Irene that Andy still believed it, or something like it.

Jenni sighed. "I've not had much to do with them, with Irene and Eddie since then. I just did what I could for the girl."

"But it wasn't her fault."

"No, but Irene was furious with her, Eddie was furious with Irene. Nancy was only ever going to be in the crossfire. They paid for her to go to boarding school here in Edinburgh. I had her in the holidays."

"And my mum wouldn't have Dad back. He lost everything."

"Tom was powerless. Don't forget that nobody except those involved knew just what had happened. Your dad resigned from school. It didn't look good. A lot of people thought he was guilty and that the charges had been dropped to make things easier for Nancy."

"And the picture?"

"The police wanted it as evidence but I managed to get it back. Despite everything I liked it and it was nearly finished. It seemed to sum up Nancy before she was – damaged. I was the one who entered it in the competition. By then nobody took much interest in a painting by an amateur who had gone to ground."

"But you showed it to Shane".

"That was a big mistake. I realised almost straight away. I was skint at the time and had some idea Tom and I could share the proceeds. I told him about Shane's offer but he wasn't having it, so I backed out, except Shane had a go at me and we never really got on after that."

"So you were in touch with Dad?"

"He went to Glasgow and managed to get work as a supply teacher. At the time I got in touch about the picture, he had moved to a school in Helensburgh. I think he was angry that I'd approached Shane. Can't blame him really. I haven't heard from him since. My own stupid fault."

Jenni had offered to speak up for him at the time of the scandal. In the end she had lost a friend too.

"He never tried to get in touch with me," I said.

Jenni was silent, looking over to her easel, maybe finding some new anger to inject into her work. "No. I don't suppose he did."

"Not even once. He was my dad."

"I suppose your mother's kept him away."

"She took his money, though. Money he sent for me."

"She did?" I nodded and she frowned. "Well, I'm surprised at that. I thought she wanted nothing more to do with him." She turned her attention back to the present and to me sitting on her sofa. "Did you never think of contacting him yourself?"

"Not when I knew what he'd done. To Nancy. And I didn't want to upset Mum. Just mentioning him used to set her off."

If I had ever thought of getting in touch with Dad it would have been to give him a piece of my mind. Even if things had been different, would I have wanted reconciliation? He might not have been a rapist, but he had an affair with another man's wife. And he had left us. For good.

Jenni was watching me. "Well, I still have that address."

"What address?"

267

"The one in Helensburgh. He might still be there, or they could forward a letter."

I took a drink and felt the whisky hit my stomach. Jenni didn't know. Why would she?

"It's a bit late for that," I said. "My dad died last year. Sorry, I should have said."

CHAPTER THIRTY

Jenni didn't cry, but her mouth fell at the corners. "Oh no," she said. "Surely not. He was no age at all. I'm sorry, Ailsa. I had no idea." In her eyes I saw deep shock at the loss of Tom, but also sorrow for the shortness of all our lives.

I told her how the letter had come and the money had stopped.

"Och, what a shame," Jenni said, "when you might have had some time together."

Some of Jenni's sorrow rubbed off on me. I felt that the man who had died wasn't the same as the one Mum had told me about. He wasn't exactly a saint, but he hadn't been a monster either. He'd been stupid and fallen victim to a woman with power, money, maybe looks too. But he'd meant no harm.

I reminded myself that meaning no harm wasn't enough.

Jenni gave another sigh and drew her cardigan around her. "If it's any help, he seemed happy enough when we spoke."

"Did he get married again?"

"I don't think so, but I think he had company. He wasn't somebody who liked to be alone."

When she got up off the sofa I could see she had stiffened with sitting and I thought again about my mum, living in the dark even then, with no idea Dad was painting anybody, never mind in the big house at Torryburn. And when the accusations flew she was no wiser than anyone else. Had he told her about Irene? Maybe she just hadn't believed him. How would she have known what to believe?

Jenni's clock had moved on beyond ten. Outside the sky and the sea were black and the lights no longer fuzzy but bright and distinct in the inky darkness.

"Where is Nancy now?" I asked. "Is she all right?"

"She's not so bad. She did a degree in art history. You probably saw her at the exhibition. She works in the City Gallery."

The tall girl in the dark suit who had taken our tickets that night. Nancy and I had passed each other without noticing. Only Danny, who must have run into her more than once, had spotted the connection with the painting.

"It's late," Jenni said. "Where are you staying?"

"I have a friend. In Colinton."

I got out my phone but Jenni saw I barely had the energy to make a call. "Why don't you stay here? Just for tonight."

When I'd sorted out my stuff she stood over me as I settled down with a blanket on the sofa. Shane might wonder what had become of me, but so what? There wasn't much he could do about it. He had reverted to what he had always been, an interlude, as I had been for him.

270

In the morning Jenni asked if I wanted to get in touch with Nancy, but I said I didn't know.

"I'll tell her you've been here," she said. "If that's okay with you."

I nodded and went to make myself presentable. It was time to tell Mum what Jenni had told me.

In the months since I had left home, I had lost my front door key.

"Oh, it's you," Mum said, when I rang the bell, like she had been expecting somebody else. "You'd better come in."

We went through to the living room.

"How are you?" she said. "Will I make you a cup?"

It took me a minute to get my bearings. The room had been painted in a shade of pale yellow. It still smelled new. Things had been moved around: the old armchair had gone and in its place there were lime green bucket seats with yellow cushions on them.

"This is nice." I could hardly keep the surprise from my voice.

"Do you like it? Liz took me to Ikea."

"Who did the painting?"

"We did it together, me and Liz. We bought special paint. Non-allergenic. It took us a whole weekend. What do you think?"

"It's good." In its way it looked better than Jenni's penthouse. The old dining table had gone and there was a new coffee table laid with two cups and saucers and a plate of biscuits. She really was expecting somebody. Mum hovered between the table and the kitchen door, unsure of how warmly to welcome me.

"I'm having a meeting. Agnes is coming this morning." Mum caught my blank look and frowned. "Agnes Crichton. She helps me with Lupus Aware. I told you about her, remember?"

I made a noise that might signify agreement. Did I remember? Had she told me?

There were other changes. The PC was in here on a proper desk with a phone next to it. On the wall alongside there was a calendar and a leaflet with *Lupus Aware* in white jangly letters on a background of red and blue. Under the desk were two boxes full of what looked like the same leaflets, packed in tight bundles. I could see there was quite a bit involved in Mum's new role.

"Are you still doing Smoothies?"

She handed me a coffee in one of our old mugs, the new ones still pristine on the table. "Och, yes. I'm quite busy. I just keep the computer in here now. It's handier."

She went to the desk and picked up the diary that had moved here too and frowned at it. She said that this Agnes would likely stay for a couple of hours, then in the afternoon she had three leg appointments.

"So, what brings you here?" she said. Not unfriendly, just curious, and her eye on the clock.

"I gave up my job."

"Why? What happened?"

She was expecting some dereliction on my part, but in terms of the job, I really hadn't cocked up.

"It wasn't going anywhere. The guy, Shane, was… cutting back."

Mum was still frowning, wondering what had really gone on between me and Shane, but I was impatient to tell my story.

"Mum, I have to tell you something. It's about Dad."

She frowned some more. "What d'ye mean?"

"I found out what really happened."

The doorbell rang.

"That'll be her now," Mum said.

I felt her relief at not having to go on with this conversation. As she went to answer the door, I picked up my bag, and took it upstairs. I could hear Mum usher in her visitor, apologising that she wasn't quite ready. "My daughter turned up. Out of the blue…" Shared laughter at the unpredictability of children.

I surveyed my bedroom, looking for signs it had been requisitioned as another office or a counselling room, but it was all just as I had left it. I rang Faye with the gist of what Jenni had told me.

"I'm at home. I need to tell Mum."

"Too right. Then what?"

"No idea."

Term had ended. Faye was off for another stint at the summer camp and asked if I'd like to go too; they might still have vacancies.

"Thanks, but I think there are things I need to sort out. Here."

I lay down on the bed and examined the not quite random pattern of cracked-ice ceiling paper, reminding myself that this was home.

I must have dozed off, because the next thing I knew I could hear farewells on the doorstep. I wandered through to the tiny room where my exercise bike still

273

lived, and glimpsed Agnes's blue Corsa as it disappeared down the road. I got on the bike and pedalled for a few minutes but couldn't work up any enthusiasm for looking at the walls.

Later we sat down to ham salad eked out with cold potatoes and a lump of cheese. Mum told me about the new brand of sugar paste she was using and the number of lupus sufferers needing her support.

"So does she have lupus, this Agnes?"

"No, but I think she knows somebody who has. She just offered to help. She has time on her hands. She's from Kirkcaldy way."

"It's a long way to come."

Mum shrugged. "This is the first time she's been. Usually we email. And she gets mileage."

I imagined Mum authorising claims and generally organising things. "And they don't pay you?"

"They do now. It just took a while to sort it out. Next month we're having an open meeting, for everyone in Fife, doctors and patients. It's to be in Glenrothes. Helen Archibald will come. She keeps in touch." She stopped eating. Her face still had a livid look but compared to how she used to be, she was full of energy. "And what about you? What are you going to do?"

"Get a job, I suppose."

She raised her eyebrows, implying *doing what exactly?*

It was a question I couldn't answer. My work experience, the bits I could own up to, amounted to very little. "I'll find something."

She opened her mouth and I felt some remark coming about my derelict degree, but luckily neither of us was in the mood for a row right then.

"I came to tell you about Dad."

Her eyes stayed resolutely on the ragged lettuce leaf still on her plate. "Oh yes."

I needed her attention. "Mum, I met Jenni Carstairs. He didn't do it. She knows what really happened."

Mum set down her knife and fork, shaking her head as if to clear away some confusing fog. "I don't know what you mean."

"Jenni is Irene's sister, like you said. When they threw Nancy out she looked after her. Nancy told her Dad never touched her. He was innocent, but Jenni couldn't say anything."

"Innocent?" Mum gave me a long look. She was right. It wasn't that simple.

"But he didn't rape her. The charges were made up. He was... having an affair with Irene Chalmers. Nancy just sort of... got in the way."

Mum folded her arms. I'd thought I would be doing her a favour, telling her Dad hadn't touched his pupil, but now I wasn't so sure. From her point of view, what difference did it make? Dad had been unfaithful, one way or another.

"Did you know about Irene?" I asked her.

"He told me that was it – the mother, not the daughter."

"Did you believe him?"

She shrugged. "Irene always had an eye for the men. I thought there might be something in it. By then, I just wanted Tom gone. Exactly what had happened didn't seem to matter."

275

Except to me.

She saw the accusation in my eyes. "And what else did she have to say, Jenni Carstairs?"

"She tried to help Dad out. But they lost touch. Jenni didn't know he had died."

I saw something in Mum's eyes then, something like satisfaction. "No. I don't suppose she would have."

Mum had found a harder edge, or had it always been there? I had meant to tell her about Dad going to Helensburgh and teaching there. Now I felt less inclined. She might even know already. I felt some need to be ahead of her.

"I saw the picture," I said.

"What picture?"

"The painting of Nancy. At Largo. You didn't know about it?"

"He told me, but only afterwards. I never saw it. I never knew whether to believe it was true. All a bit too convenient, I thought, needing to go out to the house on a regular basis."

"So what *did* you think he was doing, the times he was there?"

"I can't remember. School work, meetings, something like that."

Men with wives and young children don't just disappear for whole evenings. Not without a good explanation. Had she suspected him of infidelity, even then? Had she been mentally prepared for some kind of showdown?

"I found out about the painting through Shane. He thought it was pretty good. That it would be worth something."

Mum abandoned her meal and got up to look out of the window into the garden. She didn't want to hear any more.

They had lived together, he had fathered her child, but she had never known of his artistic ambitions, or maybe she did but hadn't believed in him. I imagined how she might have belittled his talents. *"Had you better not stick to teaching? At least it pays."*

She came back and started to clear the things from the table. "I hope it's helped you," she said. "To know what happened." It clearly hadn't helped her.

"I gave up the flat. It went with the job."

Mum raised her eyebrows. "Right," she said. "I think I get the picture."

I got the picture too. Mum wasn't going to throw me out. Nor did she want me hanging around under her increasingly active feet, absorbing her hard-earned cash.

Two days later I was back where I had started, taking money for petrol and Mars Bars. Needless to say, it wasn't long before Ian drove up in his brown van.

"Fancy meeting you here," he said, sounding pretty chipper, all things considered. "Things didn't work out then, in Edinburgh?" Considering how I had treated him he looked remarkably composed.

"Not exactly."

"Are you okay?"

"Just about. Gave up uni."

"That's a shame."

I shrugged. Another customer was coming up behind him, proffering his debit card.

"We could have a drink?" Ian said.

I was glad Ian wasn't holding a grudge. And I wasn't exactly deluged with invitations. "Okay. If you like."

"What about tonight? The King Malcolm?" The hotel, out on the dual carriageway, was part of a chain and not exactly on the youth circuit.

"I'll see how I'm fixed. When will you be there?"

"Half past seven," he said. "Try and make it."

When I mentioned it to Mum, she said there was a bus. I hoped Ian would drop me back.

When I arrived, he was already settled in a corner table with a pint. I sat down beside him.

"How's the leg?" I said.

"It's fine now, but it took a while."

Ian told me his boss had given him office work for a few weeks while he recovered and now they were talking of making him assistant manager. Maybe the accident had been a blessing in disguise.

"You're looking well," I told him. For someone who'd recently been confined to a sofa, he was definitely leaner and fitter.

"I go to the gym. At first it was part of the physio, but I like it now. The health club at Pitreavie. Do you know it?"

I shook my head. My personal fitness regime had never involved parting with money.

"The thing is, there's a girl there. She works as a trainer. We're... em, you know, seeing each other."

"Well, good for you." My reaction was sincere. I was pleased Ian had bounced back.

He checked his watch. "She'll probably be here soon. She finishes her shift at eight."

If I'd known Ian's new girlfriend was on the agenda, would I have agreed to come? But if this was his moment, I could hardly deny him. The choice of venue suddenly made sense. Pitreavie was barely a mile from the hotel.

"Thing is," he went on, "when I saw you at the garage, I did wonder if you'd want…"

It took me a minute to catch on. "To give it another go?" I had to laugh. "Well even if I did, I didn't think you'd be up for it," I said.

He grinned. "You were a bit of a handful."

I was pleased he remembered the handful as giving some pleasure, however brief.

Before I'd left, I'd searched through the drawers of my dressing table and found the ring he had given me, tucked up in its velvet box. I reached in my bag and took it out.

"This is yours," I said.

"It's okay," he said. "I didn't mean…"

"No, but it's yours. Take it back to the shop, or put it on eBay." I remembered the girlfriend, about to arrive. "You might even need it again."

"Okay, thanks." He put it in his pocket. Just in time, as it turned out, as at that precise moment the outside door opened and Laura Patterson breezed in wearing a sports vest and an incredibly healthy smile.

"Hiya, hun," she said to Ian and kissed him on the cheek. "Hiya, Ailsa. Nice to see you again."

CHAPTER THIRTY-ONE

I'd completely forgotten Laura's career plan to become a personal trainer, and even if I had remembered, would have discounted it as a bit of a fantasy. She'd always been more interested in fashion than fitness. But not, it appeared, any more. With her hair tied back and barely a scrap of make-up, she looked healthy in that just-out-of-the-shower way. She flung a serious-looking sports holdall under the table and sent Ian to the bar for a diet Coke.

"What about you?" she said. "Has he not got you a drink? Ian, you lummock, get something for Ailsa."

I suppose I had bossed Ian too. Maybe he and Laura were well suited.

While he was at the bar, she leaned forward. "I hear you've had a really bad scene."

I nodded in agreement and she tutted as if everyone knew I'd been shagging a middle-aged slime-ball.

When Ian came back from the bar I asked a few polite questions about routes to becoming a qualified gym instructor, then knocked back my Coke. There was only one thing left in my mind to clear up. I decided Laura's presence didn't matter. Not any more.

"Do you still see Andy Chalmers?"

Ian coloured. He would have heard about the scene in Edinburgh, about how I'd been throwing myself at Andy. "Not really."

"Look," I said, "I had a lot of stuff in my head. And I was drunk."

"So I heard."

"Well, however it sounded, I never really fancied Andy."

I owed him that much. As for Laura, I didn't know what Ian had told her, but whatever it was it had won me instant promotion from *persona non grata* to local celebrity. I made a mental note to tell Faye.

Having Shane's voice in my ear as I authorized the diesel pump was disconcerting to say the least. That, and the fact that he called me by the right name.

"Ailsa, it's me, don't ring off. I have a message for you." His voice sounded different, more tentative.

"Not from your wife, I hope."

He had the grace to pause. "Yeah, sorry about that. She gets a bit het up."

I rolled my eyes at the empty shop around me. "I noticed. So what's up? How did you get my number?"

"I had it from before. When you… applied." Another pause as we each recalled the peremptory interview process. "Listen. It's Jenni Carstairs. She keeps asking to get in touch with you."

"Why?"

"I don't really know, but she says it's important. Can I give her this number?"

I had no idea if Shane knew in what way Jenni and I were connected. Nor did I know if I wanted to speak to

281

Jenni again. She'd told me what I needed to know. As far as I could see, that was that.

"Look," Shane went on, "she's rung me three times. Then I had a call from the girl who works at the City Gallery. Apparently they're related or something."

Nancy. In her new guise. She must be the one wanting to get in touch, not Jenni. If she'd turned up a few months ago I would have been made up. But what was the point now?

I sighed. "Let me have her number. The gallery girl." I had no intention of getting in touch, but it was the easiest way to get Shane off my case.

"Look, I'm sorry, about… you know…"

I didn't think Shane had much to apologise for. He had put a roof over my head and shagged me senseless, just like I had wanted.

"I'm back in the flat. If you want to…"

He didn't even bother to finish the sentence. Even he knew when something was dead in the water.

A text duly arrived with Nancy's number. I saved it, filing it away like I had filed all the other stuff I had learned from Jenni, but in the end my curiosity got the better of me. Or maybe I needed to lay to rest my old memories of her, of the days we had raced hand in hand, kicking up the sand behind us. Most of all, I needed to add another piece to the puzzling jigsaw that had been my dad.

"Thanks for ringing, Ailsa." A tiny hesitation, or maybe she was waiting for me to speak. "I think we need to talk." Her voice was faint, and there was nothing in the accent or the inflection to tie her to the girl I had known. "Is there somewhere we could meet?"

282

"You mean Edinburgh? I could come on Sunday, if that's any good."

"Sunday's fine." Another pause, that hesitation I'd noticed at the start. "Do you know the Dean Gallery? It should be quieter than in town. If it's okay for you."

The Dean, where my time in Edinburgh had begun. I had come full circle, if only by coincidence. But of course she was in the art business. I thought of Shane, but even if he were in Edinburgh, there was little likelihood he'd be at work on a Sunday.

We settled on noon, but I made a huge effort to get out of bed in good time and arrived way too early. That was fine. I wanted some time to compose myself, but what threw me was the sight of Danny behind the bar, tending to his old friend the lemon squeezer.

With the academic year at an end I'd assumed the student house had disbanded. I hadn't expected to see Danny again, not here, grinning his lopsided grin.

"Hiya, Ailsa!" He was unfazed. "What are you up to?"

Last time we'd been together was at Newhaven. I hoisted myself onto a bar-stool. "Of all the bars in all the towns…"

He laughed.

"Did Faye tell you, about my dad?"

He shook his head, and so I told him what Jenni had told me. When I said Dad was innocent, he nodded in approval.

"And you were right," I said, running my finger over a light stain on the dark wood of the bar.

"How d'ye mean?"

"You did know the girl in the picture. She works at the City Gallery now. She was there the night of Jenni's exhibition."

Danny slapped himself on the forehead. "Yeh, I remember now. So that's her?"

"Yep. She did some kind of art degree. And she'll be here in a minute."

I explained how Nancy had been trying to get in touch with me. "I would have left it to be honest, but then, what the hell. She's coming at twelve."

Danny checked the time and glanced behind into the kitchen area, presumably checking someone else was on duty.

"I'm due a break. Fancy a coffee?"

I shook my head but he poured himself one from the machine and we moved to a table.

"Did you pass your exams?" I said.

"Just scraped through. Have you seen Faye?"

I shook my head. "Not for ages."

"I still don't want to go back. On the course, I mean."

"So, what next?"

"I've applied for a few jobs, but there's nothing doing so far. Needless to say, my mum's not best pleased that I'm giving up uni."

"Snap," I said and told him about my temporary solution of the garage. "What kind of thing have you applied for? Can you stay here?"

He shook his head. "I have to move out of the flat. This is my last shift. I can't afford to live in Edinburgh. There was a job in St Andrews I fancied but I'm not really qualified. Faye was going to read my application for me, but then she skedaddled."

"Do you want me to have a look?" I said.

"Could you? Just to check I haven't said anything daft."

"Okay." I gave him my email address so that he could send me the form.

It was pretty good, just sitting there with Danny in the Sunday morning silence of the gallery. I was beginning to wish there was no other reason for me to be there, when the door opened and she walked in: Danny's girl from the gallery, my old friend Nancy.

When you're five nearly everybody is bigger than you, but now that we were both grown up, Nancy was still head and shoulders above me, or would have been if I'd been standing up. Her hair was a dull blonde, almost mousey, cut short, not in an extreme way like Jenni's, but neat and tidy. She wore jeans, and a white linen blouse under a cotton jumper. Around her shoulders was a fine woollen wrap. The jumper and the wrap were in neutral colours, but it was as if the more she tried to blend in, the more she stood out. It must have been her height. Or the wide grey eyes I recognised for an instant as belonging to someone I once knew: someone who had dared me to jump higher, run faster, dig deeper. *"Come on, Ailsa."* Except now the eyes were less focussed, less bright.

I was still the only customer and so she came straight over as Danny got up and retreated behind the counter.

"Ailsa?"

I nodded but she didn't sit down, like she didn't want to presume.

"Can I get you anything?" she asked.

285

I'd worked out that Nancy was seven years older than me. If the gap had been a big one back then, for some reason it was a chasm now. Maybe it was the veneer acquired from six years of boarding school, or just the fact of her being in a steady job, but she looked every bit the young woman and I felt like a kid. I had an impulse to ask for an iced lolly or a fizzy drink.

"I'm fine," I said.

"Do you mind if I get a coffee?"

I shook my head. She was way too polite. At the counter she turned to me again. "Sure?"

I realised I was being ridiculous. "Okay, I'll have a cappuccino. Thanks."

She brought the two cups over with an air of concentration, making sure the foam didn't slop over the sides. Danny was hovering behind the counter, offering moral support, but I decided I'd rather be on my own. A hard look from me and he took the hint, clearing off into the back.

"Thanks for coming," Nancy said before she had touched her coffee. "I realise you probably didn't want to."

I thought I might as well dive in, get it out of the way. "Is this about Shane?"

"Shane Reilly?" She shook her head then gave me a sharp look. "Did you want to see him?"

I shook my head. She looked relieved, as if she wanted to think better of me than Shane's latest lay.

We drank our coffee and I noticed she kept the wrap on, even though it was warm in the café. She wore demure pearl earrings. The sun, slanting in through the high windows, made translucent pink haloes of her earlobes.

"It's about… Tom. Tom Robertson."

Then I remembered how it all began, the rock pools and the pier and the digging with our spades, mine blue and plastic, hers red and business-like. But if Faye had been right and Nancy had come looking for closure of some kind, it still made me feel uncomfortable. I could deal with the beach, I could deal with the here and now. I preferred to skip the bit in between.

"Look," I said, "it was a long time ago. I'm sure it wasn't your fault. Not really."

She smiled back at me. "No," she said, "it wasn't, though it took me a long time to realise that. I was just a schoolgirl with a crush. Other people behaved badly, more badly than I did."

I wondered if she really believed it, or if this was the mantra of some counsellor or cognitive therapist. The more I looked at her, I agreed with Jenni Carstairs that, however well turned out Nancy might be, her composure masked something else: some damage, lurking under the surface, biding its time, like shrapnel left in a wound that gives the occasional twinge of pain. And was I part of it? A last sliver of metal needing to be dug out before the whole thing starts to fester?

"I saw the picture," I said, hoping to lighten things up. "It was really nice…"

Her face darkened and I knew I had made a mistake. She didn't like the in between bit any more than I did. I watched as she took her unused teaspoon and laid it on a folded paper napkin, pushing both of them an inch further left so that there was a clear space between them and the white cup and saucer.

"Well, it was a long time ago, like you said."

I wasn't going to make any more gambits so I just drank my coffee and let her take her time.

"Jenni told me you'd been to see her, and I'm pleased that she told you what happened. But she was really shocked to hear that Tom had died."

She was expecting a response, but I didn't have one to make, so she picked up the teaspoon again and stirred the coffee. Around us, the café was acquiring more customers and with them, the comforting murmur of inconsequential conversation. "Just a scone." "Nothing for me." "Nice day."

Nancy went on. "Jenni knew that Tom had her address. She was angry that no one had contacted her when he died. She would liked to have gone to the funeral."

It was good to know that Dad hadn't been alone, but I didn't see how I could have helped. And I wasn't exactly grieving myself. I was getting tired of Nancy's story. I couldn't see where it was going.

"What about you? Were you upset?"

"Not really, I'm afraid. Shocked, yes, but not upset."

Listening to Nancy speak, it was hard to imagine her showing emotion of any kind, as if it had been drained out of her a long time ago.

She sighed. "Jenni decided to contact Tom's girlfriend. Just to know what had happened. Of course it was too late for the funeral and she might have moved, but I think she needed to hear it for herself. She rang Tom's old number, hoping to speak to this Ruth. Or to find out where she might have gone."

Whatever had happened to the mysterious Ruth, I really didn't see what it had to do with me. But I could see there was no point in stopping Nancy. She had

288

started, and no matter how many times she picked up and refolded that napkin, she was going to finish. Or was she? Suddenly she seemed to have a problem carrying on.

"The thing is…" She was making an effort now to preserve this calmness, as if the only alternative would be something unthinkable. "When Jenni found out, she wasn't sure if she should tell you. She couldn't work out what had happened. How the mistake had come about."

"What mistake?"

"Ailsa, how did you know that your dad had died?"

"Mum told me."

"Is that all?"

"No. I saw a letter. From a lawyer, saying the money wouldn't come any more. That there was 'no further provision' for us."

"Did it mention your dad by name?"

"It must have."

"I don't think it did."

"I don't understand…"

"When Jenni rang Ruth, Tom answered the phone. He still lives with Ruth. He's fine. He hasn't even been ill."

CHAPTER THIRTY-TWO

As I rose, my chair screeched backwards on the floorboards and fell over with a clatter that bounced around the panelled walls.

"Don't be stupid," I said. "He died."

I must have been shouting because two old ladies at the next table turned round, then looked in alarm towards the serving counter, where Danny had been conjured out of hiding by the commotion. One of them raised her hand, summoning him to deal with the madwoman in their midst.

He came over and asked us what was up.

"She's mad." I indicated Nancy. "Get her out of here."

But Nancy had her hand on my arm and Danny was right beside her. I realised that if anyone was going to be booted out it wouldn't be Miss Tall and Serene, it would be me, Ailsa Robertson, shouting the odds as usual. Well, I could shout some more.

"Leave me alone!"

I shook them off me and ran outside. Behind me, Danny called my name. Then Nancy's voice: "Leave her." It was the best thing she had said so far.

I walked around the cemetery as fast as I could, looking for a modest grave, an old grave, one that nobody visited, so that it wouldn't matter if I threw up over or behind it. As the sensation subsided, I sat down on the one that was nearest, a clean marble stone, square and flat as a table top. I sat down on it, my head in my hands, failing to make sense of anything. Only one thought emerged. Dad's death had released me from his shadow, however undeserved that shadow had been. Now he had come back, and with him the onset of darkness.

Could Jenni have somehow got the wrong end of the stick? No, she had spoken to Tom himself. As for the letter Mum had shown me, Nancy was right, his name hadn't been on it. It hadn't needed to be. Mum and I knew who was sending the money. The money. Was that it? Had he faked his death *just to get out of paying?*

And how would Mum feel about this news? When I had told her Jenni's version of events, I'd seen little sign that she regretted kicking him out, or of having lived without him for so long. She thought, like me, that we were better off without him.

Cautious footsteps on the gravel path turned out to be Danny's, but he stood a way off. I looked up. The world wasn't entirely steady.

"It's okay if you want to be on your own," he said. "We just want to know you're okay."

"We" meaning him and Nancy.

"I'm okay." I meant that he could come closer without sparks flying off me. "Is she still here?"

He came towards me. "No. But she said you could get in touch with her, or Jenni, if you want to."

291

I shook my head. Danny sat down beside me, gingerly, like he was creeping up on a suicide attempt. Too close and I'd be over the edge.

"She says you're not to worry, that he won't get in touch with you unless you want him to."

I hadn't even thought of it – Dad riding up out of nowhere. Why would he, after all this time?

He was holding a slip of paper. "She left you this."

I knew what would be on it. I shook my head again.

"You might want it," Danny said. "One day."

The idea of having Dad's phone number in my pocket or even hidden at the back of a drawer was weird. I didn't want it. I might not be able to resist the temptation to hunt him down. Then everything I had laid aside, everything I had got over, would start again.

"I'm going home," I said. I stood up feeling stiff, like an old person. Danny still had the paper in his hand. I felt sorry for him, trying to do what was right when actually there was no right thing.

"You keep it for me," I said. "In case I ever need it."

"Okay." He tucked the number in the pocket of his jeans.

"Now go back to work. I'll be fine."

He was still dithering.

"Look," I said. "You have my email, remember?"

"Yeah, I forgot."

I couldn't blame him. Our previous conversation seemed like hours ago. "Give me your mobile too. Then I can always ring you."

We did the necessary fiddling with phones.

"See you then," said Danny.

"See you."

292

I watched as he walked away between the mossy urns and marble angels.

On the station platform I had more time to think about what Nancy had told me. The idea of talking to someone returned from the grave had its funny side, if you liked black humour. What exactly would Jenni have said to Dad? *"Tom, is that you? I'm sorry, it's just that I heard..."*

She might not even have told him about the premature reports of his departure. But they had talked about me, enough for him to invite me to get in touch. *"I met your daughter, she doesn't know where you are. In fact she's been told..."*

Why had I been told?

I thought about the money, but Dad was up for meeting me. Would he do that if he had meant to play possum? Would he risk seeing me if Mum was to be kept in the dark?

As for the letter, if he hadn't been behind it, who had? You were always reading about banks who persisted in sending letters to dead folk. Maybe it could happen the other way round; they decided somebody had died when they were alive and well and living somewhere near Glasgow. Or did somebody actually want him off the planet for good?

Mum must still have the letter somewhere, filed away in her newly organised office area. I could contact the sender, find out what had happened. Then what? Was there any point in knowing? Dad was alive. Why someone had thought he was dead didn't really matter.

The immediate problem was Mum. Should she know that the letter was a fake, a hoax, or some stupid admin cock-up? Would she want that slip of paper with the phone number on? I didn't think so somehow. Like me, she had moved on. But all through my life, Mum had kept things from me. And if she already knew that Dad was still around, she had done all she could to stop me finding out.

By the time I got home, I had decided that I would keep my newfound knowledge to myself. If Mum showed any signs of softening towards Dad, or wanting to finish whatever business was between them, I could tell her then that he hadn't left this life after all.

It was easy to behave as if nothing had happened. I carried on with my shifts at the garage. Mum's two jobs gave her plenty to do and she was learning to drive. "Can we afford a car?" I asked her. "Probably not," she said, "but you never know." Maybe the charity would give her one. I admired her foresight, and I suppose I was jealous that she was learning before me. And although nothing else changed, I was getting used to the idea of having a dad, one who was like other dads, one that I might meet one day. Just not yet.

When I wasn't working, I looked for jobs and courses I might do. I thought about going back to my degree. Maybe I could move in with Faye and start all over again, but the thought of repeating my first year didn't feel right. And I didn't miss doing the reading and the essays. I wondered why I had chosen English in the first place.

But I had to find something. I was bored out of my skull. Danny had emailed me his job application. It was for the University Library, something to do with conserving photographs. It made an interesting read, not the "Supporting Statement", which was the usual kind of waffle, but the things about Danny I had never known, like his full name – Daniel Stuart Alan McLure – and his Higher results, and the fact that he was, like Faye had said, a year younger than me, two years younger than her. I remembered how she had fed him her fish. Maybe it was a wee brother she had wanted, not a boyfriend.

A few days later, when Danny emailed to say he had an interview, I rang back and invited myself along. I told him I fancied some sea air. It was months since I'd been to the coast.

Childhood journeys to St Andrews had ended on the long West Beach, or rather the sand dunes behind, a safe haven from the wind that strafes the shoreline. Some days we might have gone as far as the castle with its grisly dungeon, or looked for a place to get an ice-cream, but the rest of the town had always been a mystery, keeping itself to itself behind grey walls and university notices.

On the day of Danny's interview the weather was uncharacteristically warm, the air humid with low cloud that refused to part. Walking from the bus station to the seafront I could see the first half mile or so of the beach through a stubborn morning mist. The waves that usually raced up to crash in foamy heaps were listless, as if they couldn't be arsed to go any farther up the beach than they really had to.

The interview was at eleven. We'd arranged to meet on the corner by the Old Course at one, just to be on the safe side. Danny rolled up soon after me and we leaned on the fence, watching grim-faced Japanese tourists thump balls down the fairway.

Under his usual deodorant, Danny gave off a warm sweaty smell. I asked him how it had gone.

"Okay, but I don't have experience of conservation work. I could do a course on it, but if somebody else has already worked in the field, they're sure to get it."

"I checked out the website. I thought it was all online now?"

"Yeah, but they have to preserve the originals. People are allowed to see them, if there's a special need," he said. "It would be a great place to work."

I could see how much he wanted the job and how he didn't expect to get it. His shoulders were slumped. I put my arm around him. "Cheer up. You never know."

He accepted my hug but didn't return it, instead running his hand over my arm, as if he were unsure of something.

I stepped away. "Come on," I said. "It took me forever to get here. We might as well see the sights."

We walked away from the beach and turned along The Scores towards the castle, the sea still visible on our left between stone buildings with high hedges. Danny turned up a lane on our right and into the Old Quad, where a group of tourists was being lectured by a tour-guide. We walked on so that he could show me the library where he'd been interviewed, then back towards the sea.

"Have you seen Faye lately?" he said.

I had been about to ask him the same thing. "Not since she left Edinburgh. She's in Perthshire, isn't she?"

"Yeah. I thought you might have seen her, in between times."

Perhaps Faye was letting Danny go. Maybe she had seen what I had seen, that she was looking for the wrong thing.

By now we had reached the castle and through the haze could just make out the far end of St Andrews Bay.

"If you don't get the job," I asked him, "what will you do?"

"I don't know. Mum says I should go back to Napier. What do you think?"

I shook my head. "I'm the last person to ask."

We walked on until we were looking down on the old pier and the harbour with a sandy bay beyond it. The tide was half out and a group of three people were dragging a dinghy on a trailer across the wet sand. We sat down on a grass verge and contemplated our indistinct futures.

"I don't think I've been here before," I said.

"It's the East Sands," Danny said. "Dad used to bring us here because it's more sheltered than the main beach. He knew it from when he was at uni."

"He came here?"

"Yeh. Look." He pointed to a cluster of brick-built houses between the beach and the main road. "Those are student houses. He lived in one of them."

I was thinking how my dad had been to uni somewhere and I didn't even know which one.

Next to the student houses there was a complex of modern buildings. "That's the Gatty," Danny said. "I think it's for marine biology."

I was picturing tanks and microscopes and things that lived in the North Sea, the figures and photographs

297

I'd seen in *Scotland's Coastal Waters*. I should have borrowed that book. It had looked interesting.

"Will we go down?" I said. "Walk on the beach?"

Danny looked at his watch. "Mum's picking me up. I can't stay too long."

Neither of us moved. His hand was next to mine on the damp grass. Faye had gone, maybe for good. If Danny and I were looking for a chance to move things on, this must be it. His hair hung as it always did across his face. He was looking up at the cathedral ruins, not at me.

"Are you okay?" I said, for want of a better question.

He looked at me as if I were a problem he hadn't quite solved, or a photograph that hadn't developed as it should have.

"Yeah," he said. "I'm cool. Just thinking about those guys, the ones who took the first photographs. There are some of the cathedral."

I got up and held out my hand, but only to pull him off his backside. As we turned back past the lacy ruins of the cathedral, the haze was condensing into a heavy moisture and we walked faster. Danny, on his long legs, started to accelerate away then he turned and waited for me to catch up. If he had held out a hand I would have taken it, but both of them stayed in his pockets. The rain was turning into something serious.

"Why don't you come back with us?" Danny said. "Mum won't mind and the Dunfermline bus goes past our road."

There would be more buses going through Windygates than from St Andrews. I could save a good hour by going Danny's way. It was a good offer. And it looked like there was no need to read anything into it, not any more.

On the way back, Danny sat in the front with his mum and gave non-committal answers to the questions she rained down on him about the job. Eventually she gave up and looked at me in the rear-view mirror.

"What about you, dear? How's your course going?"

She assumed I was a fellow student. I felt guilty that I couldn't provide more of the role model she might want for Danny and stammered over a reply. "I'm er... having a rethink at the moment."

The windscreen was speckled with rain. Mrs McLure switched on the wipers and succeeded in producing a continuous smear that obscured her view completely. She sighed and hit the wash button hard until the windscreen cleared.

"I don't know. You young people. You never seem to know what you want."

We skirted Kirkcaldy town centre and were soon in Windygates. I asked to be dropped at the bus stop, but Danny's mum had other ideas.

"I bet you haven't eaten. Come in and have a cup. I've done enough driving for today, but Dunfermline's no distance. Daniel can drive you home. Can't you, Daniel?"

Danny gave a grunt of assent. "Could do, I suppose."

She drew up at the house and I climbed out of the car behind Danny. As his mum opened the front door Danny turned to watch me.

I gave him a smirk. "Is this all right with you, Daniel?"

He aimed a kick at my ankle but I saw it coming and sidestepped.

Inside, the house was bright and comfortable with pot plants on all the windows and photographs on the walls, family pictures in which I could recognise Danny and a younger sister. In the sitting room there was a recent photo of his mum and dad, smartly dressed, maybe for an anniversary. The father had curly hair, receding a bit, and a freckly complexion like Danny's. He reminded me of somebody, but I wasn't sure who. He certainly looked to be in perfect health. His death must have been a shock. Danny's mum looked great on the photo. I could see how her hair had lost its shine since then and her mouth sagged at the corners.

Through the window the steady rain was slanting in over a good-sized garden with a pond and a greenhouse. Mrs McLure saw me looking.

"Stuart's territory, I'm afraid. I keep hoping Daniel will show an interest."

Danny had flopped down on a sofa and turned on the TV. I saw a flicker of annoyance cross Mrs McLure's face. She turned back to me. "Do you have a big garden, Faye?"

I was caught on the hop. This explained why she'd thought I was at uni. But Danny, despite appearances, had been listening after all. Before I could collect myself he picked up the remote, pointed it at the TV and said, "She's not Faye. She's Ailsa."

Mrs McLure, not surprisingly, did a bit of a double-take. "Oh, I'm sorry. I just thought…"

Danny clearly wasn't going to offer any further explanation and so I stepped in. "I've known Faye since we were wee. I met Danny when I stayed with her in Edinburgh for a couple of nights."

She seemed satisfied. "Well, pleased to meet you, dear." She was heading for the kitchen, but just as she got to the door, she turned back. "Did you say Ailsa?"

I nodded. "Uh-huh, Ailsa Robertson."

"Oh really?" She smiled. "Ailsa's still quite popular, I suppose. Though you don't hear it so much these days."

She stood there looking at me for just a bit longer than was necessary so that the smile started to glaze over. She was probably still wondering about my exact status in Danny's life, something I wasn't sure about either.

As she disappeared, Danny got up and started switching leads around behind the TV. "Sorry about Mum."

"No problem. It was an obvious mistake."

"Yeah."

His mother came back with homemade cake on matching china plates.

"You shouldn't have bothered," I said.

"You young people are always hungry," she said.

I accepted a slice of sponge cake. I hadn't expected to be keeping up a conversation single-handedly. I remembered Stuart McLure had worked in Dunfermline. With Danny loading up a video game, I asked if she knew the town.

"A wee bit," she said. "I go from time to time."

"This is lovely," I said. "My mum hardly ever bakes."

Mrs M seemed to take the hint and stopped quizzing both of us. "Now, don't forget," she said to Danny, who now had his feet up on a pouffe, "that you're taking Ailsa home." She accented the "Ailsa" to remind him he had been the cause of her faux pas.

"Yeah, fine," Danny said through his own mouthful of cake.

CHAPTER THIRTY-THREE

It was a relief to get out of the mother–son conflict area. I could see that in his own front room Danny had undergone a bit of a personality change.

"Sorry about that," Danny said as we drove off.

"Don't apologise. She was nice." Not even Vi could produce homemade cake at the drop of a hat. "But you realise she thinks we're an item."

"Why's that? I told her you weren't Faye."

"I don't think that made a difference."

"How come?"

Something in the way she had looked at me over the teacups. "Female intuition," I said.

Danny grinned. "Does it matter?"

"It might," I pointed out, "if you decide to bring Faye home."

"Too right. I hadn't thought of that."

So it didn't sound like they had broken up. And if Danny had been going to make a pass, now he was hedging his bets. We headed out of the estate and onto the main road.

"I didn't know you could drive," I said.

"I learned in the summer. Mum said there should be more than one driver in the house."

"Is your mum okay then, money-wise? Faye said there was some problem."

"Oh that. It wasn't the money that was a problem, just some account she hadn't known about. Mind you, she keeps telling me to get a job."

I suspected his mum was less interested in Danny's income than in regaining the use of her sofa.

"Does she work?"

"Something part-time. I don't think it pays much."

We came to a junction and Danny hesitated. "Which road is it?"

"Hang on." I opened the glove compartment to look for a map and some stuff fell out, loose pages of glossy paper that looked like junk mail.

"It's okay," Danny said, "There's a sign here. I can see it now."

I stuffed the sheets back in. "Did you say your dad worked here?"

"Before I was born. We came a few times in the summer, to that big park."

Not the public park, but the huge estate bequeathed by Carnegie which was our only tourist attraction. If Faye and I could have bumped into Danny at the Links Market, he might just as easily have run into us in the playground or the petting zoo.

I directed him to the end of our road and explained he could carry on along the main road and turn back the way we had come.

"Thanks for the lift."

"No problem." He had left the engine idling but didn't actually say goodbye. "I've still got it, you know."

"What?"

He reached for his wallet and took out the slip of white paper he'd shown me that Sunday with Nancy, the one with a phone number for Dad.

"Changed your mind yet?"

Danny had just lost his dad. Why was I so unwilling to find mine? I took the paper from him and put it in my purse, if only to keep him happy.

"You know it makes sense," he said, and let in the clutch.

I got out of the car and something caught my eye as it fluttered onto the road. I picked it up as it settled into the gutter. It was one of Mum's leaflets, *Lupus Aware* in red and blue. I glanced along the road to the house, as if Mum might have just passed along, dropping leaflets as she went, to create some mad paper trail for lupus victims. But the street was empty and I was still on the kerb holding the sheet of paper with its familiar glossy surface. Familiar because I had already held some in my hands as they had slid from the glove compartment onto my lap. This one had stuck there until I got out of the car, the car that belonged to Danny's mum, who had a wee job that didn't really pay.

I turned the leaflet over. On the back there was a white box: *For information please ring.* Mum's details were filled in with one of those rubber stamps.

Lorraine Robertson, Dunfermline, 01383 76345
lupusaware_fife@yahoo,co.uk

Underneath there was an extra name, added by hand.

Agnes Crichton, Windygates Kirkcaldy 01592 6823

The surname might be wrong, but Windygates was a small place. It came to me that the wee blue car that had just disappeared round the corner was the same one I had watched from the spare room window the day I'd come home from Edinburgh.

The house was empty. Despite Mum's change in circumstances, Thursday was still Asda with Liz.

My head was a kaleidoscope of confusion. Agnes Crichton must be Agnes McLure. Crichton might be her maiden name, but why would she use it? Was there some minor tax dodge going on? I thought about texting Danny to tell him about our family connection, but boys, I suspected, didn't have much curiosity about their mothers' social or working lives. He would already be back in front of the telly or the X-box. Nor could I see that it mattered to Mum if her helper was someone I knew, or to Agnes that I was her boss's daughter.

For distraction I Googled "Gatty Marine Laboratory", except it too had changed its name. The Scottish Oceans Institute sounded a lot more grand, but I liked the old one. It sounded more scientific, more hands-on.

Names. I had let Shane call me Isla. Did my dad still call himself Tom Robertson? He had plenty of reason to start again as somebody new. But as for Agnes Crichton, why would she want to be somebody else?

I needed to talk to somebody. Not Mum, not Danny. That left Faye.

I rang her. "Can we talk?"

She said yes, but I could tell she was shouting above some background din.

306

"How are the highlanders this year?" I asked. "Fit as ever?"

"What? Sorry, I'll ring you back."

I pictured her with a finger in one ear.

Ten minutes later she rang me. "Sorry. Disco night for the kids. Bedlam in there. Are you okay?"

"Yeh, I think so. Just something weird happened. I met Danny's mum today. It turns out she's working for my mum. They're very cosy actually, she comes round all the time."

"From Kirkcaldy?"

"Yeh, well, Windygates. To help with the lupus thing."

I remembered Stuart had died of a heart attack. It did seem odd that Agnes wasn't working for coronary care, providing those machines with the paddles, so that someone might have been able to shock Stuart McLure back to life.

"Oh well, up to her I suppose," Faye said.

"Yeh, right."

But I was thinking that Agnes, unlike me, must have realised straight away that I was Lorraine's daughter. How many Ailsa Robertsons could there be in Dunfermline? But she hadn't let on.

I stuck to the facts. "But she uses another name here. Agnes Crichton."

"Okay, that is weird."

"I just wondered if Danny had ever said anything about her."

"Not much. Usual stuff. Sounded like a normal mum."

"She is, normal I mean. Just felt weird when I realised."

"You could ask Danny?"

It was true. Why was I asking Faye? We had a bit to catch up on. Maybe that was really why I had called her. I told her about Ian and Laura and she laughed.

"There's something else," I said. "My dad." A Pause. Faye had heard enough about my dad, but this was different. "He didn't die."

"Oh My God. Are you kidding me?"

I went over the story. How I could get in touch… if I wanted to.

"Wow. So will you?"

I'd been fingering the slip of paper all through the phone call, thin with a perforated edge, torn from some notebook or dairy of Nancy's. I'd heard so many versions of her story. Surely it was only fair to hear what Dad had to say.

"Yes. I think I will."

There was a mobile number, an email address and a postal address. I searched for the postcode online. Dad didn't even live in Helensburgh, but in some village outside.

I typed an email, keeping it as short as I could. Even then it was more of myself than I wanted to give.

Hello. Maybe we should meet.

Before I had time to change my mind, I'd hit send. It should have been harder. The next bit certainly would be.

Dad replied the next day, Friday, suggesting he could come to Glasgow, that he would be happy to. Not delighted, but happy. That was fair enough. I wasn't exactly ecstatic myself, but Danny was right. I was the one needing closure now. I agreed to meet him the following day.

308

It wasn't much more than an hour by train to Glasgow Queen Street, but it felt like forever. A forever of wondering how I would know him, how he would recognise me, a forever of thinking I should never have got on the train in the first place.

By the time I got there, my legs had gone to jelly. It was all I could do to lower myself onto the platform and wait for the crowd to push past, jostling me aside on their way to shops, museums, football matches. When they had gone I was alone, except for a schoolboy in a blazer checking the departure board, and a guitar-toting busker eating a poke of chips. No sign of a father figure. I would give him twenty minutes and if he didn't show, I'd get the next train home. No harm done.

I settled myself on the metal bench provided for those who'd arrived too early or too late. It was deadly cold under my legs and I started to shiver. I pulled up the hood of my fleece and checked my watch, thinking that twenty minutes was too long to wait, that the station bench was no substitute for a comfy seat, that a poke of chips, or just the offer of a chip, wouldn't go amiss. Fat chance. The busker threw the wrapper in a nearby bin and picked up his guitar. I took bets with myself on what tune he'd attempt, putting even money on *Your Song* or *Whisky in the Jar*. I tried hard not to see the figure that had emerged from the underpass and was standing at the top of the steps, scanning the platform. As he looked my way I wished I had a spell to make me disappear. In the end I shut my eyes. When I opened them two denim-clad legs had stopped in front of me.

"Ailsa?"

309

It was as well he stayed where he was, moving no closer, or I might have done a runner. It felt like I was ten again, or maybe only five. I wanted to swing my legs under the seat but they were too long for that and I ended up crossing and uncrossing them in a daft kind of fidget. When I did look up – I couldn't put it off forever – he nodded a greeting.

"Can I sit down?" He wasn't taking any chances. I wondered if there were books you could read on handling reunions with long lost children.

I nodded. And so now there were two of us on the hard station bench, not knowing what to say, except I was starting to cry.

"Sorry," I mumbled, delving for a tissue.

He handed me a cotton hankie. "Me too," he said.

He said we should go for a coffee. As we walked into the city centre I tried to get used to it, being next to Dad, trying to drag myself back through the years, from the day we'd sat by a steamy window, counting boats, to this one.

He asked me safe questions about the trains and what I was doing at uni. Questions that required one word answers. They were all I was up for. By the time we'd got to the department store café on Sauchiehall Street, I was just about composed. He found us a table in a quiet corner and sat down opposite me.

"I suppose you want to know where I've been?" he said.

It was easier to listen than to talk, and so I sat and drank my coffee as he told me about going to Glasgow and doing supply work until he got a proper job in Helensburgh, and how he and Ruth, another teacher, lived in this village on the Clyde. "A bit out of the way," he called it.

I was only half listening, but I was watching him, getting the feel of him. His hair was cut short, still curly but brown and grey in almost equal amounts. His face was paler than I remembered and less angular. The hands that turned his cup on his saucer from time to time had stubby fingers. Were they an artist's hands? It didn't seem important. He was a middle-aged guy. Someone's dad. My dad. As he finished his story this realisation made me frown.

"Your turn then," he said. "I expect you have things to ask me."

Not half. Like why it had taken him this long to take me for a cup of fucking coffee. I rubbed my hands over my face and shook my head for no reason except that the words wouldn't come.

"Ailsa," he said, "you know your mum would have nothing to do with me. She made it perfectly clear. No contact, no support. Things being as they were, I felt I had to go along with her. I sent her my contact details for a few years and never heard a thing. So I gave up. I lived my life without you. But we're here now. Things can change. If you want them to."

At last he smiled, a familiar smile. It gave my heart a sudden squeeze, enough to make me think the nice china cup in my hand might shatter and cause yet another commotion in a polite tearoom. My brain had slowed to a crawl. It had too much information to process, information blurred by hurt and anger and relief. Eventually something sank in.

"You said there was no support. But you did send us money."

He shook his head. "No. Never."

"But the money came. Until last year. That's how we knew…"

"I'm sorry. Lorraine wouldn't have it. She kicked me out. She would have nothing from me." There was a sudden edge to his voice. "So that's what she's had."

Whatever overtures he was making were reserved for me. Mum was another matter.

"Does she know that you're here?" he asked.

I shook my head. "She still thinks…"

He frowned and shook his head, like it was all beyond him. I supposed it was a bit creepy being told that you were dead. I hung on to the real facts and to what I could glean from them. Someone had sent us money. Mum had depended on it. I leaned towards him over the table and made myself say the words.

"If you didn't send us the money, who did?"

He looked at me without blinking. His eyes were still brown, dark brown, not hazel like mine. "I don't know."

Dad picked up the menu in its black plastic wallet and studied it. "Do you fancy a cake? Toasted sandwich?"

I shook my head. I was working out the next step of the argument. The money had been real. It had come from someone else. And so the letter from Edinburgh needn't have been a fake, or a cock-up. My dad hadn't died, but somebody else had.

Dad was still hell bent on feeding me up. "I bet you didn't have breakfast."

Typical grown up, typical bloody teacher.

"Okay," I said, "I'll have a sandwich." I was chewing my lip to the kind of pulp no chapstick could

312

rescue. "But if you know more about this, you'd better bloody well tell me."

He put the menu down and gave a smile. "That's better," he said. "That's the Ailsa I remember."

That was it. I burst into tears.

Dad said something stronger was called for and so we cancelled the food order and left. Practically next door there was a big pub decked out in Irish green and Guinness signs. From the street I could hear a buzz of voices and a TV somewhere. I stopped expectantly but Dad frowned.

"I don't think so," he said. "Let's go somewhere quieter." He turned back in the direction of the station.

Neither of us spoke and it was good just to walk, listening to the rhythm of his steps, not thinking of what had been said or what there might be still to come. After five or six minutes we reached a small pub in a side street with two doors, one saying "Lounge" and the other "Saloon".

He pushed open the door of the lounge bar. "I used to come here a lot," he said.

I'd forgotten he knew Glasgow and wasn't just a visitor here like me. It was a whisky drinkers' pub, every inch of the wall behind the bar taken up by an array of single malts. Dad ordered a pint of Eighty Shilling. When I asked for a Snakebite he didn't bat an eyelid. We sat at a small wooden table, on chairs that wobbled slightly on the uneven floor. To the right of where we were sitting the bar ran through into another room. I couldn't see into it, but from the click of balls and the muffled laughter there was a pool table in there.

When the barman went through to attend to his regulars, Dad and I were on our own.

"Why don't you tell me about yourself?" he said. "What have you really been up to?"

I could hardly start from the beginning, so I started with Ian, and what had happened since he – Dad, that is – had died.

"You've been through the mill," he said.

I said I'd been hoping he might help me come out the other end.

Dad put down his glass and looked into the last inch of beer. "Well," he said, "I don't know about that."

"You mean there's more to come?"

"It's up to you. You know what they say, be careful what you wish for, especially if it's the truth."

"Yeah, tell me about it."

There was a snack menu on the table. Dad said I shouldn't drink on an empty stomach and went to call the barman. When the sandwiches came I discovered I was famished. As we ate, the noise from the other room increased, each player being egged on by his mates.

I pushed my plate away. "Go on then. Spit it out."

"You're sure?"

I could have said no, but what good would that have done?

He began. "When I was kicked out of school and your mum heard why, she wouldn't stand for any explanation. I said it was a fit up, that I hadn't touched Nancy Chalmers. But she wasn't having it. She'd been unhappy ever since we'd been to Largo, and said she'd suspected that 'Something was going on'. To be honest, she must have been paranoid to think anything of the sort, but now she had facts – or Chalmers' version of them – to back up her suspicions."

He could see my doubts over the paranoia charge.

"I'm not making excuses – but if she hadn't been so bloody hard to live with, I wouldn't have got involved with Irene."

I gave him another look.

"All right. I suppose I am making excuses. But she wouldn't even see a doctor, not after one of them looked at her the wrong way."

"She was ill," I told him. "She got a lot worse after you left. I had to look after her, stay at home, pick her up off the floor."

"Okay," he sighed. "*Mea culpa* then, I suppose."

"They found out she has lupus," I told him. "It does all sorts of things. It made her depressed, maybe paranoid too. She's a lot better now."

"Right. That's good, I suppose."

I wanted him to get back to his story. "So she chucked you out?"

He nodded. "Told me she wanted nothing more to do with me, ever."

"So this was before the court case?"

"Yes. I did stay in the house until it was done, but even when charges were dropped she was just the same. The implication from Chalmers was that if I got lost, I'd hear no more about it. She thought, like everybody else, it was a put up job to save the girl from having to give evidence."

"So you *got lost*." It still sounded like an easier thing to do than stay around.

He shifted beside me on his seat. "Not without a fight. I tried to get Lorraine to believe me. I tried to get

Irene to do something. When none of that worked, I said I would go, but that I had a right to see you, and you had a right to know where I was."

For a moment I wished we were in a bigger place with more to distract us. The emptiness of the bar was being filled with all those characters – Mum, Eddie Chalmers, Irene – crowding in and having a laugh on me.

Dad broke the silence. "Then Lorraine said I had no rights at all."

It didn't come as a surprise. She might well have said that, thinking Dad didn't deserve to see me if he'd been messing with a girl. But there was something in the way he said it, as if I was supposed to draw a different conclusion.

Next door, the pool game ended with a raucous cheer followed by the thunderous roll of new balls on the table. No flash of lightning, except the one that split the sky in my head, cleaving the darkness, scorching a path that was far too bright. I blinked and knew what was coming. And so I said it for him.

"She said you had no rights because you weren't my real dad."

If I was hoping he'd deny it, I was out of luck.

CHAPTER THIRTY-FOUR

He leaned across and put his hand on my arm.

"Ailsa, I never really believed her. She was so angry I thought she was just saying it to keep me away."

I looked back at him. "But you believe it now?"

The lightning had gone but the patch of scorched earth couldn't be ignored. The money had come from someone else. Someone who was, or believed he was, my father.

He raised his eyebrows. Lorraine's version was suddenly holding water. "Well, I didn't know about the money. I wondered how she would manage. I even tried to find out through Jenni. She'd always stuck by me, and she said that you seemed okay. Not affluent, but okay. I assumed Lorraine had a job, that your gran helped out, or she got by on benefits. Something like that." He gave up, realising how lame this sounded.

"But you got married not long before I was born. She was already pregnant. I must be yours." I was remembering the school magazine, the shock of the dates, but as soon as I said it, I saw how it could be different. Mum might have been in a hurry to marry

Tom for the opposite reason – to cover up a pregnancy by somebody else.

Dad sighed. "At first I thought the same as you. We'd been sleeping together for over a year. But it's possible, I suppose, that she could have slept with some other man. She did have a sudden yen to be married."

I dragged my mind away from the uncomfortable area of parents and sex and tried to unravel the facts.

"And when you left she made him, the other one, cough up. I had a sugar daddy, but it wasn't you."

He turned his palms upwards, still unwilling to commit to the facts. "Could be, but I don't know for sure."

"So who was it?"

"Look. It was a long time ago. And until today I thought she'd made the whole thing up."

When Mum came up with her story, he must have thought it through then. "But you wondered. You went over it all in your head. You must have had an inkling?"

"Sorry, Ailsa. I've thought about this and I really can't tell you. It's your mum's secret. Not mine. If you want to know for sure, you'll have to ask her."

Even now he was holding out on me. He went to buy coffee and I took out my anger on the shard of a potato crisp still on the sandwich plate, grinding it to dust with the back of a knife.

"Sorry." He put the coffee down. "I've told you what I can. God knows what your mother will say."

I could see his mind was made up and so I asked him about Ruth and the place where they lived. He showed me a photo on his phone, a lighthouse and mountains in the distance. Clearly the back of beyond, it also looked like heaven.

"If you fancy a break, say the word."

Right now I had other things to think about. "Thanks," I said. "I have a job at home."

I was wondering how to tell Mum that Dad was alive, and that he wasn't really my dad. Then I remembered that Mum already knew. She was the one who'd deceived me, ten times over.

Whatever combination of adrenaline and alcohol had kept me going this far was fast running out.

"I think I'll go now," I said.

He walked me back to the station and I began to feel better. Dad was alive and real and surprisingly dad-like. As I left he patted me on the shoulder and said, "Keep in touch, Ailsa. I've missed you, you know."

It was only on the train that I fell apart again, remembering that this ordinary guy, who looked ready to give me some affection, wasn't my dad at all.

As the train rumbled through Cumbernauld, relieved of the baggage that had weighed me down I felt like a member of the *kindertransport*, hustled onto a train without papers, left off all the lists, unlikely to be taken in and cared for. Mum, of course, had the answers, but I had no illusion she was likely to come clean, not when she'd taken so much trouble to keep the identity of my real dad a secret – to the point, I reminded myself, of pretending that Tom was dead.

I hugged myself but failed to get warm. I needed to somehow work it out for myself. But by the time the train pulled in to the station, I was no farther forward.

The fresh air perked me up. The only clue I had was that Mum had been seeing Dad and someone else at around the same time. They were both young teachers working at the High. The obvious culprit would be somebody on the staff. How long was it since I had seen that photo in the library? Less than a year, but the only faces I could remember were those of Mum and Dad.

It was after six, the library would be shut. I should have asked Dad who else had been on the trip to France. But there was no need to go to the library. As I reached the corner of our road, I saw Agnes McLure's car parked outside our house, and lightning struck again.

I let myself in and Mum came to meet me in the hall. Her face was disfigured by a rash, exploding across it like the wings of a butterfly. She looked at me with something like suspicion.

"Agnes is here," was all she said.

She wanted me out of the way, but I had no idea of what had already been said. I needed to let Mum know I was on her case. The last thing I wanted was for the two of them to gang up against me.

"Oh," I said. "Would that be Agnes Crichton? Or Agnes McLure, by any chance?"

Mum startled. Under its livid colour, her expression was grim. "I don't know what you mean."

"Come on. I know who she is, so let me in."

Stuart McLure had taught geography at the High. Not for long, but long enough to have wound up with the history teacher and got her pregnant. But he wasn't really interested in Lorraine Ferguson nor she in him. She had a boyfriend already. And he might already have met a girl from Kirkcaldy called Agnes. No wonder the photo in Danny's lounge had looked familiar: I'd seen him before in the old school magazine.

Mum was still blocking my way. I pushed past her and went into the living room where Agnes was getting

320

up out of a chair. She looked uncomfortable. She hadn't bargained on my turning up.

"Hello, Ailsa," she said. "Your mum's not too well. I'm sorry, I think it might be my fault."

Mum came in behind me and lowered herself onto one of the green chairs.

"She needs water," I said, and Agnes, obedient, went through to the kitchen and ran the tap.

"When did she get here?" I asked Mum.

"Just now. Ten minutes ago."

From Mum's reaction I guessed this was long enough for Agnes to have revealed herself as Stuart's wife, although my brain was too scrambled to work out why she had done so now, after all this time.

Mum was hugging herself and shivering. The age-old reaction to rush around taking care of her had left me. This must be what they meant by compassion fatigue.

Agnes reappeared with a glass of water and Mum took a drink. I looked at Agnes to signify her presence wasn't required, but she stayed put.

"I'm sorry," she said again, her face harder than I remembered. "She had to be told. You had to be told."

"Told what exactly?" I needed to hear it from her.

Agnes composed herself. "That Stuart, my Stuart, is, was... your father."

I was lucky, I realised, to have had my question answered so soon and so easily. But if I was no longer homeless, I still felt displaced.

Agnes hadn't finished. "So you and Danny... I'm sorry. It can't happen."

Of course. If Stuart was my father, that made Danny my half brother. In the heat of the moment this had totally escaped me.

"And you think Danny and I are… having it off?" A gust of incongruous laughter threatened to burst out of me. No wonder she'd done a double-take when I announced myself in her front room! It hadn't been a big deal to Danny, or to me, that she thought we were an item. But she knew it would be a disaster. As the knowledge sank in I realised how easily it might have happened. Wasn't it what I had wanted, me and Danny? But for once in my life I had held back. I shook my head in amazement. Incest. Christ. One thing I'd managed to avoid.

Mum was levering herself to her feet, her knuckles white on the arms of the chair. She spat out the words, aiming them straight at Agnes.

"You had no right," she said. "No right to tell her about Stuart. It's my business. I would have handled it, in my own way."

Mum's deceit was out in the open – how she'd concealed the truth about my real dad, how she'd lied about Dad having died. No wonder she wanted to keep it all from me.

"It's okay," I said. "I'd already worked it out."

Mum shook with the effort of breathing. "How? How could you know?" Her voice rasped with the effort but I reminded myself this was just Mum, situation normal. She would get over it.

"I didn't go to Edinburgh today like I told you. I went to see Dad. Remember him? Or did he die last year too?"

322

Mum swayed, letting go of the chair as the colour drained from her face. Agnes and I made a grab for her but couldn't stop her crumpling to the floor.

"Don't worry," Agnes said, kneeling over her. "She'll be okay with rest and fluids."

"I know," I said. "I have been here before."

When we'd got Mum upstairs I rang Helen Archibald, who said she would come round after her surgery. Agnes and I sat together with mugs of coffee. Mum's fall had defused the atmosphere, but we were still unsure of whether we were allies or on opposing sides.

"I'm sorry," she said. "I knew it would rattle her. But I couldn't leave things as they were."

"It would have come out," I said. "Sooner or later." I was still numb. But I wasn't going to let her off the hook so easily. She had only known about me and Danny for a week or two. She'd been working with Mum for months.

"So why did you come here? It wasn't coincidence, was it? You did know who she was?"

"Oh yes. I knew all right."

Agnes set down her mug. She didn't look at me directly. I sensed a story was coming, one that out of loyalty to Stuart or from a desire to protect her own children, she had never shared.

"When I discovered that Stuart had been paying out money, it shook me up. Even without knowing where it had gone, I felt betrayed. We'd had a good marriage. I thought we'd shared everything, and all the time he'd been keeping a separate account, taking money away from me. I tried to ignore it, to pretend it wasn't true. But it gnawed away at me," she glanced at me, acknowledging we'd each had secrets to bear, "as these things do. I went back to the lawyers. Eventually they told me where the money had gone. And why."

"It must have been a shock. You must have been really angry."

"With Stuart? Yes, at first I was. But then this fling, or whatever you might call it, was before we were married. It's not that he'd been unfaithful... well, not in the way he might have been. The money rankled right enough. But I reminded myself we hadn't been badly off. And what you don't have you don't miss. I felt more sad than angry. Sad that the secret had been there, that he'd never been able to tell me about it. As for the bairn, I couldn't get my head round it, that Stuart had a wee girl, one I would likely never see."

The way she used *bairn* touched me. It reminded me of my gran. But I was part of another family now.

"So you came looking for us?"

"No. Not at first. I would have let things lie, I think. But I saw Lorraine's name on a leaflet at our health centre, and I suppose if I had any anger left it was for her. She'd kept Stuart on a string. She might have been after his money all along. Maybe I thought I'd confront her, or maybe I was just curious. I rang up and offered to help. I didn't want her knowing my real reason for being there, and so I used my maiden name.

"As soon as I saw her, I could see she had had a tough time. She spoke about you a lot. With all her problems she'd got you to university. I thought Stuart would have wanted that. And maybe his money had made up for the attention he'd never given you. By the time I left, there didn't seem much point in holding a grudge.

324

"Even so, I didn't mean to get involved. I just said I'd give her a hand with her leaflets for a couple of weeks, to justify getting in touch, and it went on from there. She seemed keen to be friends, and I suppose I was hoping that I'd bump into you eventually, to see how you'd turned out."

"It just didn't happen in the way you had expected."

"You certainly gave me a turn, seeing you there in our house. You have a look of him, you know."

Her smile was teary and tentative. How could I not return it? The thought ran through my head that if Mum were to die, Agnes might be my stepmother. I brushed it aside. We had enough to deal with here and now.

Agnes sighed and looked at her hands. "Of course, from what Daniel has told me about you and your real dad, there was more to it than I realised."

Yes. A lot more. And just to confuse me even more, she'd called Tom my "real" dad.

She got up. "I should go now. You'll have a lot to think about. You know where I am. And so does Lorraine."

She let herself out and I stayed where I was, slumped in one green chair with my feet propped up on the other, trying to make sense of it all. There was no arguing with the facts. I was impressed with Agnes and her forgiving nature. But she had her years with Stuart to fall back on. She had nothing to regret. I knew I couldn't be the same.

I made tea and took it upstairs. Mum was propped on the pillows. She still looked ghastly but I could see she was *compos mentis*.

325

She gave me the weak smile of an invalid. "What a to-do."

I handed her the tea.

"Hope there's no arsenic in it," she said.

"No," I said. "But I'm not going until you've drunk it. And you've told me why."

She drank and lay back, avoiding my eyes. "There was no reason," she said. "It just happened. When I threw Tom out I realised I had lost a financial lifeline. I went to Stuart, told him what Tom had done, asked him for money. Stuart agreed, but only on condition it was a secret. You weren't to know. No one was to know."

"You mean, you blackmailed him."

Mum looked shocked. "I just asked for help."

"And what if he'd said no?"

She looked puzzled. "I don't know. He did ask if I knew that the baby was his. I said I could get tests."

"And did you?"

She shook her head. "It never came to that." Her hands were grasping the bedclothes. She was cowed, like a kid trying to avoid a telling off. *It wasn't me.* Except in this case, it was.

"But when he died. You could have told me then. You let me think…" I walked over to the window and looked out, wishing I had taken him up on his offer. The back of beyond suddenly felt like a good place to be.

"When that letter came," Mum said, "the one from the lawyer, you caught me on the hop. I only told you the truth, that your dad had died."

"Oh, for God's sake."

It had been a half-truth. Worse than a half-truth.

"And look how pleased you were. You went out, you were happy. I thought it would only confuse things…"

"But I was only happy because you'd told me lies."

Mum shook her head. The rash that had faded since earlier was running riot again. "They weren't lies, not to me. He let me down." She put down the cup and eased herself under the duvet, creeping back into her hidey-hole.

I made sure I was close enough for her to hear. "Maybe you let him down too," I said.

She turned her face to the wall, pretending to fall asleep.

I wasn't fooled. By tomorrow she would be up and about. They would all rally round, the doctor, Liz and probably Agnes too. They would get her on her feet and back out into the new life she thought she deserved. My help was no longer required.

In the morning I was packing a bag. I'd already been in touch with Dad. I guessed I wouldn't hear from Danny for a while, not after Agnes told him about his new half-sister. Then I had a text from Faye.

"Home for the weekend. How about you?"

These days the library is open on a Sunday, but if I thought it would be neutral territory, I thought wrong. We stood in the foyer, Faye looking fit and tanned from her work at the camp. I hoped that she had a new man on the scene, but I couldn't risk asking and getting the wrong answer.

"Why here?" she said. She clocked my hold-all. "And where are you off to?"

It was obvious she'd heard nothing from Danny. I had hoped that the school display might do some explaining for me, but of course it was long gone. I played for time. "I went to see my dad," I said. "Yesterday."

"Wow. How did that go?"

"Okay. He bought me sandwiches and a snakebite. He says I can go to visit."

"Nice one. What did your mum say, when you told her he was still around?"

"I didn't."

Faye gave me a reproving look meaning *"how long do you think you can keep this up?"*

"I didn't need to tell her," I said. "She already knew. And I knew she did."

I walked ahead of Faye, ignoring her muttered objections. I pushed open the swing doors and asked the librarian about the stuff that had been on display. She disappeared into a back room to check. Faye and I sat down to wait, each of us silent, Faye sensing there was no point in trying to guess what might come next.

The librarian came back with two boxes of magazines. We sat down at a table close to the counter. "What are you looking for?" Faye asked me.

"You'll see."

I turned to the page about the school trip and looked again at the photo. It was like being in the pub with Dad, knowing what I was going to find.

"Anybody you recognise?" I said to Faye.

Faye was interested but wary. "Yeah, that's your mum. Doesn't she look young? And I suppose that's your dad?"

"Look closer," I said. "Anybody else?"

Faye scanned the hazy photo, her eyes passing over the young man with sandy curls, familiar to me from Danny's front room, where Faye, I reminded myself, had never been.

"Read the names," I said.

"Archie Bell, Physical Education, Stuart McLure, Geography." She stopped and looked at it again. "Bloody hell! How weird is that?" She looked at me. "What's goin' on, Ails? First Agnes is working for your mum, now Stuart's in the picture. They all knew each other back then?"

I sat back in the chair. "There's a bit more to it than that."

And so I told her how Dad had owned up to not being my natural father. "He didn't know until after he was accused of the rape. Mum told him he had to go. And that he had no right even to see me. She wouldn't take money from him, either. The money was coming from my real dad. And it turns out this is him."

It had run through my mind that Mum had never had a test done. Could she be wrong? Could I be Tom's daughter after all? But seeing Stuart in the photo again I thought not. We weren't exactly alike, but I could see a resemblance. I was more like him than either Tom or Lorraine.

"Fuck me," Faye said. The desk woman looked up from her screen and kept watching us, like she knew some hazardous substance was being used. "Are you trying to tell me Stuart is your dad?"

"Well, it's looking kind of like it," I said. "Agnes even came round to tell me that Danny and I are a no-go area."

Faye gave me a sharp look. "You and Danny were…?"

"No," I said. "I just went to their house one day. She got the wrong end of the stick."

"Christ," Faye said.

"Sorry," I said. "I didn't know how else to tell you."

There were tears in her eyes, angry tears. She wiped them away with the back of her bare arm. "Well, good on you, Ails. You cracked it. You got it sorted. Your mum, your dad… Anything else you've got up your sleeve?"

She kicked the chair back under the desk and ran out. I let her go.

Outside, she was leaning on the railing, scuffing her feet on the steps.

"Coffee?" I said, but even if the café had been open, I guessed too much had happened since we had last shared the corner table.

She shook her head. "Think I'll give it a miss. I'm back at the camp tomorrow."

She strode away, arms swinging. Faye whom I'd known since Primary Five. Whose only brother had died at Dunblane. She thought she had found a replacement in Danny, but now he belonged to me.

EPILOGUE

Five years on and Kilcreggan is still the back of beyond.
There are no shortcuts. Only thirty miles from Glasgow
but it takes an hour, past Helensburgh, where Dad and
Ruth work, across to the peninsula where the road turns
back on itself along the opposite coast. Kilcreggan is at
the furthest point. From the jetty the Firth of Clyde
stretches out in a choppy grey swell, past Gourock and
its lighthouse, to Bute and Arran. It's sailing country.
Some days the sea is full of boats with spinnakers up,
like tropical seabirds in the wrong ocean.

To the left and right of this crooked finger of land
there are steep-sided lochs, some always in shadow. It's
picturesque, but not like a holiday spot. The big houses
built a hundred years ago are crumbling. People don't
have the patience for the winding road or the chugging
ferries any more. Only the naval base keeps it alive and
people who wash up here from time to time, seeking
solitude and the sea. I couldn't live here forever, but
when I ran out on Mum it was perfect, and in some
ways it still is.

Dad wangled me a job in the local hotel, and every
summer I've come back. It's the only bar in the area, so

331

every night there's a crowd of locals, watching a match or just passing the time. On Fridays they have a tribute band or some local folk group. When tourists arrive it's usually by mistake because they've lost their way. We accommodate them, not for their company, since we are fine with making our own, but because they help keep the place in business.

The people who work here are a mixed bunch. One or two are locals and have lived here all their lives, but the others are like me, coming and going with the seasons. There's Nina and Bren in the bar, Sean in the kitchen. I know them all from previous summers. We're a team, except this year will probably be my last. I had to do extra Highers before I could even apply for Marine Biology, then it was four years in Aberdeen. But now I can look for a job, one that will pay me to catch bucketfuls of seawater, sieve out the life and put it under the microscope.

Last summer Tom and Ruth told me they wanted to be married. I'm sure Dad has every right to a divorce, and I can't see why Mum would object. But the implication is that I might help things along. I've taken it on board. They've been good to me and nothing is for nothing. It's the least I can do.

Danny came over to Glasgow last week, camera over his shoulder as usual. He got that job in the end because the other guy, the one with the qualifications, bailed out. After a year or so he did the training and got a promotion. He lives in St Andrews now. I was telling him that Tom has got hold of a dinghy this summer and has been teaching me to sail. We push the boat together over the stony beach and into the shallows, jumping in as the keel lifts and floats. I'm learning the words the

332

sailors call. I know to duck my head as the boom swings across.

At this Danny's eyes lit up. "That's so cool," he said. "I've always wanted to sail, but my dad wouldn't hear of it. He hated boats."

When he said "my dad" I caught his eye. Then we both laughed. Even now it still comes as a surprise.

"If you come again," I told him, "we'll take you out in the dinghy." He nodded, but it's a long way from coast to coast. I think he has a new girlfriend. The dinghy won't take more than three.

Today Nina and I were on a break, sitting on the sun-terrace, catching the rays, when a sub from the base poked its sleek black tower from under the waves and squirmed past on some unknown mission. We decided that going about in broad daylight it couldn't possibly be armed, but I was glad when it had gone around the headland, out of sight. It was in the sea but not of it. Its shiny carapace held secrets, secrets of life and death.

The sub was a crab or a mollusc. I prefer the feel of a fish: a herring, a haddock, or the firm dry flank of a salmon.

ABOUT THE AUTHOR

Ali Bacon was born in Dunfermline and graduated from St Andrews University. After short periods in Oxford and London, she moved to Bristol where she has lived ever since.

Her writing has been published in *Scribble*, *The Yellow Room* and a number of online magazines. She was shortlisted for the A&C Black First Novel Competition 2006. *A Kettle of Fish* is her first published novel.

Website: http://alibacon.com